PROTECTION

Claire Allen

headline
review

First published in 2006 by
HEADLINE REVIEW
An imprint of HEADLINE PUBLISHING GROUP

First published in paperback in 2007 by
HEADLINE REVIEW
An imprint of HEADLINE PUBLISHING GROUP

1

Cataloguing in Publication Data is available from the British Library

ISBN 978 0 7553 0743 2

Typeset in Minion by Palimpsest Book Production Ltd, Grangemouth, Stirlingshire

Printed and bound in Great Britain by Mackays of Chatham plc, Chatham, Kent

HEADLINE PUBLISHING GROUP
A division of Hodder Headline
338 Euston Road
London NW1 3BH

www.headline.co.uk
www.hodderheadline.com

For Mum and Philip and for Christian

Thank you to Christian Hansen, Joyce Allen, Philip Allen, Viv Pegram and Jane Borges for reading the book in its various early stages and offering support, encouragement and, best of all, ideas. Thanks to Mary-Anne Harrington and Susannah Godman. Thanks also to the many other friends, colleagues and students who encouraged and supported me. Thanks to Duncan and Eira for their help with Welsh. And to Mike, for being the original Tiger Valentine.

Part One

By the time he reaches the bottom of the page his hand is cramping up with the unaccustomed posture of gripping a pen. When he tears the sheet away from the pad he can see the imprint of his ungainly words printed into the surface of the sheet beneath. A ghost letter. Unerasable. His palm is sweating with the effort. He has never done this before: never, in his whole life.

The class is winding to a close and so he reads over what he has written one last time, savouring the strange authority the written shapes of his own words seem to command. His reading is still not fast and his slow, slightly laboured breathing is audible in the silence of his concentration, the breath catching somewhere beyond his throat, the result of forty years of smoking. This is his final, corrected draft and he wants to show it to the tutor before he sends it. He doesn't want there to be any mistakes. The other versions – the ones he did in his cell, straight from his head, in the early hours of the morning when he couldn't sleep – have been screwed up and thrown away, complete with the crossings out and corrections in the young tutor's much steadier hand.

He is a little disappointed with himself for needing to ask her to check it. He has been going to the classes for more than two years, now, and he had wanted the letter to be something achieved entirely through his own efforts, something he could, at last, be proud of. But he is still too unsure of himself to leave it to chance. She seems to know this, the tutor – just a girl, really – and she lets him hover as she collects her papers together, writing in the register to sign it off for the week and chatting to some of the others who are hanging back, wanting to speak to her about this or that. They fancy her, half of them. Want to get the most they can out of the presence of a woman before going back to the stifling monotony of wall-to-wall testosterone. She tolerates it well enough, he thinks, watching the gaggle of younger prisoners arranged in an eager half-moon around her. She's out of here in ten minutes. Back into her own world again. It's not like she has to be with them twenty-four hours a day, so she can afford to be pleasant.

He picks up his letter and, as the youngsters slope off, he catches her eye and she comes over to him, her coat on and her bag on her shoulder now, ready to go. Just the register and the file that belongs in the office clutched to her chest as she comes over and looks at what he hands to her.

He wonders, sometimes, whether she suspects. Of course, it is not mentioned in the classes, and the teachers are never told what crimes their students have committed. But there is something in the awkward way she is standing, holding the folder as if she needs it for protection, that makes him think she does have an inkling. How would she feel if she knew for sure? Would

4

she still let him stay that extra five minutes each time and show her what he has written?

She reads it, nodding, smiling, and then hands it back to him. 'It's finished!' she says simply.

He mutters his thanks and then, carefully, he folds the letter in two, feeling the solidity of his ungainly print in reverse through the thin, prison-issue notepaper. He hesitates, then folds it into two again, as if, with each halving, he can get closer to wishing it away to nothing. It is a strange sensation, the shame, the inadequacy, mixed in with the pride he feels at his achievement.

She touches him on the shoulder, just briefly, before she goes. 'Well done, Jim,' she says in a low voice. 'I told you you could do it. See you next week?'

He nods and clears his throat and turns back to his folding as she leaves the room. The door is propped open with the back of a chair and any minute the warden will come to chase him out and straighten up the room. He is glad she has gone. He has never felt so self-conscious about himself as he does during this weekly two-hour class. He has always been the big guy, sure of himself, sure of his fuck-the-world attitude. But in front of this girl, everything is too small, too fiddly, for his big hands. He doesn't want her to see how stupid, how slow, he is. Nervously, he opens the flap of the envelope and pushes the tiny, overfolded scrap inside. Then he licks along the gummed edge and thumps it down with his clenched fist until it sticks shut.

5

1

L iam has been seeing Julie for two months. It's a record for him: the longest relationship he has ever had. He met her in November, just as the build-up to Christmas was starting. All the shops playing carols, and glitter and tinsel all over the place. Not that he ever went in the shops, but he saw the decorations from outside and heard the music drifting out of the doors as he walked past. When Christmas arrived she hadn't got him a present; she just bought him a pint in the pub on Christmas Eve, and he liked that about her, the way she hadn't gone all lovey-dovey and bought him something meaningful like some girls did. They'd gone out for a drink and some of her mates were there. He didn't like meeting girls' friends usually: it was more trouble than it was worth. But they were all pissed and no one made a fuss, and Julie just said, 'Hey, everyone, this is Liam', and left it at that. Not hanging on to his arm and simpering and saying this is my boyfriend, rolling the word round in her mouth like it was an expensive chocolate. She'd gone to the bar and bought drinks for everyone, and when she brought him his, she said, 'Here y'are, then. Happy Christmas', and she raised her vodka and cranberry and they clinked glasses and smiled at each other without the others seeing.

She gave him a Christmas card, too. He opened it when he got home and looked at the picture on the front – some cartoon penguins with a joke written in spidery letters. Even without reading it, you could tell it was a fun card, not a serious boyfriend-girlfriend one. Inside she'd written him a message. He stood the card on the mantelpiece in his bedroom, which was really the living room, and had the front door from the street opening straight into it.

Julie lives with her sister, but her sister's never there because she's a nurse and she works shifts. Sometimes, when Liam stays the night, she comes home in her uniform at eight in the morning and sits in the kitchen drinking Nescafé before she goes to bed. Julie tells her she shouldn't drink coffee so late but her sister says it has no effect. She's always so whacked she falls asleep anyway.

Julie opens the door and beams. 'Nicky's at work,' she says. 'We've got the place to ourselves.'

She's lovely looking. She's tall and stands very upright, so she looks confident and kind of classy. All the girls in the salon where she works do each other's hair after hours and she's got a perfect bob which always looks shiny and freshly cut. When she moves, it follows the direction of her movement and carries on when she stops, curving sleekly against her cheek before falling back into position, like in the shampoo ads. It's coloured, too. A rich, mahogany shade which brings out the paleness of her skin, the few freckles sprinkled across her cheeks and the bridge of her nose which magically disappear when she puts on her make-up. Sometimes, when they're out, he can't help himself clocking the other girls in the place just for the buzz he gets from knowing she's better-looking than any of them. And the sideways looks from all the blokes. Lucky bastard, he knows they're thinking. Wouldn't kick that out of bed.

He follows her into the kitchen. She's wearing a new dress. It looks sexy because it's low at the back and he can see the channel of her spine, begging him to run his fingers down it. When she bends, the knobble of each vertebra shows briefly, and her shoulder blades, gliding just beneath the taut skin.

He is hungry for a taste of her, his desire made more urgent, somehow, because of the niggling awareness tugging at the corner of his consciousness like a persistent dog at the ear of a cushion. A letter. Addressed to him and as yet unopened, but as present in his mind as if he had torn it from its envelope immediately and read it over and over again until he had memorised every word. He just needs sex to take his mind off it.

Usually they don't bother much with food. They spend most of their time in bed and get takeaways when they're hungry. But this evening he can see she has plans. There's a load of stuff on the kitchen table: a plastic tray of mushrooms, some chicken breasts still cling-filmed into their polystyrene cradles, a bag of onions and a net of garlic bulbs.

'Jesus,' he says. 'What's all this for? Is the Queen coming for tea? Call her up and tell her not to bother. I've got a much better idea.' He catches hold of her from behind and mimics vampire-biting her neck. A load of fancy cooking is the last thing he wants. He just needs to get her into bed as quickly as possible.

9

She wriggles round awkwardly inside his locked arms, laughing, her smile perfect, showing just the right amount of straight, white teeth. 'Stop it, Liam. You're messing me dress up.' She allows him one pecked kiss on the cheek and then demands to be set free. Reluctantly, he lets her go.

'So, come on. I'm dying here. What's the occasion?'

'I just thought, y'know, we could have something nice for a change.'

'What's wrong with Chinese all of a sudden?'

'Nothing,' she says, pushing her hair behind her ear and trying not to look annoyed with him. 'I love Chinese.'

'Me too,' he says. 'What'll it be, madam? The usual?' He pulls his eyes into slits with his forefingers. 'Spare ribs and flied lice, madam? Ah so!'

'Liam! Don't. It's not funny. I'm doin' us something special.'

Liam stands there, his fingers still at the corners of his eyes, although his elbows have drooped slightly. She isn't normally so serious.

'And stop doing that with your eyes. They'll stick if you don't watch it. Didn't yer mam ever tell you?'

He lets his arms drop to his sides.

'Here, open this.' She thrusts a bottle of wine and a corkscrew into his hands and, at a loss as to what else he can do, he wrenches off the plastic covering and buries the corkscrew inside the cork, rotating it until the curly bit goes out of sight. He wishes he could get that letter out of his mind. The thing won't stop shouting for his attention. It's making him edgy.

He has another go at distracting Julie. 'Don't I get a proper kiss, then?' he says, following her to the chopping board where she has already halved an onion and is eyeing it suspiciously before she starts chopping. He can see she means business; she's even wearing an apron. He puts his arms round her and they kiss and for a hopeful moment he thinks he's in and maybe she'll abandon the cooking and they can go to bed instead. He tries to deepen the kiss, pulling her hips tighter against his own and managing to untie the apron, but she pulls herself away, saying there's plenty of time for that later. They have to celebrate first.

'Celebrate what? It's not your birthday, is it?'

'You know it's not. Stop messing. It's our two months' anniversary,' she says, as if it's obvious, and she turns her attention back to the chopping board, noticing as she does, the apron hanging loosely round her neck. 'Liam! Get that wine open. God, I need a glass with you around. She ties the apron again as she explains. 'It said in *Heat* you should mark all the stages in a relationship. It makes it last longer.'

Relationship. He hates that word. It's too long and difficult. And the 'ship' part makes it seem so inescapable, like being stuck on the *Titanic*. It's not that he doesn't love being with Julie; he can't get her out of his mind half the time, but suddenly he feels mired, as if his wheels have stuck in mud or he has sunk to the bottom of a very deep and sluggish river. He picks up the wine and pulls on the corkscrew with all his strength until the cork shifts and suddenly squeaks out of the bottle.

'Da dah!' he fanfares, trying not to let himself sound defeated. He sloshes wine into the two glasses she has set ready, filling

11

them almost to the brim, and they clink them together theatrically. He takes a gulp and gasps at the unfamiliar taste, sweet and not sweet at the same time. He's brought some lagers from the offy on the corner, and he'd rather have one of those; he doesn't like wine: it's more for girls, but she obviously wants them to drink it. Julie sips delicately at hers and smiles, her eyes seeming to twinkle with expectation, before turning back to the chopping board.

Liam sinks into one of the kitchen chairs and knocks the whole glassful back in one go. He watches her for a while. Normally, there isn't much call for talk and they don't notice if there's a lack of it, but now he listens to the scrape of the knife as she meticulously transfers the chopped onion into a pan she has set ready on the hob, and the repeated tap of the blade against wood as she starts to slice up the mushrooms and peppers.

He doesn't like it. He pours himself another glass of wine and carries it out of the kitchen, prowling anxiously around the flat. Her sister's done the whole place out with laminate flooring and uplighters from IKEA. He walks into the living room. There's a pile of women's magazines on the coffee table, and Julie's mobile. It catches his eye and he looks more closely. She's got a photo of him as wallpaper. She's always aiming it at him and taking pictures with it, can't understand why he doesn't get one. Then they can text each other. 'Yeah, all right, then, yeah,' he says with a grin whenever she mentions it, and changes the subject.

He sits on the sofa and picks up one of the magazines, flicking through it on his lap. Photos of the Beckhams and Britney Spears and someone or other from *Celebrity Big Brother*. They watch *Big Brother*, do Julie and her sister. Liam can't be arsed with it.

It's smotheringly hot in the flat; his face feels red and sweaty and his T-shirt is starting to stick to his back. He stands up, takes a couple more gulps from his glass, and places it carefully but with difficulty on one of the coasters on the coffee table. He is starting to feel a bit dizzy.

And then, suddenly, he doesn't want to be here any more. Not like this. He doesn't want to eat dinner with Julie and celebrate their two months' anniversary. The thought of it terrifies him. Sitting at the table like a proper couple, making conversation. Thanks but no thanks. He wants to get out and get away.

In the kitchen, she is poking uncertainly at the stuff in the pan with a wooden spoon. The smell of frying onions has draped itself quite authentically around the room but it isn't making him hungry. He feels sick. Beside the hob is a cook-in sauce. She has snipped the corner off, ready.

'I've got to go,' he says to her back, his voice coming out a little too forcefully, as if he's speaking from a long way off. 'Sorry. I . . .' When she turns round he has already left the room, is in the tiny hallway, shrugging on his denim jacket and cramming his feet back into his worn-out trainers without bending to undo the laces.

'What?'

'I've got to go,' he says again, his voice less certain this time. 'I've . . . I've just remembered. I've got to . . .'

She puts her hand on her hip. She is framed in the kitchen

doorway. He can't look at her now; he tries to avoid catching her eye.

'You've *got* to?' She lets the words hang there. *Makes* them hang there, the way she says them. He can hear the distance in her voice already, the hard, protective shell which always lies in waiting in a girl's voice to be used at times like this. But he can hear the hurt there too; the contemptuous veneer is not enough to hide it. And her body, squared against him in the doorway.

'I'm sorry,' he says, opening the door to the flat. There is nothing he can say, no wisecrack to make it easier. 'I'm sorry.'

She stays exactly where she is as he lets himself out of her flat and his feet hammer down the stairs. The street door slams, making the front door of her flat judder. When she thinks she has waited long enough for him to walk down the road and disappear round the corner, she goes slowly into the living room and pulls the curtain aside. The street is empty.

෴

When he is halfway down the road he remembers the beers he has left in her kitchen. Too late now. He mutters to himself and digs in his pockets for more change before going back into the same off-licence on the corner. He opens a can at the bus stop and swigs at it angrily while he sits on the bus. When he gets home there's no one in. He would have preferred it if Steve or Gary had been there so he could have dragged them out to the pub to blot out this latest disaster. He sits down on one of the plastic garden chairs that do for dining chairs in the tiny, dark

14

kitchen and takes another few gulps from the can. Where is everyone? At least if he could go out for a beer he could stop thinking about all of this. He can't stand being in an empty house. It makes him want to make noise, any kind of noise, to try and cover the silence.

'*Shit.*' He gets up, kicks his chair over and, as he is walking out of the kitchen, kicks the table leg too so that the table judders and tips and before he can catch it his can of lager falls to the floor and rolls giddily across the lino, spewing out half its contents. 'Fucking *shit.*'

In his room, he pulls off his clothes angrily and drops them on the floor before crawling under the covers and pulling them over his head.

๑๛

When he wakes up it is nearly midday. Steve and Gary still aren't around. Maybe they've been home and gone out again since he's been asleep. He feels bad going into Steve's bedroom, treading on clothes and stuff as he searches for the car keys, but from the moment he gets out of bed he knows he has to get away from here and Steve's car is the only way he can think of that isn't going to cost him. He finds the keys on the floor by the side of the bed and closes the bedroom door respectfully behind him. Outside, he pulls the front door shut and steps out of the binbag-strewn front garden into the street. Steve won't miss the car, anyway: he refuses to drive it until he gets round to taking it to the garage for its MOT and has left it parked outside in the street for weeks, growing mould on the upholstery and gathering birdshit on its roof. He wishes he'd been around to ask if he could take it but, well, he wasn't. It can't be helped.

He unlocks the door and gets in. The car stinks: a mixture of rotting, mulchy leaves, damp clothes, old trainers and something fermenting, like apple cores, overlaid with a strong tang of petrol that hangs there in the cold air. The seat feels damp and the steering wheel is slightly wet to the touch as if it's covered with early morning dew. He leans forward to breathe on the window and rubs at it with the sleeve of his jacket, but it makes no difference because the dirt is on the outside and he can't be bothered getting out again to wipe it.

He fumbles the key into the ignition and tries to remember which bits control what. He hasn't driven a car for ages. He waggles a lever sticking out from the steering wheel and the windscreen wipers start dragging and catching across the glass. A dead leaf tangled up in one of them trails backwards and forwards by the stalk until it is shaken free. The dirt outside the curved reach of the wipers is too thick to see through. He finds the button that squirts soapy water and a dribble spatters the glass half-heartedly before being swept up by the wipers and squeaked away to the side where it runs down in a muddy trickle.

He turns the key, praying it will start. The engine splutters and dies almost immediately.

'Come on, fucking *work*!' He tries again and, after a couple of wheezes, the car coughs into life briefly before puttering out once more. 'Shite,' he says, and sits absolutely still, his head swimming with expletives. He wants to get out and kick the rusting bodywork and shout. Now that he has had the idea of getting in the car and driving off somewhere, away from all the shit that's been swilling around his head since he got up, the thought that he won't be able to get the car going is unbearable. 'Come on!' he says again, giving the ignition one last try. 'Just go, will you!'

It does. He works the pedal, pumping it with the ball of his foot, and pulls out the choke, willing the thing not to die on him again, and this time it holds. Hardly breathing, he gives a few tentative revs and the car judders then settles into a more regular vibration. He releases a long, slow breath, fiddles with the gearstick as he twists round in his seat to reverse out of the parking space, and emerges jerkily into the road. The car has been parked in the same spot for so long the print of the tyres is left behind in the empty space, drawn in leaves and grime against the tarmac.

It doesn't take him long to get back into the swing of it. He's never driven this car before – Steve won't let him – but they're all pretty much the same after about five minutes. What he needs is to find the motorway and get as far away as he can as quickly as possible.

He isn't sure exactly where he is planning to go, only that it's out of Liverpool, away from the places where *he* might come looking for him. Isn't that why he's written to him, because he wants to find him? It must be.

Liam has a good memory for streets, even though he doesn't know what half of them are called. It's all visual with him, like a 3D map in his head, always has been. So he soon finds his way on to the main road, being streamed on to the motorway feeder road and out on to the M62.

Once he's on the motorway, a kind of euphoric release takes hold of him, a mixture of concentration and the buzz of freedom, and, as the car warms up, he lets the road ahead of him take him over. The dotted lines disappear off to a vanishing point that he is heading straight towards. Julie and the letter slip out of his thoughts and, in the thrum of the engine and the sameness of the road, he feels almost as if he is floating, the car miraculously driving itself. There isn't much traffic; so long as he doesn't get stopped by the police, he'll be away.

2

I t is 3.30 a.m. Marina cradles her son in her arms as his whimpers die down, pulling the nylon sleeping bag closer round his shoulders, trying to trap the warm air inside. The gentle suck suck of his thumb in his mouth soothes her almost as much as it does him. Sometimes his complete innocence of everything that's going on around him is the only thing that keeps her going.

The sucking slows and stops. She gently guides the little thumb out of his puckered mouth and under the sleeping bag. He stirs, his wet lips sucking at nothing, and then he settles. She tries to focus on the soft, almost inaudible in and out of his breathing, tries to close herself off from everything else. But it doesn't work. She can't get rid of the feeling that they are out there, waiting for her, waiting to snatch him from her arms. She hugs him closer, burying her face in the soft curls of baby hair that has not yet had its first cut, breathing in the warmth of his scalp. She will not let him go. Whatever happens, she will not let him go.

൦ᘉ

Yesterday she tried to get them somewhere to live. She sat and waited for more than two hours and eventually Oscar started to grizzle. He was hungry; she had given him a slice of bread, smeared thickly with strawberry jam, before they left Suzanne's flat, but he had licked the jam off and dropped the bread on the ground. Pride had stopped her from picking it up and brushing the dirt off. She wasn't so desperate.

When her turn came she tried to explain the situation, but the woman she spoke to didn't seem to believe her.

'There's nowhere you can go? Are you sure about that?'

'Yes,' Marina said, straining forwards in her chair. 'I wouldn't be here, otherwise, would I?'

The woman didn't look up; she studied the forms on the desk in front of her.

'Well, if what you are saying is true,' she said finally, lifting her head and looking straight at Marina, 'we will have to take Oscar into care.' Her voice was brittle, her expression glassy. Neither betrayed the slightest quiver of emotion or fellow-feeling as she spoke. There was no modulation of her tone, no 'I'm afraid' or 'I'm sorry to tell you' to soften what she was saying. Her words stood solidly like a barricade in front of Marina, as if they had been chiselled into the air between them.

Marina froze, and then her mouth numbly shaped itself around the ill-fitting sounds as she repeated what she had just heard. 'Take him into care?'

The woman's face betrayed a flicker of impatience. 'Yes,' she said, enunciating the word too clearly; it made Marina wince.

'If you really have nowhere to go.' She glanced up again, her eyebrows arched and meaningful.

'But I . . . we . . .'

'A child can't be left to sleep on the streets, can it?'

'No, of course not.'

'So, as I said, if you have nowhere to go . . .'

Marina stood up, her eyes brimming with furious tears. 'You're not taking him. He isn't yours to take. You can't have him.' She stopped, her voice choking in the snot and tears that were suddenly pouring out of her. She sniffed and wiped her nose on the back of her hand and turned to the child in his pushchair whose grizzling had become a drawn-out, rising wail. 'Come on, Oscar,' she said, her voice thickened but firm. 'We're going.' She grasped the handles of the buggy and jerked it towards the exit. Before leaving she turned back to the woman.

'Fuck you!' she said, loudly enough for everyone in the waiting area to swivel their heads in her direction and watch, blank-faced, as she wrestled the pushchair out through the swing doors.

She spent the afternoon wandering up and down the Narroway, not wanting to return to Suzanne's flat while she wasn't there. She didn't trust the boyfriend who Suzanne had let move in. The way he looked at her seemed to challenge her right to Suzanne, as if he felt he now had more claim to her than she did because he shared her bed. Like she was a commodity to be divided up. She didn't like him and he clearly resented Marina's presence.

They sat in McDonald's in the warm for as long as they could, whilst Oscar picked and gnawed at the chicken nuggets she had bought, chattering amiably to himself. She felt guilty feeding

21

him crap food but at least there was somewhere to sit down. She poured some of her tea into his Tommee Tippee cup and blew on it. She was glad, sometimes, that he was too young to tell when she was upset. Glad, too, that he hadn't understood the conversation with the woman at the housing office and had no idea how desperate their situation was. He lifted his hand to her and opened and closed his fingers. She waved back and he giggled and screwed up his face.

When he started getting restless she wheeled him into Primark and wrestled him into a little fleece jacket. She wanted to get him something warm – he was too big for the stuff he had worn last winter – but the jacket was £6, exactly half the money she had to last them for the next two days. It would have to wait. She put it back on the little hanger and left the warmth of the shop reluctantly. Outside, she weaved between the buses and the incense sellers and the guys bending silver wire into animal shapes and people's names, and pushed the buggy into the quiet of Churchwell Path, behind St John's. Oscar got out and tottered unsteadily in front, his top-heavy run making her smile.

She still breastfeeds Oscar. She knows most mothers would have stopped by now, but it makes her feel so connected with, so necessary to, her son, and he seems so happy to continue with it, that it has stayed a part of their daily ritual. This is what she likes most about having Oscar: the private things, the invisible life they share, that nobody else has any claim to.

She closes her eyes and hears her heartbeat throbbing loudly in her ears. In the darkness, fear and panic well up and surge through her body, making her heart flutter and the tips of her fingers tingle slightly. She feels spring-loaded, mousetrap-tense. It is only Oscar's weight, his sleeping body curving into hers, which keeps her from moving; all her energy seems to be focusing on one absolute necessity: that she remain completely still, that she allow her son to sleep undisturbed.

ᨀ

If they took Oscar away from her, where would he end up? A foster home, probably, with a careworn, exhausted stand-in mother who would be too busy to play with him. Or even worse, a children's home, where he would be left to cry. Where they wouldn't understand that when he rubbed his earlobes he was sleepy, that when his chin dimpled and trembled he was unsure and needed reassurance. If they took Oscar away she would have to sleep alone again. Even before he was born, when she was pregnant, she had felt as if there was someone else there. His presence inside her had kept her company. Without Oscar at night she would end up sleeping with someone, just so she wouldn't have to be alone. That was how it worked: your kid was taken away and you were told it was only for a while, just a temporary measure. And because you couldn't bear being alone you found someone. You slept with them. Because that was the only other way not to be on your own. And then you moved in with them, just for a while, until you found somewhere. And there wouldn't be room for the kid, and anyway, why move him when he was just settling in with the fosterers, when you'd have to move him again when you found your own place? Better to wait. And then you got used to being with the guy and your little boy seemed happy for the time being with his new family. And then you got pregnant again. It happened. In all the hours she has spent waiting at the housing place, she has heard people talking about it. People who have already lost kids, about to lose another one. She knows it is possible just to drift imperceptibly away from your own child.

Oscar is almost awake now. He is in that drifty, adorable state, where he can go either way. His eyes flutter open, his forehead wrinkling with the effort of trying to focus, and then they give up and float, unseeing, beneath half-closed lids. Each tiny breath is sweet, slightly milky, in her nostrils. She shifts her position slightly, and the movement is enough to bring his eyes swivelling back into focus. He pulls back from her, smiling a wide, yawny smile as his arms and legs go tense. She feels his fingers dig into her neck, his feet pushing against her belly, his whole body quivering then relaxing.

Suzanne is getting ready for work. Marina can hear her moving around in the next room. She hears the kettle click off, the fridge opening and closing, kitchen-cupboard doors banging. And voices. Dave seems to be getting up too. Maybe it is his day for signing on. She feels relief surge through her body. She will be able to get up and give Oscar his breakfast in peace, without having to hurry, she thinks. Yesterday morning

24

Dave had sat at the kitchen table, pretending to read the TV guide, but she had felt his eyes all over her as she moved around the tiny kitchen, had smelt last night's stale alcohol seeping from his pores, slowly filling the room. She had rushed Oscar through his warm Weetabix and scurried out to London Fields, smoking her first cigarette of the day wedged into a child's swing as Oscar squeaked gently back and forth beside her in the deserted playground.

Eventually, Suzanne and Dave leave together. She hears the front door bang shut and listens to their diminishing footsteps along the walkway. Once she has heard the clunk and rattle of the lift doors closing on them she pushes back the sleeping bag covering them both and sits up.

It is so cold in the flat she can see her breath. Oscar whimpers as she pulls the tiny pyjama top over his head and leaves him bare-chested as she rummages for something clean for him to wear, but there is nothing that hasn't already been worn. All their clothes are crammed inside three enormous bags piled in the corner of the room, spilling out on to the floor in a muddled, tangled-up heap. She hasn't been able to face a trip to the launderette. Maybe today, she thinks. At least it'll be warm and, if she tires Oscar out at the playground first, he might sleep for a bit.

She changes his nappy on the floor and quickly dresses him in yesterday's clothes before pulling her jeans on and opening the curtains. He stands up on the sofa and watches the world below him through the window, his small pale face suddenly serious.

'Come on, mister. Breakfast time.' The sooner they get breakfast over with, the sooner they can leave the flat.

'Car!' he says, pressing his finger against the glass.

ॐ

She has never been in Suzanne's flat alone before. She walks from room to room like a caged animal whilst Oscar meticulously chews his toast and jam. Kitchen, living room, kitchen, bedroom, kitchen. She rolls up the sleeping bag and stashes it behind the sofa, and squashes the remaining bag of clothes as far into the corner as she can. She hates leaving her stuff here when Dave's in the flat; she imagines him going through it, looking at her underwear, or hunting for anything he might make some money on. Suzanne once confided in her how, even before he moved in, her things had started to go missing. She wouldn't admit it now, though. She would lower her eyes and say Marina had made a mistake, was thinking of someone else. But Marina knows for a fact that Suzanne keeps nothing valuable at the flat any more. Her bank account cards, the earrings she got for her twenty-first. They're all at her mum's. But she let him move in just the same, knowing he was dodgy as fuck.

Marina hates living like this, feeling on top of other people, having to keep her personal things in their living room, bathing every other day so she doesn't use up their hot water. She has given some cash to Suzanne. Not much. Just to say thank you, more than anything. It wasn't enough to cover any bills. But she feels hers and Oscar's presence is difficult. She can see Suzanne's discomfort as Dave practically forces her to choose between them. It isn't fair; she shouldn't have to choose like this, but there's no point saying anything now. It's too late.

Oscar is still busy with the toast; she can hear his silent concentration as he chews and swallows each studied mouthful. She wanders back into the bedroom and, instead of walking straight out again, sits down on the bed. The duvet is in a rumpled heap and the undersheet looks a bit grubby, but even so, it looks warm and she wishes she could crawl in and hide underneath it. The room feels cosy and comfortable even though the wardrobe doors hang open and the contents of the chest of drawers are spilling out of the bulging drawers. On one bedside table are a lamp and a framed photo of Suzanne's sister with her little girl. On the table nearest Marina, a pile of change, a video-shop card and an ashtray cluster around the lamp.

She sighs. The flat is silent. She remembers the same stillness in her own flat when Oscar was tiny. When he napped during the day and she sometimes lay down on the bed and drifted off to sleep with him. Such a safe, protected feeling. And special, knowing that so many other people were at work, or battling on the tube to get home, and here she was, doing the job she was meant to be doing, right here at home, looking after her baby.

This is clearly Dave's side. The bedside table has a drawer. She wonders what he keeps in it and, suddenly curious, shuffles nearer. She will get her own back, she thinks, for the way he looks at her, for the way she absolutely knows, even though there's no proof, that he goes through her stuff when she's not there. Tentatively, she reaches for the handle and pulls the drawer open.

Inside, there is more loose change. And a spare pack of cigarettes still in its cellophane. Even so, the fruity tobacco smell has escaped through the wrapper and it wafts out at her. She can smell cannabis too. She pulls the drawer out further to find it. There are some used tissues and a couple of loose keys. The resin is tucked at the back, behind a Walkman with no front on it. A half-played tape still slotted into place. Next to it is a brown envelope, wound round a few times with one of Suzanne's hair elastics. Go on, she thinks. Have a look. He wouldn't hesitate in your bedroom. And you've already committed the crime. There aren't degrees of prying. You're already guilty. She smiles, taking pleasure in this game of self-persuasion. She couldn't care less when it comes to Dave. Before she can change her mind, she pulls off the elastic and unrolls the envelope. It's A4, folded in half lengthways and then rolled up around whatever he has stuffed inside. The self-adhesive flap, already opened and reclosed many times, peels up easily; she unsticks it and peers inside.

Money. It's money. Tons of it.

The sly bastard! She tips it out on to the duvet and riffles through it, too indignant and excited to count it properly. It's mostly in tens, some twenties, and there are loads of them. She starts again, hands shaking, counting through the notes, some of them so used and crumpled that they feel as soft as fabric.

There are just under a thousand pounds. Surely Suzanne doesn't know about this. Before he moved in, before she let him take over her life, she said there was no way he was living with her if he was still dealing. No way was she having the police coming round, searching the place. Well, how else could he have got this much money? Why else would he keep it rolled up in the back of a drawer?

Carefully, she pushes it back into the envelope, refolds and rolls it and winds the elastic band round again. She places it back in the drawer, exactly as it was and pushes it closed. Her heart is pumping against her ribs and a sweat has broken out on her palms.

Oscar is silent. She calls his name but there is no response. With a flicker of concern, she goes to check on him. He is sitting on the floor, carefully arranging his chewed toast crusts in a wavering line across the carpet. He looks up and bounces up and down when he sees her.

'Train!' he says.

'Hey, good boy. You've made a train.' She picks him up and kisses him on his jammy cheek then holds him close. 'Come on,' she says, a terrifying idea taking shape at just this moment in her head and spreading through her body like poison. It makes her tingle with fear. 'Let's go on a real train. Would you like that?'

As quickly as she can she pulls on his mittens and zips him into last year's coat. Grimly, she loads the buggy with the heaviest of their bags, fastening it in place with a bicycle bungee strap. She balances the second one on top and then pulls her own coat on and checks again in the living room and bathroom for any of their things. The toast-crust train is still snaking across the floor. Breathless now, she scoops the soggy bits of bread up into her hand and throws them into the kitchen bin.

They are ready to go.

It's an adventure, she informs Oscar in a serious voice. And because it's an adventure, he is going to walk all the way to the bus stop without going in his buggy.

She's ready, but she hesitates for a moment, wondering whether she can really do this. She has never done anything like it in her life. If she gets caught, or if Dave comes home as she's doing it, what then? What would happen? But he won't come home; he's only just gone out. And it isn't his money any more than it is hers. Why should he have it and she and Oscar not? She knows she has the greater need.

She closes her eyes and clenches her fists. She isn't going to think about it any more, or she won't do it, and her life will stay stuck in this nightmare for ever. She is just going to do it. Ready, she thinks. Now.

She takes a deep breath and holds it. In the bedroom she opens the drawer, takes the envelope and, with shaking hands, unfolds it again and crams the money into her back pocket. She replaces it with a wad of toilet paper and rolls the envelope up before pushing it into the back of the drawer for the second time. She hesitates for a moment, her hand hovering, undecided, and then she takes the cannabis too, pushes the Walkman back into place and closes the drawer. There. It's done.

Shouldering the last of their bags, she opens the door to the flat and wrestles Oscar and the buggy out in silence. With strength she didn't know she had she carries everything down all five flights of stairs without stopping to wait for the lift. She feels like she is gliding, not touching the ground. She sets the buggy down on the pavement. Oscar seems happy to be carried and, although he usually feels heavy, he seems almost weightless now as she streams up the road, steering the buggy one-handed. He has sensed something and she catches his surprised expression as he cranes his head round to see her. But he keeps quiet and allows himself to be carried. He is used to things not making sense.

They can't take Oscar away from her. They won't be able to now. They won't know where he is. She has had it with Hackney, with London, and all the shit she's been through here. As she crosses Mare Street to wait at the bus stop outside the Town Hall, she bids the place a mental goodbye. Say bye-bye, Oscar, she thinks. You won't remember this shithole when you grow up. Say bye-bye.

3

Hannah walks out of the surgery and down the path to the street. She closes the gate carefully behind her, lifting the latch and letting it fall into position with a pleasing tap before she turns and sets off back towards home.

The sun is bright, almost strong enough for sunglasses. Not that she has ever really been one for sunglasses – and anyway, it's January not July – but right now she feels she could wear them and not care one jot. Why not wear them? Other people do and don't seem to care what time of year it is or how ridiculous they look. She narrows her eyes a little and presses the button at the crossing, pulling her coat collar closed and doing up the top button.

As she walks down the main street she tries to work out how she is feeling, but she can't quite put her finger on it. She has been feeling so unlike anything at all for such a long while, now, that it's difficult to know what's what on the feelings side of things even on the most unprepossessing of days, and today has started out far from unremarkable.

She concentrates. What she can feel is like a muffled singing sensation, filling up her head and seeming to separate her from the people around her on the street doing their usual humdrum things. She is doing ordinary things too, but, just at the moment, she feels extraordinary, in some way special, chosen, like some women feel, perhaps, when they discover they are pregnant.

When she gets home she unbuttons her coat and hangs it up, walks slowly into the empty guests' dining room, takes her top cardigan off and drapes it over the back of one of the chairs, the same as she always does when she comes indoors. She notices that, even though her entire world has changed since she went out this morning, everything here is exactly the same as it was before she left. Her teacup and saucer still on the table and her breakfast plate with a few toast crumbs and traces of honey left clinging to it. She pulls the chair out and sits down heavily as a wave of tiredness washes over her. The buoyancy she felt as she walked home has ebbed away now and the weariness she has been feeling lately is creeping back along her limbs, but the strange tingle – a sense of newness – lingers behind.

She had been so convinced. So absolutely sure. She has never thought of herself as one of those hypochondriac types given to wild flights of the imagination, even if she does worry some-times. She knows how she has been feeling for, oh, such a long time now, and it had all added up in her mind to just one thing. There was nothing else it could be: she had cancer. She hadn't known what kind of cancer, had felt no specific pain in any part of her body, nor found any untoward lumps that couldn't be accounted for. And she had never got around to actually finding out anything concrete about the illness that was to become her new master. It was a difficult subject to broach with people. Not a topic spoken about easily, even to those with personal experience. She had thought she might ask the window-cleaner, who she knew had lost his wife to it a year back. They often talked on the doorstep when he came for his water. But when the opportunity arose, she couldn't ask. Not about cancer.

She goes over the moment again in Dr Mount's surgery. The moment when he told her. Her heart had lurched so sharply that her breath caught in her throat and she felt sure a gasp had escaped her, but she must have betrayed nothing at all, because Dr Mount had looked at her quite strangely and asked did she understand what he had just told her.

The tests had come back and, yes, there was something wrong. She had been quite right to come and see him; he made that abundantly clear. And she would need to start looking after herself, he said, in a slightly schoolmasterish way, as if he had it on good authority that she had not been doing so up until now.

'What is it?' she asked, dreading the answer, although there was nothing left to dread: she already knew what it was and there was nothing worse she could hear.

'Anaemia,' he said, stamping the word so firmly into the air that it almost left a mark. 'You are *severely* anaemic, Mrs Thomas.'

'Anaemia?' She had hardly any voice to give the word sound. 'Is that all?'

He seemed almost offended. 'Anaemia can be very serious, Mrs Thomas,' he said, his voluminous eyebrows suddenly lowering and pushing themselves together, creasing the patch of forehead between them into a worried concertina. 'Very serious. I don't think you realise. Especially for the more mature person.' Dr Mount is terribly proper, would never dream of cracking a joke or dealing with a patient's ailments as if they were anything but the most pressing and grave concern, and she has always rather liked this about him. Even so, if the discovery that you didn't have cancer after all wasn't an appropriate time for levity, she wasn't sure what was, and for a moment she almost felt annoyed with him. But then she remembered his profession-alism, his duty of care, the fact that she had never actually mentioned the 'C word' to him, and tried hard to listen, nodding and agreeing wholeheartedly with everything he said. Still, she clearly hadn't been able to keep the quiver of relief out of her voice and she could tell that he noticed and disapproved.

He had sent her away with a prescription for high-dosage iron tablets which she mustn't forget to take with food, a bundle of leaflets headed 'Managing Your Illness', and a referral to a dietician.

She sighs. It is like a reprieve, she thinks, leaning back in her chair and wishing she had sat down in an armchair instead of this damned uncomfortable dining chair with its knobbly bits digging into her back. A second chance. Something opening up ahead of her instead of closing down and finishing. She had been so, so sure. But aside from the anaemia, Dr Mount had said she was a very healthy woman. A very healthy woman. She mouths the words. They feel as strange as words in a foreign language, they are so different from what she has been expecting.

Well, she thinks, and then she says it out loud to the large

35

tabby cat stretched out along the wide windowsill between the net curtain and the glass, his feet hanging over the edge, his biscuit-coloured belly moving slowly in and out. 'Well, Mr Valentine, we've got more time than we thought we had. My goodness. My goodness me.' She stands up and walks over to the window. The cat gives a chirrup of surprise when she touches it and lifts its head up to look at her. 'What on earth shall I do with myself now, d'you think?' she asks. The cat blinks. As she stands there, stroking the top of its head and looking out at the sea, a brief shiver of possibility thrills across her shoulders making her shudder, and she carefully buttons up her cardigan.

4

It's the tail end of the morning rush hour when she reaches Euston and the commuters pouring from the platforms are fighting against time, trying to overtake their own lateness. People are moving about the concourse like marbles being tipped madly this way and that in a tea tray, pouring in hurried diagonals across the shiny floor towards the exits. The few who are not caught up in the rush stand wary and bewildered, scruffy islands of jobless or homeless lassitude trapped in the steady stream of men and women in suits. Marina sets Oscar down on the ground and tells him not to let go of the buggy.

She hasn't been here for years. Not since she last went home to see her parents. Before Oscar. She aims the pushchair towards the middle of the concourse, and sets a determined road through the wall of people coming at her. In the centre, she gets snarled up in a kind of huddle – an immoveable block of people surrounded by luggage, heads all raised expectantly towards the departures board. She stops and looks up too. She hasn't thought, yet, where she wants to go. Oscar stops obediently beside her, the knuckles on his clenched fist squeezed white.

She needs to get out of here as quickly as she can, she knows that much. Who knows who she might bump into in a place like this? So many people about. Any number of them could be on the lookout for her. Dave's mates. If he's got home already and gone looking for the money, he'll know it was her and he'll get everyone he knows after her, for sure.

As she scans the board, a platform number appears with a minute flick, and instantly the slick of people surrounding her starts moving and dividing, half of them staying where they are, the other half drifting towards Platform Seven. It's a Wolverhampton train. She has never been to Wolverhampton, has no desire to go there. But she has to go somewhere. As the knot of people thins out she casts about anxiously, feeling suddenly conspicuous. There're a couple of guys with their heads together, one with his back turned, but the other one keeps scanning around the place for something or someone. She has to leave. Now.

She looks back at the departures board. There's a train to Glasgow running late and one to Liverpool. Liverpool, she thinks. It's leaving in ten minutes. Her best friend from school went to Liverpool University. She hasn't seen or spoken to her for years. But they had been the best of friends once. Had shared everything. They could start again, couldn't they?

She frees herself from what is left of the crowd, pulling the buggy backwards carefully, trying not to let the overhanging bags catch against people's legs, and scurries towards the ticket windows, keeping her head down in case anyone recognises her. There are three or four people in front of her in the queue and she can feel the minutes ticking away. If she doesn't get on this train she can't hang around here; it's too risky. She holds her breath, willing the woman in front of her to hurry up.

When her turn comes she whispers 'Liverpool' to the woman on the other side of the glass and the woman just stares at her. She tries again. 'Liverpool, please.' There's someone behind her in the queue now and she doesn't want them to hear.

'What?' The woman fiddles with her microphone, as if it's that that's at fault, but Marina says it again and this time she hears her.

'And when will you be returning?' she asks, her voice automatic, its dips and modulations garish and false.

Marina grabs Oscar's free hand and pulls him closer to her. He keeps holding on to the buggy with his other hand and it tilts dangerously as he is pulled away from it. The person behind in the queue grabs the handle as it is about to fall and holds it upright.

'I just want a single,' Marina says. 'Just a single.' The woman looks like she is about to protest, as if she might try to persuade her out of going, but she says nothing and the printed ticket is ejected from her machine. Marina hands over the money with a trembling hand, glad that the woman cannot see the bundle she has pulled it from. Nobody carries this much money around with them. Especially not in a bundle in their pocket. She feels as if everyone in the station is looking at her, pointing at her, accusing her. But the woman takes the money and swings the ticket and change round to her on the little turntable between them without interest. Marina scrapes everything up and stuffs it into her jeans pocket. Briefly, she notices the stranger's steadying hand on the buggy handle, and pulls Oscar closer.

ᘒ

It was her husband Evan's idea, of course. Moving away from London. It would be a fresh start, he had said. A way of moving on. Hannah knew what that meant. She had spent nine months as an inpatient at a private psychiatric hospital and she saw the embarrassed glances thrown in her direction by people they knew – his colleagues at social functions, the neighbours – who had been left to wonder where she was. She's been in the loony bin, they were probably thinking. He had to have her put away. Poor man. Such a burden. Such a responsibility. She had to go in for her own protection. Who knows what she might have done to herself.

As if it had ever been that dramatic: Hannah holding a kitchen knife to her own throat, locking the doors from the inside and turning on the gas. It hadn't been like that at all. Her madness had been far more mundane.

But Evan had decided she would be better living somewhere quieter, and he found the guest house as he was browsing through a list of properties for sale in North Wales, near the town where his father had been brought up. Right away he had known it was the answer to their problems. Too much spare time on her hands was, he informed her levelly, at the root of her malady. She had developed a brooding disposition in the months following their marriage, and hadn't this coincided with her leaving her job? Hadn't she been a busy, neat little person, perfectly self-controlled, when he had first known her? It was this fretful state which had built up and led her to her illness, her incapacitation. Leaving London, he repeated time and time again, would be her salvation. She would have something to occupy her during the day and she would be away from the cramped city existence he felt did her no good at all.

When he was dying, and she sat day after day at his bedside, watching him fade, she tried to pinpoint the exact moment he must have begun to hate her. She didn't care. She didn't hate him, because, for her, hatred was a backwards swing from love, which she had never felt for him either, but when she returned from the mental hospital she had thrown up more defences, immuring herself in her fortified keep, peering at him through the arrow slits. By sending her away, he had alienated her further than he knew. He had pushed her beyond any calling back. Whisking her away to some windswept resort she had never heard of on the far side of Llandudno – where in winter the wind could blow you nearly flat, and where even the name of the guest house, *Swn Y Don*, when Evan translated it into English for her, resonated with the sucking, chocking, echoing sounds of the sea at night – was merely widening an already uncross-able gulf between them.

ॐ

The letter arrived yesterday. When Liam woke up, it was there in the wire basket on the back of the front door, which opened straight into his bedroom; he could see it even without getting out of bed. He almost ignored it; there was always some kind of crap in that basket – pizza and Chinese takeaway leaflets which he never bothered to clear out for weeks at a time. Sometimes gas bills sat in there so long they sent people round to cut them off. Steve was always going on at him about it, but he didn't see why he should have all the responsibility just because the letter box was in his room. It was bad enough having people walking through the front door all the time when he was in bed, coming home at four in the morning and fumbling with keys, then tripping over his mattress and waking him up. He wasn't going to start being Mr Postman, too. But yesterday, as he was getting ready to go round to Julie's, something made him open the flap of the wire cage and pull the envelope out.

It was addressed to him. His name anyway: Liam Kelleher. The address written under his name was wrong, but it had been crossed out and another one scribbled beside it. That one was crossed out, too, but the third one was the address of the place a few streets away where he'd lived for a bit a year or two ago. Someone there must've remembered where he'd moved to and pushed it through the letter box. It was only luck that the letter had got to him at all.

He never gets letters. He doesn't even get his giros in the post any more since they changed the rules. He'd had to open a post office account, sweating over the form, eventually handing over the crumpled sheet of paper with half the words crossed out, or with thickened, strangely shaped letters, where he had changed them halfway through.

He tore open the envelope and shook the contents out on to the kitchen table while he ate a piece of cold pizza left in its box from the night before. Another envelope fell out, a much smaller one, made of thin, almost see-through paper. It, too, had an address on it, in handwriting not much better than his own, although it was joined up at least. Joined-up writing is something he has never managed.

He sat down hard on one of the garden chairs when he had carefully spelled out what this joined-up writing said. Underneath a neat 'Liam James Kelleher' was an address he scarcely remembered, he had lived at so many others since. It was his nana's address. His nana had died when he was fourteen years old, more than half his life ago. And nobody had ever called him his full name. Nobody except his dad.

Well, whatever it is that his dad wants, he is going to be well away from here before very long, and there's no way he'll be able to find him. How can he? Liam doesn't even know himself yet where he is going.

5

Her parents had called her Maria. When she left home she added the N because she didn't want to be Maria any more; she didn't want to be the person they had created. And she had always liked the sea. Marina seemed appropriate. She had called Oscar Oscar simply because she liked the name. It wasn't tainted with anything. There was nobody else she knew or knew of called Oscar, and she liked that more than anything.

He is asleep in the seat beside her. As the train hurtles northwards, she counts the money again, holding it low in her lap, frightened another passenger will see it and know it isn't hers. There is nine hundred and forty pounds, plus the change from the ticket in her pocket. It feels dangerous to have so much money on show. She unzips the corner of one of the bags of clothes and digs inside it until she finds what she is looking for. Carefully, she extracts a long, striped sock, the type that pull right up over the knees. It comes free reluctantly, like a worm being prised from its hole. Once it is out, she pulls the sides of the bag close again and holds them together with one hand while she does up the straining zip with the other.

The sock is long enough to tie round her middle. She pushes the money inside it, leaving out just a couple of notes and the coins, which she stuffs into her back pocket. She pushes the dope into the sock, too, and then ties it round her waist underneath her jumper. The carriage is almost empty. Feeling more relaxed, she lifts Oscar into her lap and pulls up her jumper to nurse him. The money, the feeding: they have two secrets now.

As she feels him falling into the silent, mesmeric rhythm of his slow sucking, Marina starts wondering about Lisa, her friend in Liverpool. She imagines turning up on her doorstep with a child and seeing the surprise on her face. It occurs to her that Lisa might not still be living in the same place. She was in a student house with friends last time she saw her, in a little terraced street a bus ride from the centre. How stupid, she thinks. Of course she won't still be there. She would have finished university nearly two years ago; she could be anywhere. For all she knows she might have moved on and not be in Liverpool at all any more. After such long silence, why would she bother to let her old friend know?

She looks out of the window. Nondescript countryside streams past, vaguely hummocky, under a heavy sky. A man walking along a path through a field watches his dog dancing ahead of him, its lead dangling loose in his hand.

Why is she on this train? She leans her head against the window, letting the vibration judder her brain, the sound of it filling her head. What was she thinking of? Even if Lisa is still in Liverpool, it will be impossible to find her. And even if she

45

could, pride would stop her from asking for help: they will be practically strangers.

She closes her eyes and keeps them closed until the train slows and stops. Crewe. A few bored-looking people stand about on the platform.

Something else has occurred to her, something she ought to have thought about earlier, too. Mightn't there just be a chance that Dave might know someone in Liverpool? He seems to know people all over, and London's full of scousers. Going there is too risky. She needs to be somewhere small and safe, out of his reach, not stuck in another city, with danger lurking round every corner.

The train is still sitting at the platform, waiting. There might just be enough time. Marina makes a snap decision: she will get off here. She drags the bags and the folded pushchair to the doors as quickly as she can, terrified the whistle will blow at any moment. But the train must be running early, because it seems quite unconcerned as she hurls her belongings out and steps down on to the platform.

She settles Oscar into his buggy and wheels him towards the waiting-room café while she thinks what to do next. It has been raining here and wet footsteps have been walked inside, muddying the floor. She finds a table, piles all their stuff on a chair and sits down to roll a cigarette. The air is stale and close; it smells of exhaled smoke and chips. The place is crammed with little metal tables and chairs which scrape on the floor each time someone gets up or moves out of the way for someone else. A couple of kids are running round, clattering into the chair legs and shrieking. A train thunders on to the platform, its vibrations shivering across

46

the floor and through the hard seat into her body, rattling her already aching head. She wishes the kids' parents would shut them up and make them sit down. A voice over the tannoy outside announces the train's destination is Holyhead. She can't bear to sit in this place any longer. That'll do, she thinks. She can get off somewhere along the way. Anywhere, it doesn't matter, so long as it's not a big town. She stubs out her cigarette, loads herself up with all their stuff again and wheels Oscar back out on to the platform. 'C'mon, we're getting on another train.' Tiredness has pushed her into the shortcut of bald statements now. There's no playing, no shall we shan't we. She drags everything to the nearest carriage door and hurls it inside the train. A guard is walking the length of the platform, slamming doors, coming closer, as she hauls herself and Oscar in and sinks gratefully to the floor.

6

Hannah's first thought after Evan died had been to sell up the B & B. To retrace her steps and go back home to London. But reflection warned her she had been away for too long. London might not welcome her home after so many years away. The city had a strong hold on those who lived there; by God, she knew that. It was like quicksand. But it was a fickle place which, once rejected, could maintain a healthy grudge that might easily outlive a person. Her presence there had been erased, forgotten, her trace of footprints washed away by successive tides. Other people had taken her place. She was getting on for seventy and London was not an old person's place. Besides which, she had got used to the more stately pace of things up here, had grown accustomed to the space, the broad, clean planes of colour when she looked out of her windows at the sea and the sky. In London, she would have nowhere to breathe freely, nowhere to walk without having to stop every ten paces and wait for traffic to let her pass. Even the language feels familiar now, not like it did at the start. The strange cadences, the lilting swing of Welsh voices, had felt so wrong when she first arrived from London. Now, she greets the green-grocer, the girl in the bakery, the butcher's delivery boy, with a confident '*Bore da*,' and takes her purchases away with a '*Diolch*, let's hope the weather improves, now?' She can detect the hint of an accent there in her own voice, a slight lift at the ends of her sentences, where it has matched itself to the surrounding timbres over the years, echoing what she hears, following the steeply slanting contours of the hills which encircle the town. In London she would stand out; she would be a foreigner.

But there were problems with staying, too. Even before Evan died, something had started to happen. Gradually, year by year, bookings during the busy holiday periods had begun to slow down. It wasn't too noticeable at first. Just an empty room here and there which meant that the vacancies board was never still, always being flipped over in the window as people came and went and rooms were filled and vacated.

Eventually, though, even Evan couldn't ignore what was happening, although he had stifled any attempt of Hannah's to express her concerns for as long as he could. They were experiencing a low period, he at last conceded, but instead of doing anything about it, 'The tide will turn' became one of his favourite phrases. 'The tide will turn and they will all come running back; we just have to weather these lean times.'

It made Hannah worried. In the past, when they were solidly booked every Easter week and throughout the long expanse of July and August, she had thrived on the industry it took to keep everything going. Evan was still working at a firm over in

49

Llandudno then, and the hotel was left entirely in her hands. She didn't have a spare moment in the day which wasn't taken up with cooking, changing bed sheets, dusting dressing tables and airing rooms ready for new guests. Every morning she would be up at six to do the breakfasts and she didn't stop until almost ten o'clock in the evening, after she and Evan had eaten their meal together at the kitchen table and she had cleared away the dishes and washed up. It was exhausting work but she was happiest this way, burning away like a combustion engine, feeding off her own fire and then extinguishing herself utterly when she finally came to a halt and slid into bed, too tired to think of anything at all.

She liked it best when children came to stay and the place was filled with their bright, singing voices. In the hustle and bustle of the brief crossing of their lives and hers she had spent the most fulfilled times of her life, watching them as they played Ludo and Snakes and Ladders in the guests' lounge when the weather was bad, smiling sympathetically at mothers who had come on holiday hoping for a bit of peace and quiet but found none. Sometimes, gratefully, they left Hannah in charge of their little ones whilst they went upstairs for a bath and a change of clothes. Hannah was a willing participant in their children's games, allowing herself to be prodded and poked and climbed over, kneeling on the floor with them to play tiddlywinks and clock patience. But time after time, the weeks would draw to a close, parents would pack belongings back into suitcases, line them up in the hallway and it would be time for them to return home. Evan always seemed glad they were leaving.

When the flow of guests began to dry up, Hannah had wondered out loud whether they shouldn't update the place a bit. She had been looking in brochures, and most small hotels just did Bed and Breakfast nowadays. Guests didn't want full board any more. Dining out at restaurants was more the thing. And all the places in magazines had ensuite bathrooms and TVs in the bedrooms. Could they afford something like that, she had asked Evan, anxious to woo the dwindling numbers back again. She feared the expanses of idle time their absence created. But Evan insisted that for a certain sort of guest (and she knew that by this he meant the child-free elderly couples he favoured) dinners must be provided, the communal bathrooms on every floor were perfectly adequate and television sets in hotel rooms were an unnecessary indulgence – the guests were supposed to be on holiday, after all, and they could watch TV in the lounge if they absolutely had to: it was provided for their use. Hannah hadn't dared to say that nowadays TVs had remote controls and that the old Baird set in the corner of the lounge wasn't exactly inviting to children. That, surely, was the point, as far as Evan was concerned. To keep little meddling fingers and unruly manners well out of the way.

Still, his wilful blindness to the need for modernisation didn't stop him coming home angry from his walks in the hills each time holidaymakers, rustling along in bright waterproofs carrying maps, asked him directions to the stone circle or the Jubilee Path. Why were they not coming to stay at *Swn Y Don*, he demanded, and Hannah could only shrug and shake her head.

She saw them too, on the beach, kicking footballs around; and on the promenade sitting side by side on benches eating sandwiches and scowling at the sea. She took to walking herself in the afternoons, since there was less work to do, and she sat on the promenade too, watching little boys on bikes with stabilisers, little girls on roller skates, and felt sad that none of them would be returning to her dining room for their dinner but would be spending their evenings elsewhere.

୭

So when Evan died she didn't sell up and go back to London. The day after the cremation, she started packing everything he had owned into cardboard boxes. She opened the wardrobe and lifted out his shirts and suits and packed them up, hangers and all. She paired up shoes and boots, removed pictures of locomotives from the stairwell and sifted through the bookcases for the pristine-spined volumes he had read carefully night after night of their married life, propped upright in the bed beside her. His smoking apparatus – the pipes and pipestand, the tobacco and pipe cleaners – she tipped straight into the bin because she had always found them a revolting habit and couldn't face the thought of cleaning them. Finally, she dug out some crumpled tissue paper saved from innumerable Christmasses and separately wrapped each of the Toby jugs he had inherited from his parents and made room for them in one of the boxes.

She watched as volunteers from the charity shop carried the

boxes out one by one and loaded them into the back of their car. Within a week there was nothing of Evan that remained. She spread out her clothes to fill the wardrobe rails and the chest of drawers, rearranged her books on the shelves and put her favourite vase where the Toby jugs had been ranged in ugly battalion for so long on the dining-room dresser. After the volunteers had driven away with their last carload, she closed the door and stood in the hallway, widowed but, for the first time in her life, alone and answerable to no one. Outside she could hear the wind. She bent over to drag the heavy draught excluder across the door and smiled to herself. As a special treat she was going to light the fire early and have a bacon and egg sandwich for supper. Well, why not? There was nobody else to please, now.

As winter gave way to spring and the crocuses in the front garden poked their first tentative leaves through the surface soil, the slow trickle of bookings for the Easter holiday began.

The first phonecall shocked her out of her elevenses one morning. She was taken by surprise. There hadn't been a guest since before Evan died and she had been rather enjoying the peace and quiet. She wasn't sure, afterwards, whether it was the shock that had made her lie, or the tone of the man's voice. What time was breakfast served until, he demanded, and was there a decent restaurant in the town? As if she knew. She hadn't been to a restaurant in years. When Evan was alive she would have replied nicely that there were a number of inexpensive restaurants in the town but that most guests found they preferred to eat in, as the price per night was inclusive of dinner. But this time she didn't feel like it. 'Oh,' she said. 'I'm afraid we're full that week.' And that was that. From then on, if she didn't like the sound of someone, she just said there were no vacancies.

7

Oscar won't stop grizzling. She has tried to feed him, tried rocking him to sleep, tried singing to him and pointing out the things passing by outside the window, but nothing has worked. The train isn't full, but there are a few people in the carriage and she can sense their irritation, can feel their annoyed glances in her direction. If only she could calm him. They are still miles away from Holyhead at the very tip of Anglesey, have gone past the seaside resorts of Rhyl and Prestatyn, and the hump-backed shape that sticks out from Llandudno is slowly receding. They are all places she remembers kids from her class going on holiday to when she was a child. She has never been to any of the places herself.

'Look, Oscar. The sea. Look.' She holds him up at the window for his first ever glimpse, but he turns his head away and starts to scream, kicking his legs into her thigh and punching his little fists so that they thump against the glass. She sits him in her lap again and tries to contain him, but there is nothing she can do when he is like this except put him in his buggy and push him along until he quietens down. The motion seems to pacify him, has an almost hypnotic effect, stopping tears almost instantaneously and surprising him into sudden tranquility.

OK, she thinks. If that's what you want. She puts him down on the seat beside her and clambers over him into the passageway, trying to ignore the sound of his screaming. She pulls their things down from the overhead rack and puts them ready by the doors before coming back for Oscar. The train shifts gear slightly and seems to be slowing. When the next station comes, they will get off, no matter where they are, and she will wheel him in his buggy until he stops howling.

The train eases itself into the station and squeezes its brakes with a long, low squeak. When it stops, she lifts everything down on to the platform and slams the door. She waits until the train pulls out of the station and slides away from them. It is their last link with London, she thinks. Now we're on our own.

She has always loved the seaside, could never get enough of it as a child, but was scarcely ever taken there by her parents, who seemed to disapprove of children having fun that was unadulterated with some other purpose. They had scowled at parents who let their children run around naked, splashing in the sea and building sandcastles which were obliterated within the hour by the incoming tide. Marina had watched them enviously through her fringe as she hunted for the seashells her father had pointed out to her in the *Discover the Seashore* book he had brought along specially. Well, her parents aren't here now. She and Oscar can do exactly as they please.

꙳

When Liam's mam died, his dad had run away, too. Maybe it's in the blood, he thinks grimly. But to write him a letter, after all these years. Why? He is as dead to Liam as his mother is; they both went away on the same day. Why should his dad choose to come back now and not his mam? When he was six there was very little difference between being in heaven and being in prison. From what his nana said, one was for very good people, and the other was for very bad people. That was one thing he had always known for sure: his dad was a very bad person.

He has been thinking about all this as he drives. Despite the distraction of the road, he can't keep the thoughts from coming back into his head and staying there. But the car has been acting strangely for a few miles, hiccoughing as if it is drunk, and then lurching into a series of long spasmodic shudders. He is on a narrow cliff road when it finally gives out – a deserted road, skirting round a bulging mountainside which seems to hang over the sea. He tries as hard as he can to keep going but when the car eventually stops shaking it is only to sigh gently into a stall and roll to a standstill in the middle of the road. He tries the ignition a few times but nothing happens. This time it is completely dead. He sits and listens to the silenced engine roaring in his ears. Now what? He has absolutely no idea where he is; he must have been driving for two hours, near enough. Maybe longer. He never bothered to check the petrol. Maybe it's run out. Fuck knows.

And now he is in the middle of nowhere, halfway up the side of a mountain. On his left a jagged granite massif rises upwards almost vertically, its grey surface slick with night frost that has melted in the weak sun. To his right, the tarmac edge of the road gives way to only a few feet of stony soil before the rock drops away steeply. Beyond it lies the sea, impassive and still. Miles of it.

After a moment or two, he clambers out of the car. There's no point sitting there any longer; it's gone as far as it's going. The air outside is colder, damper, full of the sea. He stands up and walks a few paces, shaking the cramped feeling from his legs. It is so quiet he winces at the amplified slam of the door, his trainers scuffing loudly, sending little stones bouncing across the road. He looks around, but the curve of the mountainside makes it impossible to see where he has come from or what lies ahead. Out at sea, its outline as distinct as if it had been drawn with a freshly sharpened pencil, an oil tanker sits on the horizon.

There is nothing to do but to keep going on foot. He zips his top up to the neck, pulls the hood over his head and buttons his jacket. He will have to leave the car where it is. It's in a dangerous place; anyone coming, from either direction, won't see it until they're almost on top of it, but there's nothing he can do; there's nowhere to wheel it off the road, other than over the edge, and Steve wouldn't be too impressed with that. Anyway, he hasn't seen a single car for ages, not for miles; it's like he is on a dead road. He gives the car a final, resentful glance and then walks quickly away.

As he rounds the corner, the arched mouth of a tunnel appears, straddling the thin ribbon of road as it swings outwards, following the contours of the rock. He hurries through, a second, echoing set of footsteps seeming to tap against the walls in unison with his own.

Out the other side, he can see a town ahead. Row after row of grey slate roofs hunkering down in the shadow of the hills that crowd around, almost pushing them into the sea. He can see a few curls of smoke rising in wisps from one or two chimneys, but other than that, the place seems absolutely still. It doesn't look too far away, though. He could walk there at least. Try to figure out where he is and what to do. He pushes his hands into his jeans pockets, feeling their cold against his legs through the thin material, and keeps walking.

ᕉ

When he reaches the fringes of the place he sees a sign and goes to look at it, but the long word printed on it means nothing to him. He can't even begin to unravel it. He guesses he must be in Wales, although he doesn't know for sure. He has never been to Wales before, although he has seen it on clear days from Liverpool and knows it isn't too far away. A distant outline of grey bumps from certain high vantage points. He once spent the night with a girl who was from there. She lived in a high-rise in Birkenhead and pointed the hills out to him from her bedroom window. Long words and hills, and that one drink-fuelled night: that's all he knows about Wales. It's not much.

He shudders. It's too cold to hang around out of doors. Even the town seems to turn its back on the sea and huddle into itself for warmth. What he needs is a pub where he can get a few beers down him. That'll warm him up.

When he sees one down a side street he pushes gratefully at the door and the welcome fug of cigarette smoke and low voices snakes out through the gap and wraps itself round him, winding its warmth and comfort round his frozen arms and legs, drawing him inside.

He walks up to the bar where a few old men stand in a huddle with their backs to him. Their voices are gruff, roughened by decades of smoking and drinking, the same as old men in Liverpool, but the strangely tilting way they speak, as if half of their words are on a slant, makes them seem softer, younger, more like women's voices.

Liam digs his hand into his pocket for some change. 'I'll have a lager, please, mate,' he says to the barman, who doesn't seem to have noticed him standing there. The heads at the bar swivel round as one to face him as if waiting for him to say something more.

'All right.' He nods at them. They blink. One of them half clears his throat and half returns the greeting and then turns back to his friends and gradually, guardedly, the buzz of their conversation rebuilds itself. In one corner, on a TV fixed up by the ceiling, a try is scored in a rugby match and the barman flicks his tea towel jubilantly and exchanges a few words with them.

'Er, I'll have a pint when you've got a minute there, mate,' Liam says again. He rests his elbow on the bar and glances up at the screen.

'Follow the rugby, do you?' The barman looks pointedly at him as the angled pint glass he is holding under the beer tap slowly fills.

'Er, no. No, not really.' Liam looks at the change in his hand, less of it than he thought he had, and sifts out the coppers which he puts back in his pocket. 'I prefer the footie.'

The barman doesn't answer. Liam hands over his money and takes a few deep mouthfuls from the top of the pint. The place is emptier than it seemed. There are a couple more blokes watching the telly, their chairs pulled out from the table so that they sit side by side, arms folded, their legs splaying out in front. Liam sits a few tables away from them, where he can still see the telly. He takes another few gulps from the pint and it's almost half gone. He's going to need another one.

ॐ

Now he's got some beer inside him and has relaxed a bit, the stuff that was bothering him in the car snatches its chance and starts up in his head again.

He hasn't heard from his dad in all these years. Why has he made contact now? When he first went to prison his nana said he wouldn't be let out until Liam himself was a grown man. And that would be too soon. As far as she was concerned, prison was too good for the likes of Jim Kelleher.

He remembers his dad much less well than he remembers his mam. When he closes his eyes he can still see her as clearly as if he last saw her yesterday. Her pale, lightly freckled skin; her long, straight hair, dark brown and shiny as a conker, and the fringe in a dead straight line across her forehead. He had thought she was so beautiful. Long-haired people were always beautiful in his child's understanding: you couldn't have one without the other. That was why all the girls in his class were growing theirs. They wanted to be air stewardesses and for that you had to be beautiful.

His dad, on the other hand . . . Most of the time he was in the betting shop or the pub. He didn't have a job like his mam did, but he never looked after Liam even so. When his mam was at work and there was no school, Liam went to his nana's and he had his tea there. His mam picked him up on her way home.

He was a big man, he can remember that much: broad-shouldered with thick, freckled arms – the freckles so numerous and large that they overlapped each other – and reddish-fair hair, not like Liam and his mam. This had pleased his nana: that Liam looked so much more like Bernadette. It meant he had less of his dad's bad blood, wouldn't go the same way. Liam remembers seeing his picture in the *Echo*, and on *Look North* after the trial. That photograph, in grainy black and white, has stuck better than any flesh-and-blood memories. And it had made him cock of the school for nearly a whole week, his dad being on the telly at teatime. Even if it was because he'd killed his mam. There was a kind of glory to it.

And now he has written him a letter. This man he scarcely remembers. He has sat down with a pen and a blank piece of paper and written a letter to his son. Well, it's more than Liam could do.

He wanders back to the bar and orders another pint. 'Listen, mate,' he says to the barman when he carries it over. 'I'm starving. There's no chance of us getting something to eat in here, is there?'

'Don't do food here, I'm afraid, young man.'

'Ah, go on. Just a sarnie. I'll pay you for it.'

'Like I say. We don't do food here. Now don't you go starting any trouble.'

'All right, keep yer hair on. I was only asking!'

'And the answer's no. I think you'd better just drink up and clear off, lad. My customers don't come in here for trouble.'

'Neither did I. I just come in for a drink, that's all. I'm not starting nothing!' Liam can feel irritation ballooning in his chest. He's hasn't done anything wrong.

'Well, I suggest you drink it up quick and bugger off.'

Liam takes a deep breath. He can feel his hands curling into fists. 'Fine. Fine. I'm going. I can see when I'm not wanted.' He stays where he is, his anger temporarily immobilising him, and drinks the whole pint down in one go. Some of it overflows the rim and runs down his chin but he keeps going; he isn't going to leave until he's drunk every last drop. He slams the empty glass down on the bar and walks out wiping his chin with his sleeve. 'Fucking wanker,' he mutters. He pushes through the door as noisily as he can and lets it swing shut behind him.

ಲಾ

Evan Thomas walked into Hannah's life when she was a few months off her seventeenth birthday.

63

He was a tall, thin man, not yet thirty, although his hairline was already well receded and he was thinning at the crown. His manner, too, made him appear older than he was; he had a certain air of deference towards women which smelt false to the other two office girls Hannah worked with. They didn't say so out loud to her, but she overheard them talking about him once. It seemed to go down all right with other men, though. All the solicitors in the firm seemed to think very highly of him.

She had been working as a clerk in her uncle's firm for just over a year when he first appeared, taking up a vacant accountant's post for a couple of days a week. The other three days he did a similar thing elsewhere.

His interest in her seemed to be sparked almost immediately, but she didn't take it seriously at first. She simply assumed he looked at the other girls the same way he looked at her and put it out of her mind. Still, she preferred the days he wasn't at the office and she didn't have to be reminded of things she would rather put out of her mind. She couldn't relax, somehow, when she knew he was around, even if he didn't intend to cause her any trouble.

He took her completely by surprise one evening on a day he wasn't even meant to be there, appearing so abruptly from a doorway which let on to the stairs that she gasped and put her hand to her mouth. She was in a hurry to get home, but Evan Thomas seemed oblivious to her anxiety to be gone and, standing so that he blocked her way, he asked if he might have a private word with her. Since she couldn't get past him, she stayed where she was and nodded meekly, her stomach plunging violently.

What kind of private word? Surely there were only two sorts, and she never had any dealings with him professionally so it couldn't be to do with her work. Besides, judging by how he was standing so uneasily on the stair below her, it was the other kind of word he meant to have with her now.

She stared at her feet and waited for him to say his piece, dreading what was coming.

He invited her to the cinema.

She accepted automatically – it never occurred to her to do otherwise. He appeared to be satisfied and stepped aside to let her pass before following her down the stairs at a trot.

'So, I'll pick you up from your house, shall I?' he said, catching her up at the street door.

'Oh, yes, of course.' She stuffed her arm inside her coat sleeve and told him her address. She didn't want him to know where she lived, didn't want him to know anything at all about her, but she hadn't the energy to say no, nor the right words to shape into a refusal. He held the door open as she fastened up her buttons and picked up her bag. He watched her intently, his eyes everywhere at once. She thanked him for holding the door and ran down the steps and away.

❧

When she got home she was appalled. Why on earth had that yes pushed itself so willingly through her lips? Later, she lay in bed trying to think how she could stop him arriving the next evening to pick her up, but she had no idea where he lived, nor what his telephone number was. And even if she did know it, she wouldn't know what to say. She had no choice: she didn't want to spend the evening with Evan Thomas but she was going to have to endure it.

She made her announcement that evening over the dinner table in a voice that betrayed nothing. Her father's stony silence as she explained who Evan Thomas was and how she knew him was cut short by his curt bark of a cough when she had finished speaking. She noticed her mother's empty fork hovering in mid-air, as if she were waiting for a judge's verdict. The meal continued with just the sounds of knives and forks scraping against china until her older sister, Celia, looked sideways at her father and then began chattering about something or other, Hannah didn't hear what. She scarcely ate anything on her plate. After dinner, a low murmur from her father's study suggested that he was speaking on the telephone. Celia and Hannah dealt with the dishes in the kitchen and Celia elbowed her gently in the ribs.

'Cheer up, darling. He'll let you go, you know.'

'I know,' Hannah said weakly.

For several hours, until she fell into an exhausted, troubled sleep, she lay in bed ricocheting between two horrors – the date itself and the possibility that Evan Thomas might want to repeat the experience and make it something more serious. She knew where that would lead, and there was nothing she wished for less. She must have been sighing and tossing about under the covers because eventually Celia sat up in bed and put her light on.

'Come on, Hannah. You've been miserable all evening. It'll be all right, you know. He won't be able to tell, if that's what you're worried about.'

Hannah shook her head slowly and sighed deeply. That hadn't even occurred to her. Celia climbed out of her own bed and tiptoed across the room to get in with Hannah. She put her arms round her sister and Hannah felt them, tight and comforting, around her middle.

'You've got to get on with your life, you know. In the end.' She kissed the hair at the back of Hannah's head and squeezed her hard. Hannah felt herself relax a little, as if her older sister were squeezing out some of her sadness.

'So, what's he like, then, your Evan?' she asked at last. 'I'm dying to know. Is he delicious?'

Hannah couldn't help herself. It was the way she said it – *your* Evan – as if he were already a part of her. It made her shudder. She started crying and the more Celia tried to comfort her the more she cried, until her face ached and felt puffed up and ugly. When Celia eventually fell asleep she kept as still as she could so that she wouldn't wake her up.

ଛ

The next evening Celia fussed round as Hannah slowly got herself ready.

'You can't wear that,' she said. 'It's an office blouse. You need something pretty. Here.' She dug inside the wardrobe and pulled out a couple of blouses Hannah had occasionally seen her come home in after an evening out. Celia was crafty; she went out on

67

dates all the time, but she always made it seem as if she was going out with a group of girls. If he suspected, their father never did anything about it. Celia had always been fearless and maybe he knew he could never control her like he could Hannah and their mother so he didn't try.

A faint smell of scent and cigarettes still hung in the weave of the fabric. Hannah fingered the silky material and looked blankly at her sister.

'Oh, come on. Buck up, Hannah. It's meant to be fun, you know! You just need to look pretty and relax and you'll have a whale of a time.' Hannah knew Celia tried her best to understand, but she found it difficult. How could she not? Hannah refused to talk about anything; she just closed herself up and Celia hadn't the skill or the patience to coax her out again. She knew her sister cared deeply for her, knew how strong the instinct to protect her was, but she had almost given up trying. For her, life was so much more simple. Hannah could remember when things had been simple for her too, and she and Celia had been much closer, real pals, always laughing together and sharing their secrets. Celia had always been the passionate one, wincing at the way their father spoke to their mother, bursting into the bedroom red-eyed and furious when their mother begged her not to challenge him. She was always as quick to tears as she was to laughter, and she seemed to provoke their father deliberately, sometimes, because she didn't seem able to contain what she felt about things, and Hannah had always been there for her, more even-tempered and patient, calming her and listening to her fiery outpourings every time she erupted. Since Hannah's illness, though, Celia had lost her little ally.

Hannah knew her sister was taking such an interest now for her sake. A date was something to be encouraged; it was a normal, healthy activity, and if Hannah was to be drawn out of herself, this was a way that Celia understood.

Her entire upper body disappeared inside the wardrobe again and she lifted something out on a hanger. 'Here we are. This is pretty. It must still fit you, surely. I can't remember the last time you wore it. Put it on and let's have a look.' She was holding out a white summer dress with a pattern of tiny red poppies dotted all over it like spots of fresh blood. Hannah had made the dress herself when she was still at school. It was pretty, with a plain bodice and a full skirt which she had made fuller with stiffly starched petticoats. It was the first really good dress she had had and when it was finished she had been justly proud of it and had stood in front of the mirror smiling rather shyly at the young woman she was becoming.

Hannah knew exactly how long it was since she had worn the dress: one year and five months ago she had worn it on a trip to Epping Forest. As her sister dangled it in front of her the room seemed to fill with stone and she sank down on to the edge of her bed, a screen of red dropping in front of her eyes, cutting her away from herself. Celia rushed to her side and wrapped her arms round her.

'Oh, don't be so unhappy, Hannah. You do deserve to have some fun, you know.' She rocked her in her arms, squeezing hard. Hannah sat within her tight embrace, momentarily protected like a wizened nut in a shell, feeling nothing.

In the end she wore her office skirt with one of Celia's blouses.

And at the end of the evening, just as she had feared, Evan walked her home and asked if he could take her out again. She was trapped. Because she hadn't been able to refuse the first time, now she couldn't refuse without giving offence. He would think he had done something wrong. And people, her father, might want to know why, what was wrong with him? Why had she said yes and then said no? Why so particular all of a sudden when she was in no position to be so? And the girls at work might call her cheap, leading him on and then dropping him like that. Running hot and cold. With him working at the office, too, so she couldn't escape from him, it was just easier to say yes.

When she got home she ran a bath even though it was past ten o'clock and the hot water had long been used up. She washed in an inch of barely warm water, needing to wash the evening and the lingering presence of Evan Thomas away before she went to bed.

8

The guests' lounge is a sea of chairs and sofas all of which have seen better days. They sit empty, their flattened velvet pile and collapsed seats whispering of past, more occupied times. A sofa covered with a once bold Liberty pattern of enormous blue hydrangeas sags wanly, its cushions frayed and patched. The worn arms wear differently patterned covers as if they were slings, covering the bald spots. In the window sit two armchairs, faded by the sun, their stuffing slowly dropping, in horsehair clumps, on to the pale green carpet beneath them. The nests of tables have not been unnested for years; they sit, carefully stowed, on either side of the fireplace. In the grate the brass tongs set stands rigidly to attention and the coal scuttle sits empty as the wind buffets and ricochets inside the chimney, sending the occasional huff of air into the silent room and the faint smell of coal dust. It is all too old and tired, Hannah thinks. No wonder nobody wants to come here any more. There are places in Llandudno that have their own gymnasiums and swimming pools. People expect that sort of thing nowadays. They want something modern.

She walks to the window and looks out at Conwy Bay. The

tide is out and the sands are deserted apart from a pair of tiny silhouetted figures with scissoring legs. The familiar coast curves round towards Llandudno and the rocky Great Orme and she follows the line of cables marking the route of the funicular tramway up to the top. Slowly, she scans across the horizon until she reaches Puffin Island and the stretch of Anglesey that she knows is Beaumaris. She has been there, and from the seafront has looked back at her own stretch of coast, seeing it as a stranger might see it, with its backdrop of scarred and quarried hills. It seems strange to her, now, how much she had hated this place, with its strange-sounding names, when Evan first brought her here. She knows the view of the bay from the windows as intimately as she knows her own face. And the hills behind the town, the steep climb up to the moors and the Druid's Circle. She used to climb up there in the wind and rain when she was young and breathe in the sense of freedom.

So did Evan. He was a great walker. Never together, though. Not once in all the time they were married. She turns back to face the room with a shudder. It is two years to the day since Evan disappeared up there. He was fit for seventy-seven. Light but wiry. He could still make it up and down in just over an hour and be home in time for an early lunch.

She had lunched alone that day, wondering what was keeping him, but not worried as she munched her cheese and crackers. Periodically during the afternoon she glanced at her watch and then looked at the heavy sky. At about four o'clock a heavy fog came swirling in and the tops of the hills disappeared from view. She rang Billy, who ran the pub Evan sometimes stopped off in

72

after his walks, but he hadn't seen him. When it started to go dark, he knocked and said he was going out to look for him. A couple of regulars at the pub stood slightly behind him, one at each shoulder. They nodded at her when she said hello. They were all wearing woollen hats and held powerful torches in their gloved hands. It was easy to get lost in a fog, they said, when it swung in like this from nowhere. 'Spins your compass out of true, it does,' one of them said. 'Clogs up your sense of direction. We'll have him fetched down in no time, see, Mrs Thomas. Don't you worry.'

They did find him, discombobulated and hypothermic, wandering hatless on the moor near the Druids' Circle in search of his wind-claimed cap. It took him nearly a fortnight to die of the pneumonia his adventure rewarded him with.

ॐ

Having an official boyfriend meant that every Friday evening she had to sit in a coffee shop with Evan until it was time to go and join the cinema queue. She enjoyed the coffee, and, once they were in the cinema, she gratefully lost herself in the film, but the interlude between the end of work and the dimming of the auditorium lights was excruciatingly long and she couldn't bear the inactivity, the sitting there doing nothing with someone she had so little interest in.

Evan found it most rewarding to talk to her about his work, and she sat politely as he detailed the vagaries of small-business finance, her head angled slightly to one side. She preferred to sit facing the front of the shop, because that way she could see the rest of the coffee shop and could watch the passers-by through the window. After a few weeks she started recognising people: other couples idling away a spare hour before the cinema, chatting about work and friends; groups of girls who reminded her of Celia – high-spirited and independent – passing round rouge and lipstick; hollow-cheeked young men in carelessly belted, slightly shabby gaberdines, who sat alone drinking their coffee black and sugarless. They were the most interesting and she would stare at them intently, wondering about their lives as Evan's long-winded explanations spooled out, barely grazing her awareness.

They saw a film every week. Hannah didn't care what; she let Evan choose. Sometimes he chose what he himself preferred; sometimes, indulgently, he selected a film he thought she might like. Regardless of what it was, Hannah immersed herself gladly in each new world which unfurled itself in front of her eyes, grateful for the release it offered from her own life. Sometimes, she all but forgot Evan was there and her heart sank when the film ended and she was dragged out blinking on to Tottenham Court Road, dodging out of the way of taxicabs as they sheared through the enormous rain puddles in the gutter which had collected as she sat in the flickering darkness. She watched *Singin' in the Rain* and *The Importance of Being Ernest*. *High Noon* and *Ivanhoe*. She saw Elizabeth Taylor, Gregory Peck, Ava Gardner, Deborah Kerr, Burt Lancaster. Winter turned into summer and then back into winter. She saw the brutalised face of a gangster's moll, after Lee Marvin had thrown scalding coffee over her in *The Big Heat* and shuddered inwardly. She saw tiny human beings achieve the impossible and reach the summit of Mount Everest. She watched aliens threaten to take over the world and then succumb to the common cold, although, as they filed out of their seats when *The War of the Worlds* was over, Evan pronounced the film ridiculous and a waste of the five shillings he had spent on the tickets.

∽

One Saturday morning, he arrived before eleven o'clock. It was a week before her eighteenth birthday and he had arranged to take her out for lunch. He was supposed to be arriving at twelve and she was still soaking in the bath with a sprinkling of Celia's lavender bath salts when the doorbell rang. Celia made her unbolt the door and she sidled in and sat on the linen basket. She waited until Hannah had stepped back into the bath and resubmerged herself.

'Evan's downstairs talking to Father,' she said.

Hannah straightened her legs and pushed herself upright, her shoulders and arms shooting up out of the water, slopping some over the side of the bath in a foam-flecked arc which splattered against the tiles. 'What for? Why's he here so early?'

'Mind out.' Celia dragged the mat closer to the bath with the toes of her outstretched foot to soak up the splashed water. 'He's probably asking for permission to marry you,' she said, in a matter-of-fact voice.

∽

He took her to the Regent Palace Hotel.

'Don't look so worried,' he said. 'We're grand enough,' and

he crooked his arm at her so that she had no choice but to link her own into it and walk through the vestibule into the hotel arm-in-arm with him. He led her into a vast area flooded with milky light and sat her in a leather armchair to wait while he went to the reception desk. She stared up at the enormous leaded dome-light in the ceiling, wishing she could defy gravity and solidity and rise up into the air and somehow move through the glass and fly far away. Instead, she felt the heaviness of the structure, the weight of the lead and the glass suspended over her head.

Evan was in a frivolous mood that made her feel uneasy, and he suggested they have a drink at the bar before eating. She perched on a too-high stool sipping the sherry he had ordered for her. Celia's words were still echoing in her mind and, when they sat down at their table and ordered, she could hardly eat a thing for worrying. He chose for her, and it seemed to annoy him slightly that she scarcely touched what he had selected. He asked her more than once whether anything was wrong, in the kind of voice that didn't invite an honest reply.

'I'm fine, quite all right, really. Just a little overawed by all this,' she said, lifting her hand limply from her lap to indicate their plush surroundings. He smiled indulgently then, and she noticed with a plunge of her stomach how his canine teeth poked over his lower lip, giving him a wolfish, slavering look.

The Louis XVI dining room held its light dusting of lunchtime diners in a kind of muffled suspension. The few people dotted around the vast room made hardly a sound, and what little murmured conversation there was got tangled in the low-hanging

76

chandeliers and absorbed into the carpet, the geometric pattern of which spread out dizzyingly in all directions. At the far end, a jazz trio played soothing music, but that, too, seemed to be drunk in by the thirsty furnishings so that Hannah could hardly hear anything but the low thunk thunk of the double bass's resonant strings. The air stood thick and porridgy around her. Evan insisted on pouring her another glass of wine after their plates had been taken away and he seemed to be working up to something. Hannah hastily excused herself and half rose from her chair. As if summoned, a waiter came running to assist, but Evan waved him away. He had reached his moment and there was no escaping it. He looked at Hannah peculiarly and she sank back down on to her seat, dreading what was coming. He drew something from his pocket and held it in his closed fist on the table in front of him. Then he cleared his throat.

His words washed over her and she fixed her stare on the table she could see just beyond his left shoulder. The way the cloth was so carefully draped, its pristine edge turned into waves, folding in on themselves and back again, like the waves in the sea, like marble cake, like . . . She felt sick.

'Hannah?'

'Hmm? Oh . . .' He was waiting for her to speak. 'Oh, I'm sorry. What did you say?'

He smiled and reached across the table to cover her hand with his. It felt clammy and hot. She wanted to pull hers away but she let it stay there.

'Darling,' he began, and the word didn't seem to fit his mouth properly. It spilt out and made his face look messy and wrong, so that she had to look away, embarrassed. He repeated what he had said and she tried to concentrate this time. Her head was swimming with the wine she had drunk but she focused on the stem of the glass in front of her. 'Darling. Hannah. Will you do me the honour of becoming my wife?'

She stared at the wine glass, noticing how the stem flared out gradually and then suddenly melded into the upended bell shape that held the wine he had poured for her, waiting for her to pluck the glass between her fingers like a poppy and raise it to her lips. The jazz band finished their number and after a few moments they eased themselves into something with a more up-tempo beat. The music drifted across to her as if it were crossing the vastness of a desert. She moved her hand, still trapped underneath his, and he took this as a signal to clasp it more tightly.

'Hannah?'

She gulped a lungful of air and made herself look at him. 'I'm sorry,' she said, as firmly and loudly as she could. 'I need to excuse myself.' She pulled her hand away, and squeezed awkwardly out of her imprisoning seat, dragging the tablecloth a little in her haste and spilling her wine. She was halfway across the room by the time the waiter reached the table and attempted to clear up the mess with a napkin.

ॐ

He banged her head three times against the wall, as if to emphasise the last three words as they hissed through his teeth. 'You will *marry – this – man.*' She could feel flecks of spittle land on her face as she breathed her father's whisky breath. She couldn't see round the edges of his face, couldn't see the walls of his study beyond it. He was still speaking, and she could feel the sting in her scalp where his fingers were pulling her hair tight. She lost count of the bumps against the wall. Each one hurt less, seemed just to fill her head with a swimmy vagueness which made her feel almost happy. A few stray words reached her through the fug: 'supercilious . . . count yourself lucky . . . will not shame this house again . . .' And then it was over. Her scalp burned as he released it. Automatically, she straightened her blouse and tucked it into her waistband where it had come loose. Her head was singing now, buzzing madly, freely. She heard his voice tell her to go to her room and she fumbled with the doorknob. Her outstretched hand was dancing like a firefly; she couldn't keep it still. Maybe it wasn't her hand at all. She turned to see if there was someone else behind her who it might belong to, but there was only her father, standing on the red rug, watching her.

She climbed into bed fully clothed, without removing even her shoes. Time seemed to have stopped dead. The late afternoon sun was shining through the pattern in the heavy lace curtains, throwing dusty beams of sunlight across the room. Dizzy, when she looked at them she saw bright white bars, caging her in. She watched the thousands of airborne swirlings of dust swimming around in each one and listened to the changing sounds in her head. The singing became a surging which pulsed with each heartbeat, gradually quietening to a breeze rustling through long grasses as she lay on her back looking up at the sky through the branches of a tree in summertime.

She didn't think she had slept, but she came to suddenly, lying on her side facing the wall. Her head was aching terribly. She rolled on to her back and the sudden pain as her head moved against the pillow made her suck in her breath and sit up, disorientated. Tentatively she reached round to the back of her head and touched it. It felt the same: her hair was still there at any rate. She moved her legs one at a time, placing her feet side by side on the floor, and stared at her shoes. She remembered what had happened now and she needed reassurance, needed to see herself before she grew too scared to look. Shaking a little, she sat at the dressing table and pulled at the hinged sections on either side of the mirror, readjusting the angle until she could see her back view. Her hair was in a mess, but there was no blood, nothing noticeable.

She shrank back on to the bed and lay there listening. She wondered where everyone had gone; there were no voices carrying from downstairs and the street outside was as silent as if it was the middle of the night.

ॐ

Reading has never been Liam's strong point. When he was at school, he just didn't get it. He was fine with the theory: he saw that the alphabet was made up of different letters, and that these letters could be put together into different configurations to make words, but after that he got lost. He could spell the words out, letter by letter, but he couldn't run the letters together and blur them into a word. It just wouldn't come, no matter how many times the teacher said *c-a-t cat* and *h-a-t hat*. When he tried to picture the words in his head he could only see the objects themselves, the skinny marmalade cat with the manky eye that lived in the flat downstairs, and the hat his nana wore for church.

He couldn't even recite the alphabet in the proper order. Round and round the class they would go – A B C D E F G H – and when it came to him the snake of letters would stop dead. The teacher would glare at him and the rest of the class would hold their breath. The teacher would ask him 'What comes after *Haich*, Liam? Eee Eff Gee *Haich* . . . What's the next letter?' The more he needed to know, the further away from him the right letter spun, and he would shout out anything, grasping at the letters that came within reach and cramming them into his mouth so that he could spit out their sounds, hoping against hope that they were the right ones.

In the end he just sat at the back with the other divvies and kept quiet. Every time one of them got something wrong, the kids in front would turn round mouthing 'mong', and sticking their tongues into their bottom lips to make divvy faces at them, but he didn't care. The teacher didn't bother so much with the thick kids so he didn't have to waste his time trying any more.

ॐ

He wonders whether, if he could read better, he would have opened his letter by now. He isn't sure. All his life, his dad has been the big baddie, the one that killed his mother for no reason.

81

Because he was drunk, because he was angry, because he was out of work, because he was so bloody useless he was just one big waste of space. Who knows why he did it? His nana had never asked questions like that, and why should she? He had killed her one and only child, her pride and joy, and that made him a monster. For his nana, it was as simple as that.

He wanders towards the seafront. As the expanse of beach opens up before him he starts to remember things that don't fit. Things he never mentioned to his nana. One of his earliest memories is of going on the train to Formby with his mam and dad. It wasn't far. When they got there his dad bought him an orange football and they kicked it to each other on the sand and then his dad lifted him over his head as if he was as light as a feather and sat him on his shoulders and he had never been so high up in his whole life. He had hold of both Liam's legs with one hand and he had the other arm round his mam. She was so close, Liam could reach out and touch the top of her head, on the little line right down the middle where all her hair seemed to grow from. It just doesn't fit, this memory; it troubles him. He wishes he could forget about it.

ை

It is the baby she notices first, because of the pushchair, parked just inside the shelter but visible from further down the promenade. It is one of the modern folding kind everyone has nowadays, with chunky wheels and a rain hood, and a kind of hammock slung underneath the seat for bags and paraphernalia.

As she walks closer, the unmistakeable shape of a baby, well wrapped up against the weather, comes into view. Hannah slows her pace.

There is a girl, too, hunched at the far end of the bench, leaning her head against the wooden side of the shelter, fast asleep. Lined up beside her on the bench are two or three bulging bags, the sort Hannah associates with launderettes and poverty.

Curious, she slows her pace. The child is quiet. He is probably asleep like his mother. She thinks 'he' even though she can't really tell from where she is. The girl has pulled the pushchair in as close to herself as she can, and, although she is asleep, her foot is hooked around one of the front wheels.

As Hannah draws level with the shelter she stops and deliberates. It wouldn't be wrong, would it, to sit down at the other end of the bench, just for a moment or two? Now she thinks about it, she is feeling a little breathless and could probably do with a rest. She hovers for a moment, unsure what to do – she doesn't want to startle them – and then she decides, walks quickly to the bench before she changes her mind, and lowers herself on to the seat.

Yes, it is a little boy, she is sure of it. Now she is sitting on the bench, the sleeping child is almost facing her and she can see cowlicks of butter-coloured hair curling from under a little red hood. His head is drooping over on to one shoulder, and the straps that hold him in place seem to crisscross his body like so much parcel tape. On each of his hands is a tiny mitten and on his feet he has little shoes with velcro straps. Oh, he looks angelic, so small and helpless and perfect. Hannah pulls off one of her gloves and rummages in her handbag for a tissue.

83

She turns and glances again at the girl. She looks young still, but not too young. Not a teenage mother. Nevertheless, there is something of the runaway about her, what with the bags and her fast asleep out here in the cold. She looks away; it feels too intrusive to stare at another adult for too long, and she turns to the baby again. He must be a year old, maybe more. In between babyhood and toddling. His cheeks are round and a little pink, maybe from being out in the cold, and Hannah imagines the chubby arms and legs, the little round tummy inside all his clothes.

She glances up the promenade. There is nobody around; it's too cold in January for most people. But there have been muggings, robberies, recently, and the two of them look so defenceless, both fast asleep like that. Hannah can't quite bring herself to get up and walk away. Who knows what could happen to the child while the girl is asleep? And yet the longer she sits here the more uncomfortable she feels, as if she is taking advantage, somehow.

The tide is coming in and she watches the scalloped edges of the front running waves slide gracefully closer, eating up the sand. Two gulls strut towards her on flat, yellow feet, their heads side on, eyeing her hopefully.

She is still in a whirl after her visit to Dr Mount. She had thought a brisk walk along the prom might help to calm her down. This second chance her life has handed her is so awash with possibilities she doesn't quite know what to do with herself and walking is the only way she knows of stopping everything crowding into her head at once.

As she goes over the moment in the doctor's surgery one more time, a teenager whizzes past on roller skates – not the old-fashioned, strap-on kind she used to play with, but bright-coloured ones with boots attached. The two gulls unfold their wings and rise, screaming, into the air. Hannah watches them as they wheel out over the water, dropping down low until they almost skim the grey surface, then lift upwards again on the wind currents.

The gulls' cries nudge against the slipping edge of Marina's sleep and, grudgingly, she wakes up. Although short, it was a deep sleep, and she comes to slowly, as if surfacing from the seabed, miles down. Her body is so saturated with the sea cold that she feels half-mermaid, her legs numbed into one useless, scaly trunk, her skin salty and wind-toughened, her hair coarsened and knotted up by the rough, briny tousling. She hunches forwards, unstraps Oscar and lifts him into her lap, rocking him as she tries to shake away the mixed feelings of abandonment – still buzzing through her body, intoxicating as firewater – and guilt at having left Oscar unguarded.

For a moment she doesn't notice that there is anyone there, but then, with a start, she sees someone sitting at the other end of the bench and automatically she wraps her arms more tightly around her child.

The woman offers her an apologetic smile. 'Sorry,' she says. 'I didn't mean to startle you. I—'

'It's OK,' Marina says. 'Don't worry about it.'

She stands Oscar on her knees and dances him up and down a few times to try to wake him up, but his legs dangle limply and he looks sleepy and cross and when she pulls him close and presses her face against his, she feels the cold in his cheeks. She shoots the old woman a quick, nervous glance, wishing she would go and sit somewhere else. She doesn't like the fact that she was sitting there while she was asleep. It feels creepy. It is only an old woman, but it could have been anyone.

'It's rather bracing, this afternoon, isn't it?' the old woman says. Marina would prefer not to get into a conversation, but she sounds friendly enough, and it's better than sitting there in silence.

Marina nods and shivers. She hugs Oscar again and cups one hand around his head. He has started to make the little bleary, grumbly noises that always come before tears. He never likes waking up. She looks sideways at the woman, wondering how long she has been watching them. She can't think of anything to say to her. She smiles awkwardly and starts feeling inside one of her many coat pockets.

The woman looks a little unsure of herself, and seems half inclined to get up and go, but then she changes her mind, turns back and speaks again.

'Have you travelled far today?' she asks.

'From London,' Marina says. She bounces Oscar on her lap. 'Hey, hey, hey,' she says in a falsely cheerful voice. 'Guess who's at the seaside?' She fumbles again in a different pocket and pulls out a dummy which she wipes on her sleeve and then puts in her own mouth before slipping it into Oscar's.

The woman watches her intently, almost hungrily, as she tries to soothe away his sleepy tears. 'Which part of London?' she asks when he is quieter. 'I used to live there.'

'Hackney,' she says. 'Shithole. Sorry.' She puts one hand to her cheek, half embarrassed at her lack of manners, half not caring. 'We were glad to get away, weren't we, mister?' She hides her embarrassment in Oscar, nuzzling his teary cheek as she speaks.

The woman smiles. 'It's a long time since I've been to London. I'm sure it's very different now. What brings you so far from home?'

For a moment Marina isn't sure what to say. She certainly can't tell her the whole truth, but the woman looks harmless enough. She is probably just being nosy. In the end she just says that they needed to get away, that things weren't going well, and leaves it at that. It gives nothing away and it's not like it isn't true. There is a slightly uncomfortable silence before the woman speaks again.

'Do you have anywhere to stay?'

Hannah says it on the spur of the moment. Suddenly there seems no good reason not to, and once the offer is made it hangs there in the air between them and she thinks well, why not? Why not offer a room free of charge if someone needs it? It's not as if there isn't one going spare. She rummages in her bag and pulls out one of the leaflets from Dr Mount's surgery and hurriedly scribbles her address on it. 'You don't have to decide now,' she says. 'Have a think about it. Here.'

The girl seems unsure, and Hannah feels a worried pang, like a warning that she has done something foolish, but it's too late now. She can't withdraw an offer once it's been made, so she hands over her address and leaves in a rush.

As she walks back up towards home she starts to panic. What

has she done? She knows nothing about this girl. She could be into all sorts of things. She could be on drugs, anything. Heaven knows, she can understand the need young people have to escape from their lives sometimes, but she is frightened by drugs, by the hold they maintain over people, by the things they make them do. What if this girl is addicted? What would she do, if she turned up and started taking drugs in her house? But then, that little boy. She remembers him, and smiles to herself, thinking what Evan's reaction would be if he were still alive. A non-paying guest? With a crying baby? What in heaven's name was she thinking of? Had she gone mad?

ೞ

The night before she and Evan left London, she waited until he was asleep and then crept out of bed. The window at the top of the stairs looked out over a tangle of railway tracks and the orange glow of night-lit roads. She dragged a chair across the carpet and unhooked the catch. For an hour she balanced on one foot breathing in the city as she leaned out as far as she dared. This she would take with her, this single hour. Nothing more. She had been out of hospital for less than a month.

ೞ

On her wedding night, she had claimed she was too tired for anything, and locked herself in the hotel bathroom. When she came back to the bedroom Evan was fast asleep, buttoned into a new pair of maroon pyjamas that still held their original folds and she slid gratefully beneath the covers, taking care not to wake him up. The next night he fell silent and sulked, turning his back and making a show of reading his book. But by the third night she knew she would have to let him do it and as she undressed in the bathroom and slid her new nightdress over her head, she resigned herself with a shiver.

He would be gentle, he assured her, fiddling with the tie of his pyjama trousers before positioning himself carefully astride her; she needn't be afraid. He dropped the pyjamas and she turned her head to one side and stared hard at the pattern in the wallpaper as he pushed himself into her as cautiously as if he were lowering himself into a scalding bath. She could feel his lips wet on her skin and fought the urge to push him away from her. When he finished, with a kind of judder that made the tendons in his neck go stringy and a vein down the centre of his forehead stand out, he disengaged himself immediately and tied up his pyjamas with his back to her before lying down again. She sat up and got out of bed. In the bathroom she shivered on the lavatory until she felt sure he was asleep. It wasn't meant to be like this. She knew it wasn't. With Evan, it was all wrong.

From that point onwards, she tried as far as she could to disguise his weekly exertions within the rest of her marital duties, alongside cooking his breakfast and scrubbing the folds of his shirt collars until they were white. This way, even if she did dread it, it was only the same bored dread with which she approached everything else.

But there was something else. Without her job at the solicitor's office, she had nothing to occupy her mind and she began to drift. It wasn't noticeable at first, but soon she knew something wasn't right. Sometimes Evan would seem to come striding through the front door almost as soon as he had left for work in the morning, and she would still be upstairs in her dressing gown deciding which clothes to wear and which to put in the laundry basket. Other times she would catch herself standing in rooms with no memory of going into them, or of what she was there for. Evan began to notice the change too. Was she ill? he asked her. Did she want him to send for the doctor? But there was nothing actually wrong with her. She had no other symptoms, so what would be the point?

9

Technically speaking, the first non-paying guest was actually a cat. Evan had been one of those men who, for no reason beyond their own disagreeableness, thoroughly despise cats. If he saw one in the street he would hiss at it. And if a cat spotted him first, it knew instinctively – cats just did, Hannah was sure of this – and turned tail before he came any closer. Until he died, Hannah had to content herself with the cats she met when she went out walking, and the ones who wandered into the back yard over the wall and came to the kitchen door for scraps when she called to them under her breath.

This cat moved in on Valentine's Day, a fortnight after Evan's ashes had been presented to her in a little plastic tub which she had shoved into the sideboard in the back room, and promptly forgotten about. He was a tiger-striped tabby who arrived leggy and lean, a young cat just growing out of kittenhood, who couldn't get food into his growling belly quickly enough. She had never seen such urgency as she saw in the angular features of this little prowler who sat mewing on the kitchen windowsill until she let him in. Before long he was her constant companion, trotting after her as she moved from empty room to empty room. She called him Tiger only because it was the first thing that occurred to her, because of his markings, and because some part of her still believed Evan would come back and chase him away as soon as he realised his game, so there was no point giving him a proper name. By the time she realised he was there to stay, the throwaway name had already stuck, so she gave him a surname, Valentine, by way of compensation.

What Tiger Valentine's game was would have made the living man jealous. The little urchin was claiming Evan's recently bereaved wife, moving in on a woman in a weakened state, who was too enfeebled to know her own mind, to say no, really, she wasn't ready for something so soon. Had Evan been watching his wife he would not have recognised the nightly bliss which was played out on his own bed, against his own pillows, scarcely cold. It had never happened there before. The skinny cat would jump up on to the bed and sit bolt upright as his new mistress got ready, never taking his eyes from her as she moved about the room. His brow looked permanently furrowed with his kitten-fresh tabby stripes, and he seemed to watch her with a worried, protective air as she sat in the chair and brushed her hair, as she dipped her fingers into pots and smeared night cream on her hands and face before getting into bed. Even once she was in bed, his worry lines didn't uncrease immediately. He remained straight-backed, his thin tail straight out behind him, until she tucked the covers around herself, placed her open book face down in her lap and reached out to him. Then he would come, purring, and allow himself to be tickled and stroked, petted and patted and calmed. Only after this, would he stretch beside her, on her dead husband's side of the bed, and fall asleep as she read, his feet and whiskers twitching in his dreams.

ᏮᏩ

As soon as she arrives home from her walk, Hannah sets to work with an intense kind of energy she has not known for years. She has been given a new start, and what better way to begin her life again than to have a thorough clear-out? It will give her a bit of time to think. She has too many strange emotions and sensations fizzing round in her head to make any big decisions straight away. She has already done something silly, offering a room to that girl. What was she thinking of? Still, she won't come; she'll find herself somewhere else to stay, somewhere with some other young people. But Hannah must try to keep hold of herself, and not do anything else she might come to regret. She must keep her head. And she doesn't need to rush into anything; she must remember that, now. She has plenty of time. As Dr Mount said, she is a very healthy woman.

She hangs her coat up in the hall and Tiger Valentine follows her down the narrow passage to the back room, where, for so many years, she and Evan ate their meals together. Hannah associates the room with Evan, even now. It is dark and rather gloomy, the mean window and the cold, tiled floor making it feel somehow unyielding and male. All the furniture has the same, awkward, brown heaviness that, to Hannah, makes it feel uncomfortably cramped and oddly Spartan at the same time.

When Evan was alive he spent so much of his time in here, sitting at the table poring over his accounts in the evenings after she had cleared the dinner things away. And he is still here, she remembers suddenly, in the plastic tub he came back from the crematorium in, pushed inside the bowels of the enormous sideboard, with its ornate carving and all its drawers and cupboards, and forgotten about. She turns to face the ugly piece of furniture. Somewhere inside there, mixed up with the tablecloths and teapots and the boxes of old photographs and God knows what else, the ghost of her husband still lurks.

Well then, she will begin with this room, she thinks. She will empty out that blasted sideboard and get rid of Evan once and for all.

❧

By the time Glynnis, the home help, arrives at three o'clock, the sideboard is already half emptied. She takes over immediately, tutting at Hannah for not waiting until she got there. Hannah finds her bluntness an irritation sometimes, and is on the point of reminding Glynnis that she isn't in the first flush of youth herself, but a glance at the stout woman's meaty arms as she lifts out an entire dinner service without losing a single side plate, makes her think better of it.

Tiger Valentine watches nervously from the doorway as more and more folded linen, dusty boxes and cases of cutlery are disgorged on to the table, throwing out an old, musty smell that catches in his whiskers and sets him on his guard. He keeps himself half hidden, crouching low on his haunches but not quite sitting. There is too much activity all of a sudden and he can never settle when Glynnis is around; she is forever waking him up and shooing him away.

Hannah, hovering at Glynnis's elbow, tries hard not to lose heart, but there is so much more stuff in the sideboard than she had bargained for. Glynnis, bent double, drags another box out and, perched on top of it, is the tub containing Evan's earthly remains. Hannah's heart sinks. She can't let Glynnis see it; she is a happily married woman and would most certainly disapprove. Concealing her anxiety behind a purposefully brisk tone, she instructs Glynnis to carry some of the boxes through to the dining room. She slips the plastic tub on to the mantelpiece, out of the way, while she is gone and winks at Tiger Valentine, who has taken the opportunity to sidle round the perimeter of the room and jump up on to the windowsill, concealing himself behind the net curtain.

The boxes, she supposes, will have to be gone through. She can't just throw stuff away without first at least knowing what it is. There might be something important there. Lord knows what paperwork Evan has squirrelled away. He never involved her in anything like that. So it will all have to be gone through.

'Oh, do let me give you a hand,' she says, as Glynnis returns for another box. Her round face is flushed quite pink.

'You go and sit down, now, Mrs Thomas,' is all Glynnis says. 'It's best you don't get under my feet.'

೧

95

When Evan died so quickly, so suddenly, he left his life in the middle of things. There were unopened bills on the mantelpiece, unread books on his bedside table. In the chest of drawers in their bedroom lay several pairs of his socks still joined together with plastic tags. Knowing the kind of person he was, Hannah knew the unfinishedness, the relinquishing of control, must have tortured him.

Perhaps it is this experience of his death, as much as her own unexpected reprieve, that is influencing her now, giving her such a need to do something worthwhile. Certainly, when her time eventually comes, she does not want to go as Evan went, putting up his puny fists in pathetic challenge, filling his fevered mind with poppycock ideas of cheating his grave of a body and fighting his way out. Now that she has this second chance, this extra time, she feels she must make the most of it. It is golden time, the most precious she has ever had, because she wasn't expecting it, and because it is hers alone. So much of her life feels as if it has been stolen from her, it would be a crime if she were to waste what remained.

She doesn't quite know what happened after Evan died. She had gone for too long being told what to do by other people, having her life decided for her; that was probably it. After the initial flurry of legal matters had been dealt with and the funeral was over and his clothes and odds and ends got rid of, she seemed to have let herself slip. She was so unused to looking after herself and making her own decisions. It wasn't the practical things. She had always done the cooking and cleaning and shopping and looking after in that sense. But pension books and paying the bills and budgeting: Evan had always taken charge of these things. She didn't know how to manage them. Not once, she realised shortly after his death, when brown envelopes started dropping through the letterbox, had she had been responsible for paying a bill. Not once, in sixty-five years.

She can see now that she had allowed it all to get on top of her. She had felt very low for a while, and hadn't really been looking after herself properly, skipping meals and leaving the curtains drawn all day. No wonder Glynnis is bossy with her. And then, of course, the cancer had come along.

She can see, now, how silly she has been. If only she had gone to see Dr Mount earlier, she would have saved herself all those months of worrying. Keeping it to herself, ashamed of it, almost. As if it was her own fault she was ill. As if it served her right. How had she allowed herself to become like this?

ை

While Glynnis makes herself busy with a duster upstairs, Hannah forces herself to make a start on her throwing out. She unrolls a black rubbish sack from the roll under the kitchen sink and carries it into the dining room, where an assortment of battered shoeboxes and bulging brown envelopes tied together into bundles with string, has been neatly piled on one of the tables. She sits down and makes a space so that she can see what she is doing, and picks a box at random. There are a couple of perished elastic bands around it which break as she pulls them off and shrink slowly on the tabletop, like dying worms, unearthed and exposed. She lifts off the lid cautiously and peers inside.

It is full of cards: postcards, birthday cards, Christmas cards, Get Well Soon cards. She pulls a few out. *Congratulations on your Fortieth Wedding Anniversary! Happy Retirement! Merry Christmas, December 1963.* She pulls one out. The picture on the front is a robin perching on a snow-laden branch, the edges of the snow still sparkling with a few remaining specks of glitter. She runs her finger over the surface, discoloured with ancient glue, and the glitter comes away, sticking to her skin.

'Everything all right, Mrs Thomas?'

Hannah jumps; Glynnis is standing just behind her, staring at her outstretched fingers with the bits of glitter still stuck to them.

'Oh,' she says. 'Yes. Look at all these old cards. Aren't people silly, keeping things like this for so long?' She brushes her hand smartly down the front of her skirt a few times, as if to dislodge and brush away the years along with the glitter. She is angry at herself for feeling sheepish. She can tell Glynnis disapproves of her getting up to all sorts, as she calls it, when she should be looking after herself. Hannah isn't sure how Glynnis comes by most of her information, but there isn't a thing that goes on in the neighbourhood that passes her by, and, by some means or another, the news has already reached her that Hannah has been to see Dr Mount this morning.

'I'm fine, Glynnis,' Hannah tries to reassure her now. 'I was having a check-up. Nothing more than that. I wish you would believe me.'

But Glynnis doesn't believe her; she chooses not to believe an awful lot of what Hannah tells her. She lifts her eyebrows a little and her wide forehead concertinas into sceptical furrows as she bustles out of the room.

∾

After less than a year of marriage, Hannah had given up all pretence of normality and had stopped getting out of bed at all. When Evan returned from the office she would be lying where he had left her, in a turmoil of sheets made prematurely stale by her prolonged rest.

The visit to the hospital was just that, he had reassured her – a visit. To ease their minds that there was nothing seriously wrong. He told her to put on a good dress and they drove out of London into the promise of a particularly warm early summer morning. Hannah blinked in the sunlight and shielded her eyes. Evan told her to roll down the window and breathe in the health-giving country air.

The hospital was built in spacious grounds, encircled by a ha-ha, so that the view of the long, symmetrical building was not obscured as they approached it. Apart from a small copse of ash trees to the right, and some flower beds directly in front of the gravelled parking area, there was nothing but carefully tended lawn radiating from the house in all directions. A central copper-green dome curved against the blue sky. To the odd Sunday driver that passed by, the building might appear to be the country estate of some aristocratic family or other.

Everything was neat, opulent. Well-ordered. She fiddled with the brim of her straw hat, pulling it down lower over her eyes as Evan slowed down and the car shuddered over the cattle grid that crossed the ha-ha.

As they turned down the driveway, the tyres crunched loudly on the gravel and Hannah was relieved when they stopped and the noise stopped too. She couldn't bear loud noises; even the sound of her own voice made her wince and when she spoke she lowered it to scarcely more than a whisper.

Evan led the way, striding up to the door and giving the bell a firm push as she slowly clambered out of the car. Once inside, they were escorted to a small room whose walls were lined with a mixture of upright chairs like dining chairs, and a couple of Chesterfield sofas. Through the windows, the curtains framed the view of the driveway they had just driven up, cleanly bisecting the lawn. Hannah worried about how they stopped the gravel from getting lost in the grass and blurring the neat edges.

Evan preferred to stand while they waited, occasionally pacing up and down, pretending to study the framed pictures on the wall. Hannah perched on a chair and closed her eyes. She tried to imagine she was at home in bed, with Evan safely away at his office. A clock ticked importantly on the mantelpiece and chimed the quarter hour. A floorboard squeaked slightly as Evan shifted his weight. Hannah hoped the consultation wouldn't take too long.

When they were called in, Evan did most of the talking, although a lot of glances were sent in Hannah's direction. Then he was sent out whilst she was given a physical examination and some more questions were asked as she was made to breathe in deeply and then out again. The doctor's fingers were warm, but the stethoscope he pressed to her chest and then to her back was cold against her skin and she flinched at its touch. He apologised, disengaging it from his ears and letting it drop so that it hung around his neck.

As he shone a light in her right eye, then her left, she noticed the slight medical smell he gave off, tinged with shaving soap; it seemed so out of place in a building which seemed on the surface to be so unlike a hospital. His breath smelled faintly of potted shrimps and he had a healthy cluster of grey hairs poking out of each nostril.

When he was satisfied with his examination she was asked to go with a nurse while he spoke to Evan. She thought she would be taken back to the waiting room, but the nurse went a different way and led her down a passage and into a room with a bed and a chest of drawers. Through the window, she saw the same view of the lawns and the stripe of grey road down the middle. The ha-ha meant that there was no clear dividing line, at this distance, between the grounds of the hospital and the outside world. Everything looked the same. And there were no locks on the doors, no grilles over the windows or padlocked gates. Her stay here, the nurse explained in a voice that sounded as soft as muslin, would be entirely voluntary.

10

Once she is alone again, Marina unzips her parka and pulls Oscar inside it. As she lifts her jumper she feels the chilly air on her naked skin and flinches, but then Oscar's cold cheek presses urgently against her warmth and his mouth, already sucking as she pulls the dummy free, finds her nipple and clamps on to it. She pulls her jumper down over his head and zips the parka up as far as it will go, tucking his legs inside it until she looks pregnant again, the bulk of her child curled tightly against her stomach.

As he sucks she blows into her balled hands, curling her fingers as far into the middle of the ball as she can. It reminds her of the rhyme she chants to Oscar: *Here's the church and here's the steeple. Open the doors and see all the people.* Oscar has never been inside a church; she wonders why she sings the rhyme to him. If she ever went home again her parents would find it unforgivable that she had denied her child something so fundamental. She shivers and pulls her hands inside her sleeves.

The woman is called Hannah. Hannah Thomas. It is an honest-sounding name. Quite no-nonsense. She looks at the piece of paper in her hand as if it can help her decide. She wonders what prompted her to make the offer. Maybe she is lonely and wants someone to talk to. Maybe she's a loony who goes round offering rooms to everyone. But she didn't seem mad. She seemed nice. A double room, she had said. The thought of the long, nourishing sleep she could have in a double bed in a room of her own hovers temptingly in Marina's mind as she wraps her arms more tightly round Oscar, trying to draw up some of his warmth into herself.

∽

Even in January, a few brave traders have opened up shop to pick up what small amount of passing trade there is, eking out a living for themselves in the closed season. Near the promenade a couple of caravans cluster together as if for warmth, their windows steamed up from the open vats of boiling water and fat, cooking chips and hotdog sausages. The smell of frying onions and cheap burger meat makes Liam feel almost nauseous with a sudden, urgent hunger. He has eaten nothing for twenty-four hours. He edges closer, fumbling in his pockets for change, his mouth filling with anticipatory saliva.

'A couple of burgers, mate,' he asks, nodding at the sizzling hotplate. 'How much?'

'Three pounds.'

'*Three?* Christ, they must be good. I've got one forty-seven.' He slaps the handful of coins on to the counter. 'Just give us one?'

'If you want one, it's one pound fifty. You've not enough.'

'You're joking, yeah?' Liam pulls his head back, cocking it slightly to one side. He can't tell if he's being serious or not.

The man shrugs.

'Oh, come on. It's a few fucking p we're talking here. Give us one, can't you? I'm starved.'

The man shrugs his shoulders again and leans forwards as if to slide the serving window shut. He's in a white coat, Liam notices, like a fucking gourmet chef. Quickly, he scoops his money back into his hand.

'Don't worry, mate. I'm going. I get the message.' He shoves his fistful of change angrily into his pocket and stalks away. He is still sulking, staring out to sea, clenching and unclenching his jaw, when a voice behind him makes him turn round. It's a girl.

'Hey. I got the burgers for you.' She holds a paper bag out to him. For a second, he doesn't understand, and he stands there looking at her, not knowing what to do. She looks uncomfortable, scared, even. She pushes the bag at him again, more urgently, and he takes it from her and looks inside. Two burgers nestle together, bleeding tomato sauce into the paper serviettes they are wrapped in. He looks back at her and raises the bag in an uncertain salute of gratitude.

'Thanks.'

She doesn't take her eyes off him. They look dark and watchful, as if she is waiting for something bad to happen and doesn't know when it will strike.

'I said yes to ketchup,' she says at last, her gaze still unbroken, her restless eyes hungry, expectant. 'I hope I did the right thing.'

'Oh, yeah. Most definitely,' he says, feeling a smile tweaking at the edges of his lips despite his bad mood and her anxiety. 'Most definitely.' The smile spreads across his face and he forgets the mealy-mouthed vendor in the caravan. 'Cheers.'

She stands and watches him as he rustles one of the burgers out of the bag and takes an enormous bite, forcing a dollop of ketchup out of one side of the bap. It follows a lazy arc down towards the tarmac. He swallows the mouthful half-chewed. 'It's good,' he says. 'Ta very much,' and he takes another bite.

She has a child with her, just a little one, and it starts pointing at the big red splat of tomato sauce that has landed on the ground by his foot, jigging its legs up and down in a speeded-up war dance of delight and laughing like a demon.

'Glad someone's happy,' he says.

The girl almost smiles this time, although she still seems uneasy.

He moves on to the second burger without pausing for breath. She stands there, half watching him eat and half watching the kid, which is squatting on its haunches, its enormous, nappy-wrapped behind almost touching the ground, as it examines the ketchuppy blob with a stream of high-pitched yelps and squeals. Liam eats as quickly as he can, feeling a bit self-conscious with her just standing there. He crams the last bit into his mouth, chews it once, and swallows it down almost whole like a seabird would, feeling it edge uncomfortably down his gullet.

'Cheers for that,' he says again and grins and pats his belly. 'Bloody tight arse, that fella, though.'

At last, the girl gives him a proper smile. Thank God for that, he thinks. He doesn't like it when he can't make a girl laugh;

there's got to be something wrong with him if he can't get her giggling. It's usually so easy. She is pretty when she smiles, and it seems to relax her a bit. He holds out his hand with mock formality, feeling more sure of himself now she isn't so tense. 'Liam Kelleher,' he says. 'Nice to meet you.'

She shakes his hand. 'Nice to meet you too,' she says. She doesn't offer her own name. To stop the baby poking its fingers in the tomato sauce she picks it up and holds it so that it can look at the sand. A seagull spins past, its wing tips almost fanning the child's face, and the child waves its arms in fright and cranes round to hide against her shoulder. Now that he has finished the burgers, maybe they will go. Suddenly, Liam doesn't want them to. He tries to string the conversation out a bit longer.

'So, what is there to do round here?' he asks.

The girl shrugs. 'Dunno. Not much probably.' She isn't giving anything away. She shifts the baby's weight to her other arm as if she feels happier with it between them, a human barrier. He wishes he could think of something else to say to her.

A sudden gust of wind bowls up from behind and the baby shrieks again. The gust swirls itself into a miniature tornado, gathering up strewn polystyrene cups, leaves and ripped open sugar sachets and sending them into a frantic, rattling spiral. It hurls grit into his eyes and he turns away, pulling his jacket tight across his chest and shivering. The girl hugs the baby close and jogs it up and down to comfort it.

'Oooh, let's go and find somewhere warm, shall we?' she nuzzles into its neck. She turns to Liam. 'Sorry, we've got to go.'

'Right, sure.' Quick, think of something to say, he thinks, as she turns to go. He takes a couple of steps towards her, not wanting to seem like he is bothering her, but if she leaves he will be on his own again. 'Do . . . Do you live round here, like?' he asks feebly.

The defensive look clouds her eyes again. 'No,' she says. 'Not yet, anyway.' She leans over the pushchair, pulling straps round the kid's body and clicking the fastenings into place.

'Bye,' she says, straightening up.

He shrugs and smiles. 'Nice to meet you. Thanks for the burgers.'

'That's OK,' she says. And then, after a pause: 'I owed someone a favour.'

He watches her hurrying away and wonders what's wrong with her. Or is it him? Has he has done something to frighten her off? But he can't have, because as he watches, she stops suddenly and runs back to him as if she has forgotten something, leaving the kiddy's pushchair standing in the middle of the promenade. She is out of breath when she reaches him, unable to speak, and she holds out her closed fist as she pants, waiting for him to understand and hold out his hand. When he does, she drops something into his palm and turns to go without waiting for his reaction. He looks: it is a tightly folded bundle of notes. There's thirty, maybe forty quid there.

'Hey,' he shouts after her, starting to run in the same direction. 'Hey!'

She stops and turns round, that weird, closed-up look on her face again.

'I . . . thanks. Thanks, this is great.' He doesn't know what to say. 'I don't even know your name,' he blurts out, feeling that somehow this is not right.

She stands there, seeming to debate with herself, still unsure of him. 'Marina,' she says at last, in a tight voice, and then she turns and walks away.

∽

He feels even more aimless after she has gone than he did before. Their meeting seems to have left him a little unhinged. Now he is alone again, everything seems worse, as if she had somehow helped him forget about the cold and the broken-down car and the letter in his pocket: all the crap that's been happening to him since yesterday. He wanders up and down the promenade all afternoon with the notes clenched in his fist inside his pocket, trying to figure out what to do next. He wonders why she ran back and gave him the money like that, after seeming so wary. And she had bought him the food, too; she obviously wanted to help. Maybe she was as lost as he was in this place. Maybe she had taken pity on him because she could understand how he was feeling. But he wishes she had hung around for a bit. He wouldn't have tried anything, if that's what she was scared of. He could just do with another person around right now, to take the edge off his misery.

11

Hannah can't settle. Alone in the house now that Glynnis has gone home, instead of getting on with her sorting, she loses heart and wanders into the back room again. Evan is still squatting there on the mantelpiece, safe inside his pot. She will have to dispose of him somehow.

Upstairs, she opens the door and peers into Room 3, the best room, which has two huge windows overlooking the bay. Years ago, she kept these two front windows ablaze with colour in the summer, with windowboxes full of fragrant wallflowers that stood out cheerfully against the sober grey walls. She kept everything perfectly neat and well-maintained then, as if proving to the world that she could manage, that she wouldn't let herself be defeated again. Everything just so. Evan had prided himself on her recovery, which he felt he himself had brought about. She never let him into her confidence, never displayed any outward sign that this was not the case and that she still felt wretched, but was just more guarded about showing it. She had continued taking the tablets they had given her at the hospital, grateful for the torpid blankness that filled her head and allowed her to get on with things mechanically. Evan had made arrangements with a local private clinic and her supply of the pills was refreshed each month without her having to think about it.

Nowadays, the windowsills at *Swn Y Don* are bare, save for a few plastic pots half filled with waterlogged soil and the twiggy remains of long-dead plants. She can't get that girl out of her head. If she does come, she could put her in here. But is it a place for a child, so dull and colourless? Perhaps she should get some flowers, just in case, and find a nice bright bedspread. She opens up the linen cupboard on the landing and peers inside to see what she can find.

๑

The chiming doorbell makes her jump. Even though she has been half awaiting it, half dreading it, the girl's arrival sends her into a fresh tizzy of anxiety as she hurries down the stairs.

She recognises her even through the frosted glass in the front door, can make out the long, dark hair and the huge khaki-coloured coat that, on the promenade, had seemed much too big. Her stomach gives an unexpected leap of pleasure as she opens the door and bustles the girl inside.

She watches closely as the child is unbuckled from his seat and the girl lifts him into her arms. She follows Hannah into the guests' lounge and sits him in her lap, looking around the room slightly ill at ease as Hannah fusses round, offering something for the child to drink, asking if he is warm enough. She insists on making a pot of tea, for something to do rather than

110

because either of them wants it. She is so unused to having guests, she has forgotten what it is like.

She carries the tea in on a tray, again noticing how old and shabby the place looks with young people there. The child, acclimatising and curious about his new surroundings, wants to explore, and the girl watches him as he makes his way from chair to sofa and back again.

'He's adorable,' Hannah says softly, as much to herself as to the girl. She can't quite believe how glad she is that they have come. It is such a long time since there have been children at *Swn Y Don*.

The girl smiles. 'Say hello, Oscar.' She lifts him up by his outstretched arms and walks him across the room towards Hannah.

Oscar. She likes the name: it is original, self-contained, something he will grow into and make his own. She shakes his little hand theatrically. 'Nice to meet you, Oscar.' The girl's name is Marina.

When Oscar starts whining and grabbing at the tongs set in the fireplace, Hannah has an idea. She goes into the dining room and picks up a handful of the old cards she had been about to throw away.

'Here,' she says. 'Maybe he would like to look at the pictures.' She passes the cards to Marina, who immediately kneels on the floor and spreads them out on the rug. In a flash, Oscar forgets the coal scuttle and squats beside his mother, his face a picture of concentration as his eyes take everything in. He grabs at the cards and picks up one in each hand, his chubby fingers so new and pink against the sad old pictures, crumpling in his eager little fists. He lifts one to his mouth and clamps his teeth on to the corner and Marina pulls it away, giving Hannah an apologetic look.

'He puts everything in his mouth. I'm sorry.'

'Oh, he can have them,' Hannah says. 'Don't worry. I was only going to throw them away.'

When they have finished the tea, she shows them upstairs to their room. She has found a yellow bedspread and carefully laid it over the blankets, and, although she has no flowers, she has put a potted African violet in a saucer on the dressing table. She leaves them to settle in, pulling the door gently closed as if on her own children, put to bed for the night, and goes back downstairs smiling.

ᕬ

There may as well have been a ten-foot wall around the hospital with barbed wire at the top, as far as Hannah was concerned. She drew no comfort from the relaxed regime operated there. If she discharged herself, where would she go – back to Evan, who had taken her there in the first place? She sat in an armchair wrapped in the quilt from her bed, scarcely able to turn her head or blink. Every evening a nurse came and gave her more tablets to swallow. She never refused them or asked what they were. Through the window, she saw cars coming and going, up and down the long, straight driveway. Sometimes, she didn't bother to open her eyes for hours at a time and she would listen to the sound of their engines growing louder as they approached, and fainter as they drove away across the ha-ha, back into the world outside.

Displeased with her lack of effort, after a few weeks the staff started to make her do things. They sat her in a wheelchair and wheeled her out into the hospital garden on nice days and sat her under a tree. She watched some of the other patients fiddling about with trowels in flower beds and vegetable patches but she didn't see the point in what they were doing. They pulled up radishes and picked the runner beans dangling from green teepees made of sticks. Someone carried a bunch of sweet peas over and handed them to her. 'For your room,' she said. 'Smell.' Hannah lifted the bunch to her nose and breathed in. The fragrance reminded her of something but she couldn't remember what it was. She thanked the girl and clutched the stems tightly in her lap until the nurse came to take her inside. For the next few days, every time anyone came into her room, they exclaimed, 'What a glorious scent!' and she smiled obediently.

She lost track of time. Nobody, not even her husband, came to visit her and she didn't care. After her first electro-convulsive therapy she was excused activities and allowed to stay in her room for the rest of the afternoon. Her sweet peas had wilted, their shrivelled blooms lying in a ring around the water glass the nurse had put them in. She slept and when she woke up it was evening and they had been cleared away, a fresh bunch already in their place. The therapy seemed to have interfered with her senses, disturbing their equilibrium as if it had magnetised them and pulled everything in the wrong direction, and

113

even though the nurse said the flowers smelled just as lovely as the others, Hannah couldn't smell a thing.

She sat up slowly to take her medication, and a loud throbbing started up inside her head like a hammer. She clapped a hand to each temple. She could scarcely remember what had caused the pain. When the nurse handed her a glass of water to swallow the tablets, her hands were shaking so much she couldn't hold it. Confused tears ran down her cheeks. 'What happened?' she asked.

They kept it up, the charade that it mattered how she filled her time and, day after day, the curtains were wrenched open to let in the morning, and she was badgered out of her narrow bed when she would much rather have been left to sleep all day. Periodically, she was taken for her therapy and each time she resisted it more. She started to wonder whether this was how the cure worked: by giving the patients something to hate and shocking them out of their deadness. It was the tail end of summer before she knew it, and when she started going outside without being made to, and noticing how the roses were starting to go blowsy and drop their petals, the doctors decided it might be time for her to go home again.

12

Liam has nowhere to go, so he finds an off-licence in the town and buys some cans of lager with the girl's money, before wandering down to the beach again. The day is sliding towards evening and the chilly wind has a seriously cold bite as the low sun sinks lower in the sky, turning the air a lilac-tinged grey. The sand is dark and waterlogged, but he finds a washed-up plastic oil canister that has obviously been used as a buoy at some time, a frayed piece of rope coiling behind it, half buried in the sand. He sits down on it, pops the ring pull on one of the cans and takes a long, thirsty swig.

The sea has gone right out, so far that it is only just visible – a narrow strip of luminescence on the horizon. Even as he watches, the day is draining from the sky, the light being sucked slowly away until, at some point soon, it will disappear altogether, leaving him in the dark.

೦൦

His mother was twenty-four when she died. She had scarcely

had a life. Liam tries to think back to when he was twenty-four himself but he can't remember anything about it. What has he done with his life?

But his mother had been so overwhelmingly alive, had really tried to make something of herself. She hadn't had a good education, and there was precious little money around, but she didn't let that get her down. Liam remembers her going off to night school sometimes, taking him round to his nana's first. He had felt sorry for her at the time; he didn't think grown-ups had to go to school, but maybe some of them did. She didn't seem bothered by it, though. She seemed to quite like it.

His dad didn't like her going. At first Liam was glad of this, and he thought his mam should be glad, too, because if his dad went up to the school and had a word, maybe she wouldn't have to go any more and he wouldn't have to eat so many spaghetti hoops at his nana's. But she shouted back at his dad when he complained, saying she wanted to go, why couldn't he just let her.

Sometimes, when just the two of them were at home together, his mam would sit reading a book. Not just any book, but a kind that Liam had never seen before, with lots of pages and dead tiny writing with no pictures. And she didn't read it out loud like she did when she read him a story, but kept it all in her head, so that it looked like she was doing nothing at all. He would stop in the middle of whatever he was doing, his toy cars forgotten, and he would watch her, fascinated. She sat there, absolutely still, the open book held lightly in her lap in both hands. Sometimes her lips moved slightly, and her face looked strange and far away, but she never made a sound. If he watched for long enough she would lift one hand and turn over the page, and he would hear the dry paper rasping against her fingers in the silence.

If she ever read books when his dad was home, he got angry. One time, he pulled a library book out of her hands and stood there in front of her, tearing out all the pages, throwing them around the room so that they fell down on to the floor like leaves falling off the trees. She just sat there and let him, never saying a word.

His mam worked in a fruit and veg shop. It was a very ordinary job, but she said she was lucky to have it, and she made it sound like magic, all those boxes of fruit, each apple and orange in its own little cardboard compartment, wrapped up in blue paper. She would bring the empty apple trays home for him to play with, and sometimes she brought him a wrapped-up apple in her bag. Stuff that was past its best found its way home, too. Bendy carrots and muddy potatoes that had started growing roots. Anything like that she took round to his nana's and it got used up in a big pan of scouse. If she brought speckly bananas home she would let Liam peel the tired skins off a couple and would mash them up with sugar to make banana sandwiches for their tea.

ॐ

Liam shivers. He hasn't thought about any of this stuff for years. It's the letter that's done it. Bullying him into thoughts he would rather not be having, memories he would rather forget. But what does it say? For the first time since receiving it, he wants to know. He needs to find out what his father is planning. Because if he is out of prison and coming to find him, he wants to be ready. There's no way he is going to let himself be taken by surprise, like his mam was. No way. He resents the fact that he feels so powerless all of a sudden, can do nothing to stop his father if he wants to look for him. All he can do is run away.

໑

His mam and dad always fought with each other, ever since he could remember, but their fights got worse after she started going to college, as if it was that in particular that got him mad. She never stopped going, though. It was as if a part of her enjoyed how much it bothered him, as if she felt it gave her something over him. From his bedroom Liam heard their voices and other noises he hadn't heard before: bumps and thuds and stifled cries. His mam started phoning the fruit and veg shop to say she was ill, and staying at home instead of going to work. Sometimes Liam's nana came and took him to school, but sometimes she didn't, and Liam would stay at home all day, too, throwing nervous glances at his mam's puffed-up, sad eyes, the skin around the rims all red from crying. His dad would sleep in bed until the afternoon and then go out without saying where he was going. On days like that she wanted Liam close to her. 'You look after me, don't you, Liam?' she would say. 'You're my little guardian angel, my little soldier.' That was why he was called

Liam, she told him once. Names were important. Liverpool was a scary place sometimes, she said, but she was lucky because her little boy's name meant *protection* in Ireland, where she had her roots, and that meant that she would always be safe.

୶

He gets up, feeling uneasy. He doesn't like thinking about the past. Doesn't like things which remind him of it. But he can't help it: in this place it seems to just creep up without him knowing. He looks at the glinting, pale line of the sea and, without deciding anything, he starts walking towards it. The sand is hard and pressed flat, like fresh plaster. His legs feel heavy and awkward with the aching cold that has seeped into his body while he has been sitting still.

He wonders about the girl from earlier. Tries to figure out why she took it upon herself to feel sorry for him and help him out the way she did. People don't usually do him favours. Not like that, anyway. It's different when he's out on the pull, and trying to impress. Girls fall over themselves then. He knows how to charm them, how to win their confidence. But it wasn't like that this afternoon.

As he walks further out, the texture of the sand changes. Hard ridges massage his feet through the worn soles of his trainers. On one side a shallow skein of water threads its way down towards the sea, like a miniature river, widening and merging with another one and opening out into a wide, shallow pool. Some gulls, picking amongst the stones around its edges, fly off as he approaches, their white feathers almost luminous in the now purplish dusk. He watches them getting smaller, until they are just tiny grey and white dots against the sand.

Well, she wouldn't have been so kind to him if she knew how he had treated Julie, would she? If she knew the way he had run away just when she was doing something really nice for him.

He looks down at his feet. The sand has become wet and shiny, lying beneath a thin layer of water like a skin. His footprints wash over and disappear almost as soon as he steps out of them and he can feel the cold water seeping through his socks where his trainers leak. He stops. The sand all around him is pockmarked with worm casts, tiny squiggles of sand in neat little piles, like little brown buttons stitched on to the ground. He turns round and starts retracing his steps back up to the town.

∽

Oscar is lying asleep right in the middle of the bed in his cleanest pair of pyjamas. Marina doesn't feel like sleeping. Glancing at her son curled up against a feather pillow which is almost as big as he is, she pulls a chair over to the window and opens it slightly. There is a bruise-coloured darkness over the bay now, and the light is dropping away moment by moment, almost perceptibly. She retunes her hearing, sharpens it whisker-fine, until she imagines she can hear the whisper of the waves riding piggyback on the still air. Remembering something, she unties the sock from round her middle and pulls out the lump of hashish she stuffed inside it earlier with the money. Even before she has unwrapped

120

the cling film it is wrapped in, she can smell the pungent, familiar reek, and feel its texture, slightly softened by her body's warmth. She balances a Rizla on one knee and crumbles a corner of the resin along its length before adding threads of tobacco and rolling it into a thin cigarette. She pulls a lighter from the back pocket of her jeans, rasps the wheel and holds the flame to the end of the joint she has rolled, inhaling deeply. The tobacco catches and crackles faintly as it starts to burn. She closes her eyes. The wind is buffeting against the buildings, brushing round their man-made corners and slipping over the slanting rooftops and the sound seems to enter her head. She lets it fill the cavity she imagines inside her skull, slowly, like smoke curling around the inside of a bottle before leaning towards the window and exhaling the smoke in a long, slow stream. She squeezes her lungs empty, and then waits for one, two, three counts before opening her eyes and drawing in a new breath.

It feels so strange, being in an almost deserted building. In London, she has always felt crammed in. Every inch of space is taken up, is someone's little corner to hide away in. Every building secretes hundreds of invisible people. She has seen evacuated tower blocks spill out string after string of silhouette figures like streamers – all holding hands and snipped out from folded sheets of newspaper. Something from nothing. Huddling together and waiting, gazing up at smoke billowing from shattered windows as wailing fire engines drown the scene in noise. Here she can hear the emptiness. Every move she makes feels enormous, amplified by the hollowness of the unused room.

Remembering London brings the events of the day back into

her mind and her relaxed feeling starts to ebb away as she thinks about what she has done. She feels safe for the moment, but how long will it be before Dave catches up with her? Surely she won't be able to hide from him for ever. Suddenly, her escape feels all too easy, and she starts to doubt its solidity. What if Dave followed her to Euston and on to the train? What if he knows she is here? What if he is here, too, in this town, waiting out there in the growing darkness, watching her, just biding his time?

She finishes the joint quickly and screws out the stub on the outside of the sill, peering out into the street. She is being crazy; there is nobody there. How could there be? And he couldn't have followed her; she listened to him leaving the flat. But he must know by now that the money has gone, must know it is she who has taken it. Quietly, she pulls the window closed and looks across the room at Oscar asleep on the bed. If only she could guarantee that she could keep him safe for ever.

∽

Hannah has found her wedding photographs. She pushes her spectacles down her nose slightly so that she can see more clearly and picks one up to examine it.

Her wedding dress was smart but plain; her father had set a limit on how much could be spent on the material. Duck-egg blue, she had chosen, when she went out shopping with her mother, and her mother had gone back the next day and spent half the housekeeping money on lace in the same colour for the collar and cuffs. That was kept a secret from her father. They knew it was better that way. As far as he was concerned, enough time and money had been spent on Hannah already and she was lucky to have anything new for her wedding day. Was lucky to be having a wedding day at all, after what she had done.

She looks pretty in the photograph. Her hair is freshly waved and she is smart, slim, her lips parted slightly in a demure smile. But there is a pallor in her cheeks beneath the rouge, and the dress is loose around her waist and across her chest. At the end of each sleeve her tiny wrists poke like pale twigs from the lacy cuffs. She was awfully thin when she married. She is standing a little in front of Evan. She remembers now, how the photographer suggested her husband put his hand on her waist. But Evan's hands are pinned firmly at his sides, and both of hers are bunched tightly, protectively, in front of her stomach, clutching her wedding posy.

She puts the picture down. After she had accepted Evan's proposal things moved very quickly. A date was set, and her mother said to her one evening, her mouth full of pins, that perhaps things had all worked out for the best. Hannah, standing with her arms out on the kitchen table in her half-finished wedding dress, said nothing, but she sensed relief in her mother's voice, as if something heavy was being lifted away.

Two years after starting work as a clerk at her uncle's firm, her last day came and went. She would soon be a married woman and married women didn't work. She wondered what she would do with her time.

On the afternoon before the wedding, Celia helped her to

pack her going-away bag. She pulled open the wardrobe and dragged out its entire contents, laying skirts and dresses across the two single beds, holding up outfits against her sister, trying skirts with one blouse and then another. They had precious few clothes, even between them, so it would be impossible for her to pack anything which Evan had not seen before, but they were at least good quality, Celia insisted, and with a little bit of imagination, she could make him believe the outfits were new. Men were easy to fool, she said, in a knowing voice. Hannah couldn't see why it mattered.

She was lost in this whirlwind of preparation. She was trying desperately to be happy and hopeful about her impending marriage, but the closer it came the further it seemed to drag her from the truth, as if it was a false wall being built up in front of her and pasted over to conceal what was too ugly, too shameful ever to be looked at. Suddenly she felt constricted and choked by the oppressive closeness in the bedroom, with the curtains closed against the daylight, so that she could try things on, and the dusty mothball smell yawning from the open wardrobe. And yet again, Celia was holding her home-made summer dress in her hand, dancing it on its hanger.

'You've got to take this, Hannah. It's so pretty. Why don't you wear it any more?'

'It's too small,' Hannah said in a weak voice. She couldn't tell Celia the real reason. She couldn't say anything. Just the sight of the dress made her clamp up into a tight ball of unhappiness and there was nothing she could do to make the feeling go away. She wanted to hurl all the clothes away from her and pull open the curtains and windows and let in some air, some light, but she couldn't move.

'Try it on,' Celia persisted. 'Let's see.'

Without protest, Hannah took off her skirt and stepped into the dress. Celia jiggled it up over her hips, eased her arms through the armholes, and fastened it up at the back.

'There,' she said. 'It's perfect. Rather loose, if anything. You've lost weight.' She shuffled Hannah to one side so that she could see herself in the oval mirror on the wardrobe door.

Hannah looked at herself. The dress wasn't as long as she remembered it, or perhaps she had grown taller during the last two years. The skirt came to just below her knees. Celia handed her the underskirt and she pulled it up underneath. It rustled and scratched against her thighs. She felt her bottom lip trembling and couldn't do anything to stop it.

'Hannah! Hannah! Stop this, you silly thing.' Celia turned her sister round and put a firm hand on each shoulder, trying to shake her free from the sadness that had suddenly gripped hold of her. 'Oh, I'm such a klutz. I didn't mean to get you all upset, honestly, darling.' Hannah cracked then, saw in the mirror how the skirt of her dress ballooned around her as she dropped to the floor, her chest heaving with the sobs she couldn't suppress any longer.

ॐ

The boy was called Simeon. His mother, a Jewish woman from Whitechapel, had been killed in one of the final rocket bomb attacks of the war. She had been visiting her family and was just setting off for home. An hour later and she would have been on the other side of London. When Hannah met Simeon he talked to her about existential philosophy. He had just been reading Jean-Paul Sartre. Hannah had only been in the library to return her brother's overdue books and felt instantly in awe of him. She had scarcely even heard of Sartre, but he seemed genuinely interested in her nonetheless, even though she knew she had nothing of interest to say about anything at all. He followed her out of the library and insisted she sit with him on the bench outside while he smoked a cigarette. Hannah fell in love with him there and then. He was so unlike anyone else she knew. As she listened to him speaking she felt everything all at once: she was energised by his passion, his inquisitiveness, his hunger for knowledge; she was lulled by his assuredness, the feeling he radiated of absolute certainty. He was twenty-six and she told him she was eighteen.

They went to Epping Forest. It was summer and she was wearing her new dress. Her mother had helped her to make it, slightly disapproving of the amount of material the skirt used up, but impressed with the results despite herself. All the young girls were wearing dresses like this now, the full, swinging skirts somehow rebelling against the make-do-and-mend war mentality which had dragged on until the end of the forties. The new styles seemed to presage something hopeful. They made the dress in the snatched hours between school and her father's return from work, in the same way most of Celia's more flamboyant dresses had been made, pedalling furiously on the treadle of the old

Singer sewing machine. It was better this way. Their father disapproved of extravagance.

How good she felt, walking hand in hand with Simeon down the shady pathways, the skirt of her new dress swinging gently from side to side as she walked, the underskirts that kept it so full brushing against the backs of her bare knees at each step. She tightened her grip on his hand. He stopped, mid-step.

'Hey,' he said gently. 'Hey, come here,' and he pulled her towards him and kissed her on the forehead. 'Hey.' His voice was low, his breath warm in her ear, as his hand traced the curve of her waist, moved slowly up to her breast and rested there. She stayed so still she felt she had turned to porcelain; she imagined her arm cracking and breaking off if she tried to move it. His hand moved slowly back down to her waist and stopped again when it reached the outward flare of her hip. She felt herself prickle all over and she shivered.

He led her away from the main path and on to a less clear track. From here, they broke off again and butterflies and bees flew up out of the long grass as they disturbed them with their trespassing feet. In a daze, Hannah watched him shake out the blanket he had brought and smooth it on to the grass for them to lie on.

There was never a moment when she felt what she was doing was wrong, or when she felt compromised or taken advantage of. He did everything so carefully, so gently, never avoiding her eyes. And yet, he did it skilfully. Until she felt him pushing at the place between her legs, she was unaware that she was naked there. She felt a momentary startle, the beginnings of embarrassment, but then she noticed that he, too, was revealed to her and the feeling subsided; they were skin to skin, with nothing between them. At his pressure she opened her legs wider and felt something push inside. Strange rather than painful. His body heavy on top of hers, moving, and the same movement inside. Not one moment, though, when it felt like it shouldn't be happening.

13

The clock on the mantelpiece chimes the quarter hour. Hannah takes a deep breath and sits up straight in her chair. There are only a few more things left to sort through. She pulls the nearest of them towards her, a black box file like the ones Evan once used to keep all his accountancy records together. She pushes a button on the side to open the lid and lifts the metal hinge holding the contents in place. There has been no sound from upstairs, but she wonders whether her guests are feeling hungry yet. It must be nearly teatime.

Only half concentrating, the rest of her mind raking through the kitchen cupboards and wondering whether she has anything suitable to give a baby, she lifts out a handful of papers and sifts quickly through what is there, before sliding the lot into a fresh bin bag. It is more old stuff, bits and pieces from her parents' house. She has no idea why she still has it, why it wasn't thrown away when she and Celia cleared the house after their mother's funeral. There are dividend statements from some stocks and shares cashed in more than thirty years ago. Copies of her parents' birth certificates and a yellowed booklet of operating instructions for her mother's new twin tub, bought in 1965.

And then she stops. She feels a sudden lurch in her chest, as if something, some creature, has just pounced at her out of the darkness.

An address in the top corner of a letter has caught her eye. It is from the Salvation Army, and is paper-clipped together with a bundle of other letters. She takes a sharp breath before she pulls off the paperclip and glances at the letters underneath. They are all from the Salvation Army, and they are all addressed to her father, dated 1951, when she was fifteen years old.

ॐ

It is possible to become pregnant the first time you have sexual intercourse; she knows that now. Although there wasn't just the once. He never took her to Epping Forest again but there were a couple of other times. Just a couple. There was no way of knowing which was the one that did it, and for a long time she didn't know she was pregnant at all. Years later, she hated herself for this, for wasting precious months in ignorance.

It was her mother who recognised the unmistakeable swelling of her belly and gently coaxed the truth from her daughter as she soaked in the bathtub one Sunday evening, her pale stomach nakedly giving up its secret as she tucked her knees under her chin and wrapped her arms around them. Her instinct, straight away, had been to protect, to shield herself and as her mother spun the evidence before her into pregnancy, a baby, ruin, she pulled her knees in as tightly as she could, until she felt the curve of her protruding belly pressing against the tops of her thighs, which had been scalded red by the bathwater. Her mother had sat on the edge of the bath and stroked her hair for a few breath-held moments before standing up and leaving the room without another word.

∞

She was shaken from her bed very early one morning not long afterwards. It was not yet dawn and all she could see of Celia was a humped-up shape under the quilt. Hannah was hurried out of sight before the disturbance woke her sister up. Downstairs, her best clothes were waiting, ready-ironed, and a suitcase had been packed for her.

'Where am I going?' Her voice was still thick with sleep, her head muddled and heavy. 'Mother?' Her mother was standing in the corner, her eyes suspiciously red. But she was silent. She wouldn't answer her daughter's questions. She dropped her eyes to the floor. 'Mother?'

Her father waited in the hallway as she dressed. Frightened to disobey, she did as she was told without another word. As her father led her out of the house her mother reached towards her and clasped her hand briefly before being sent back inside.

A taxicab was waiting. They sat in silence for the whole journey. She and her father, side by side. The muscle at the side of his jaw rippled continually. She knew he was not to be spoken to in this grim mood. She dared not question where she was being taken.

The cab took them to the train station at London Bridge, soaring over the swollen Thames just as a grey light was fingering its way upwards from the east and climbing into the city sky. Her father paid the driver, took the suitcase from him and led the way into the station at a clip.

At the ticket office he bought one ticket, not two. A single. So that was it. He handed it to her and she followed him to the platform as slowly as she could. She wanted him to keep walking away from her until the platform reached a vanishing point and he disappeared, but he turned round in irritation and waited for her.

He was sending her away. She had not dared to think too much about what her pregnancy might mean. Somehow, she had trusted that they would come up with something gentler than this. But her father was not a gentle man. Reluctantly, she joined him at the platform edge. He scarcely acknowledged her presence and she wondered whether he actually hated her. Without turning to meet her gaze he said the train was due in fifteen minutes and that he would wait until it arrived. She wanted to tell him to leave, that she could manage quite well on her own now, but it occurred to her that he was not staying to be helpful or to say goodbye, but to make sure she actually boarded and didn't come running back home again. For the full fifteen minutes he stood at the edge of the platform, as if the train's arrival was imminent. After a few minutes she crept away and lowered herself slowly on to a bench, her eyes staring sightlessly at the ground, unblinking.

He sent her to Chatham. He had a relative, a cousin, who lived there. Hannah had never met the cousin, or his wife, but it was with these conveniently distant members of the family that she was sent to stay until she was ready to give birth. Her family, she realised with a creeping sense of horror, were ashamed of her. Or her father, at least. Her mother, she couldn't be so sure about – like Hannah, she always did as she was told. But she had not stood in the way, had not tried to stop him taking her away in the taxi. So perhaps she, too, was ashamed.

When the train arrived she climbed in and took the suitcase from her father's outstretched hand. She would be met at Chatham, he said, and slammed the door. She nodded, kept her head lowered and went to find a seat. She deliberately looked away from the window when the train started to move. She did not want to see her father's diminishing figure standing there watching her leave. She didn't want to see London sliding past and away from her, as if, by not acknowledging her departure, she might avoid all that was to come.

ॐ

She feels a sudden jolt as she comes to and realises she's sitting in the dark. The letters from the Salvation Army are spread out on the table in front of her, the paper clip still between her fingers. She pushes them together and crams them back inside the box file, out of sight. She sighs heavily. Oh dear, she whispers, and she lifts a shaking hand to her mouth, feeling the possibility of tears trembling in her chin. How cruel that she should find these letters like this, without any warning. And today of all days, when everything has gone so unexpectedly well. Oh, she is disappointed. She feels really punctured, like a popped balloon, one minute so round and proud, the next a damp bit of coloured rag. And angry too. What on earth did her father keep the letters for? She would have thought they were the last thing he would want to hang on to. Had he planned to torture her like this, from beyond the grave? Slowly, she stands up and tries to massage the stiffening ache out of her neck. Perhaps she needs to go to bed and try to forget about it. After a good long rest, she might not feel so raw.

The curtains are still wide open and the glass in the enormous, exposed window looks as fragile as a thin sheet of ice, the only thing between her and the glowing darkness outside. She shivers and goes to pull the curtains across before switching the lamp on. Just as she reaches her hand out, a movement in the street catches her eye and she pulls her hand back and retreats a little behind the bunched fabric.

There is somebody there. A man, she thinks. Just standing there, looking. As she watches, the familiar fluttering of a new anxiety starts up somewhere between her throat and her chest. The figure comes closer and leans in over the front gate, peering up the steps on to the raised front patio as if he is looking for something. Definitely a man, a young man. He seems up to no good; he has on jeans and a denim jacket, scruffy-looking, and one of those worrying hoods they all seem to be wearing nowadays, pulled up tight over his head so that she can't see his face. Hannah keeps absolutely still, her last in-breath held and trapped tight behind clenched teeth. She wonders whether she should go and warn Marina, but then the thought occurs to her that he might be something to do with her. What if she is on drugs, after all? What if she knows he is out there? What if she is quietly waiting for him upstairs? Hannah looks out of the window again, but he seems to have lost interest in her house, and is walking slowly back down the road, looking around him all the time, still on the lookout for something.

Hannah watches until he is out of sight and then pulls the curtains tightly closed, making sure she leaves no chink that can be peered through. In the kitchen, she snaps the blinds down as quickly as she can. She spoons some catfood into a saucer for Tiger Valentine, reassured by the fact that he is behaving perfectly normally, miaowing up at her, his tail proudly vertical as he weaves back and forth, his claws scratching against the tiles as he rubs his mackerel stripes against her ankles.

෧

Marina has closed the curtains, although she has left the window open a crack. Mainly, she is worried the joint has left a smell in the room. The landlady, Hannah, didn't mention smoking, but she is pretty sure she wouldn't want dope smoke hanging in the curtains and catching in the carpet of her best room, even if nobody does want to stay in it any more. Partly, though, she wants to be able to let the stillness of the vast, clear sky suspended over the bay seep into the room overnight to purify her and somehow leach away her worries, her crimes.

Carefully, she climbs on to the high, springy bed, and sits cross-legged with the sock full of money in front of her. Oscar has thrown off the covers in his sleep and is lying on his back, his arms and legs flung out like a starfish. He has a faint rosy glow in his cheeks which she hopes is the sea air and not a fever. She looks at the sock; she feels branded by the stolen money, feels it is obvious to everyone that she has it and that she is a thief, no better than the thief she stole it from. She picks the sock up and shoves her hand inside. The bundle of notes is slightly curved into the shape of her body. She flattens it between her hands and spreads the notes out singly on the bedspread. They surround her like pale greenish petals, accusing and yet vital. She thinks. Anyone would have done the same. She looks at Oscar, his little chest rising and falling, rising and falling, fast in the artless, trusting sleep of the very young. She took the money for him, so that he would not have to be separated from her. And for herself, too, she forces herself to admit that, because even if Oscar would be all right, would survive elsewhere, with another, replacement mother, she knows that she would not, that for her it would be unendurable.

She has thought about this such a lot over the past weeks. What it must be like for a child who does not remember its own mother. She has tried to dredge up her own earliest memories and has been just about able to recall events from as early as three years old. But Oscar is not yet two. If she were to lose him now, he would have nothing left of her, save his biology. And

136

he wouldn't remember anything about today, the day his mother stole him away from London. It is funny, because young children seem to exist so much more earnestly in the present moment than adults. And yet, once past, moments which have been so absolute leave nothing of themselves behind. Perhaps that's the deal, she thinks. Maybe the experience itself is the exact price of a memory.

Well, if Oscar ever returns to London, he will experience his own birthplace as a newcomer, a stranger would, with no awareness of the thread that already ties him there, the invisible looping back on himself as he scuffs unconsciously over his own tiny footprints.

She gathers the money together again, pushing it back into one, untidy pile, as if clearing fallen leaves from a pristine, pocket-handkerchief lawn. One or two of the notes are brand new and still have the crispness, the sheen of recent minting. But most of them are tatty, well used, with tiny rips and frays like war wounds. She imagines the procession of pockets and palms, wallets and purses they have been pushed inside, the strings of items they have paid for. Packets of biscuits and nappies side by side with wraps of cocaine and heroin and lost bets at Ladbrokes. All those purchases. So many prices paid.

She rolls the whole lot up and pushes them back inside the sock.

At least she has helped someone out, though. That guy on the promenade. Without her he would have gone hungry, she thinks. She wonders what he was doing there. His accent wasn't Welsh. He sounded more like a scouser. He looked like he was in almost as much trouble as she was. Maybe that was what made her run back.

Without disturbing Oscar, she pushes the sock under a pillow, wriggles out of her jeans and jumper and climbs into bed beside him, trying to rearrange the covers over his starfish limbs. Outside, a train rattles past and the sea moves closer to the shore, flinging spume, like an advance battalion, in light, frothy clusters on to the wet sand ahead of the surging waves. She watches the curtain stirring slightly at the open window, feels the cold sea breath on her shoulders, before switching off the lamp and submerging herself in the bed's beckoning warmth.

∾

When all was said and done, Liam had not done the one thing his mother had asked of him. He hadn't kept her safe, had he? After everything she had done for him, all the selfless love she had showered him with, all the special time they had shared, the secret time that was just theirs, he couldn't keep his promise. When she died, he couldn't forget what she had told him about his name, and it caused him so much pain he stopped talking, and refused to answer to it any more. He closed himself up and sat in front of his nana's telly, ignoring her when she spoke to him, pushing her away when she tried to comfort him. His name was a mockery, and when she insisted on using it he flew into a screaming rage, shouting and kicking until his head felt like it was going to explode, and his nana, at her wits' end, sent for the doctor.

When he eventually went back to school, it made no difference; he just sat there, blank-faced and silent. He had allowed his father to do something so terrible to his mother that she was gone for ever, and he had done nothing to stop him. That was the only thing he could think about. When the teacher put reading books in front of him, hoping he would absorb something of what was going on around him and remember at least some of his lessons, a swimmy blankness came into his head and he let it fill him up inside. Outside, the world carried on as normal. The teacher's voice droned on in the classroom, the smell of mashed potatoes and thick, skin-covered custard pervaded the corridors at dinner time, the bland school dinners food in the canteen tasted grey in his mouth. While the other kids played right up until the bell for afternoon lessons, he leaned against the wall and let the sounds of breaktime drift across to him: the slap and drag of a skipping rope against the ground, the scuffling shoes, as girls threaded themselves in and out, singing breathlessly as the rope churned round and round. He watched the intricate hand-clapping routines and two-balls juggling that they did in pairs, heard their sing-song voices dancing in the air: 'A sailor went to sea, sea, sea, to see what he could see, see, see . . .' He put his hands in his pockets and fingered the soft material on the inside, rubbing it between his finger and thumb for the small comfort it offered him. Sometimes the other boys would talk about him, stopping in the middle of their games and huddling together so that all he could see was a row of backs. He knew they were talking about him because they kept

139

turning round and looking at him, their eyes full of secrets, but he didn't care.

For a while he hated his mother for dying and leaving him. Then he hated her for making him fail, for giving him a name he couldn't live up to. Much later, he hated her for being so stupid that she thought a name, a stupid little word, could save her. When his nana died, he was almost relieved that he would no longer have to listen to her going on and on about how wonderful her Bernadette was, as if she could bring his mother back to life with the power of her memories. Liam knew better. By the time he was fourteen, he had everything sussed out. He knew you couldn't put your trust in anything or anyone. Eventually, whoever it was, they would fail you.

He ran away when his nana died. He knew it was going to happen, this time. He had watched her grow thinner and thinner, her skin become greyer and greyer. Before she got too weak, she went to Lourdes to be healed. Her church had had a collection to raise the money. She came back tired but filled with fresh hope, smiling and calling herself a pilgrim. Her cheeks had hollowed more even in the few days she had been away, and her smile etched deep creases down either side of her mouth, making her look like a ventriloquist's dummy. She went into hospital soon after that and never came home again.

While she was in hospital, Liam stayed next door with the Donaghys. Mrs Donaghy was a good samaritan, that was what his nana had told him. But he couldn't stay with her for ever. She had her own family to support, and there wasn't room for another. After his nana had passed away, the authorities came and spoke to Mrs Donaghy. Liam stood in the hall and listened through the closed kitchen door. They had run out of options. There was no one left who could take him. They regretted to say it but Liam would have to be placed with a foster family, one that took kids long-term, because he was too old to be adopted.

After Mrs Donaghy had shown the lady out, she gave Liam a hug and went very quiet for the rest of the day. She didn't even tell her own kids off when they started fighting over the TV channels, leaping up from their chairs and diving at the little black and white portable, popping the buttons so that it kept jumping from ITV to the BBC and back again.

◌

The foster mother had a large family – a mixture of her own children and children who had no parents of their own, or whose parents couldn't look after them. Liam supposed he was both those things. There were one or two older than him and the youngest was four. Some of them had lived with her for years and at times she seemed hard-pressed to remember which were her own and which were not. She was nice like that; in a way, she said, it didn't matter. They were all God's children.

He slept with three other boys in a tiny room with two sets of bunk beds, one on either side and just enough room to walk down the middle. Their clothes were kept in a chest of drawers on the landing and an extra wardrobe in the girls' room. The girls' room was bigger and sometimes the boys argued that it wasn't fair, but the foster mother said girls needed more space and that was that.

There were no night lights kept on all night in this house, like he was used to at his nana's. Once the foster mother came and turned out the big light at the switch by the door, there was only the light from the landing to see by, slanting through the gap in the slightly open door. He lay on his back on the top bunk, staring through the greyness at the swirly texture he could still just about make out on the ceiling.

Each time he woke up in the middle of the night, it was pitch dark. The foster mother switched out the landing light when she came to bed herself. Night after night he lay there, desperate for morning to come, listening to the silence in the room, not daring to get out of bed and switch the landing light back on again.

The night he wet the bed, he woke up almost immediately and lay in his cold pee for hours, terrified of the dark, terrified, too, of what would happen in the morning. He prayed he could keep it hidden from the other kids, hoped against hope that Gareth, who slept in the bunk below, wouldn't find out and spread it round the school. It was a new school; his old school hadn't let him stay once he moved off his nana's estate. Different catchment area, they said. He didn't care; he hadn't liked it there anyway, but he didn't know anyone at his new school. Now he would get known as the kid that pissed his bed. No one pissed the bed at fourteen and got away with it.

He didn't like Gareth. He had been winding him up since the day he moved in, kicking the underneath of his bunk and laughing that Liam had only been given the top bunk because he was a weed. It was true: Liam was a full year older but he was a good three inches smaller.

The next morning, while Gareth was lying with his legs in the air, kicking at the diamond-shaped mesh that held Liam's mattress, he noticed the dark-coloured stain. The mattress was so thin the pee had soaked all the way through. Liam scurried into the bathroom red-faced. At the breakfast table he could eat nothing. He could see Gareth and the others smiling inwardly, and knew that it would be all round the school yard within minutes of them arriving, if he didn't do something to stop it.

The walk to school passed through some council houses with a patch of grass in the middle. There were signs up saying No Ball Games, like there had been on his nana's estate, but they always kicked a football around there anyway, until some window or other shot open and they were yelled at until they ran away. Liam trailed miserably after the other boys, following them round a corner and through the maze of railings that were meant to stop kids with bikes from riding over the grass. Gareth and the two older ones dropped their bags and started kicking their football between them, and then they started doing kick-ups, taking it in turns to have the ball. Liam dropped his bag on the ground too, and walked towards them.

Gareth turned round and looked at him. The sneery look was still there, hiding behind his normal expression. Liam could see it, could feel his derision, making the back of his neck and the tops of his arms prickle.

Gareth arched his eyebrow. 'What's up?' he said, 'Want yer nappy changing?'

A silence fell. And then it happened all at once. Liam launched himself at Gareth with the force of a rocket, squeezing his hands into fists and hurling them into whichever part of Gareth's body seemed softest and least protected. The rest of the family, excited by the prospect of an impromptu fight, closed around them in a tight circle, urging 'Scrap! Scrap! Scrap! Scrap!'

Liam felt a fist meet the corner of his mouth but he couldn't feel any pain. It stoked his anger even more, fuelling his arms which were working like pistons, punching and punching his fists into Gareth as if they could keep on punching for ever.

For a moment, Gareth managed to free himself and he staggered backwards, winded.

'Scrap! Scrap! Scrap!' came the cry. There seemed to be more kids surrounding them now, like it was a proper organised fight. Gareth had red coming from one of his nostrils, and his already-sallow face had paled to almost the same colour as his white hair, so that the blood stood out all dark and horrible. He dragged his sleeve across his face and, when he saw what was smeared there, his expression hardened and he seemed to draw some fresh reserves of strength from the air as he took a deep breath and squared his shoulders.

Liam waited. He waited for Gareth to come towards him, letting fly, and then he caught him, full in the face. This time, he felt the pain. Gareth's teeth split his knuckles and his fist turned red with his own blood. It was the end of the fight. The onlookers regrouped themselves around Gareth, who had dropped to the ground and was rolling around howling, and Liam seized his chance. He ran. His legs were trembling but he willed them to hold him up. He ran across the grass, grabbing his bag as he passed it, and shot blindly up the first street he came to, not caring where it led.

He thought they would be straight after him, but there was no sound of running or shouting from behind. He didn't let himself stop and check until he had zigzagged down another street and then another. When he did stop, his legs buckled beneath him and he sank to the ground, the sound of his heart and his panting breath deafening him to anything else. If they were following, he could do nothing about it now.

He examined his fist. Across the middle two knuckles a jagged, messy cut marked the point where Gareth's front teeth had made contact with his skin. He could almost see the bucktooth shape in the outline. It had started to hurt: a stinging, throbbing pain which got worse when he lowered his arm and his fast-pumping blood rushed down to it. He lifted it up again quickly and held it against his chest. Other places were hurting too. He lifted his other hand to his face and touched the tips of his fingers lightly against his cheekbone. Something felt wrong there, and the skin round his eye felt puffed-up and tight. If he breathed in too deeply his chest hurt. He wanted to lie down and close his eyes right there, but he couldn't, not in the middle of the street. And he couldn't go back to the foster home either. Not now.

When he stood up unsteadily and started walking, he didn't know where he was going, only that he was not going back. He wove through street after street, not looking where he was going, not caring that he wouldn't be able to find his way home. He didn't need to. He was on his own now. Gingerly, he lifted the strap of his bag over his head so that it hung across his chest and limped grimly onwards.

∾

Fresh memories keep butting into his mind, pissing him off. Why won't they just stay put, where he has left them? Angry, he lashes out and kicks at a litter bin as he passes it, but it is fixed to the ground and his foot bounces off, the bin unaffected.

'Fucking useless cunt!' He drains the last of his beer can and crunches it in his fist and then, turning to face the sea, hurls it as far as he can. He watches it fly out into the darkness and disappear.

He is back in the spot where he met the girl. He has been looking everywhere for somewhere to spend the night, somewhere with a bit of shelter from the cold, but his wanderings round the town's streets have come up with nothing, and he is tired of looking, and fed up with the way things are turning out. When he sees the burger van an idea takes shape instantly. It's all locked up for the night. There's a padlock on the door and another on the hatch at the front, but it's worth a go: it'll be warmer in there than it is out here. He tries the lock on the door first, poking up inside it with the tweezers of the penknife he has fished from one of his pockets, but it won't catch; he can't do it. His fingers are so numb he can't hold the knife properly; it keeps slipping from his grasp and falling on the floor.

After picking it up for the third time he gives up on the padlock itself and goes for the screws attaching the hasp to the doorframe. It takes all his concentration to make his fingers do what he wants them to, and by the time he has fumbled two of the screws out his patience has run dry. He wrenches the door, his foot wedged against the frame, and pulls the last two screws out by force. The door flies open and he climbs inside, triumphant.

The trailer has been cleaned up, but the stink of frying onions and burger grease is strong. On a shelf along the back wall are catering-sized jars of pickled onions and pickled eggs, suspended like slithery eyeballs in the cloudy vinegar. He pulls the eggs down and unscrews the top, his mouth watering at the sulphur and acid tang which wafts out at him. He sticks his hand in the bottle and pulls two eggs out, the vinegar dripping off his fingers and running inside his sleeve. After the eggs, which he crams into his mouth whole, he helps himself to a can of coke and a bag of crisps from one of the boxes with holes cut in one end. As he crunches and swigs in alternate mouthfuls he looks for the controls to the griddle, but when he finds them and presses them nothing happens. Bastard's probably run off a portable generator, he thinks, and that wanker's driven off with it. There is a pile of newspapers under the counter. He hunts around for a lighter or some matches, so that he can make a fire, but there's nothing. He'd burn the whole trailer down if it would get him warmed up. Defeated, he spreads the newspapers on the greasy floor of the trailer instead, and lies down on top of them. If he could go to sleep for a bit he might be able to forget about the cold. He pulls his knees in as close to his stomach as he can and closes his eyes against the darkness.

శు

He ended up breaking into somewhere that other time, too. He spent the day wandering the streets, feeling the blood drying on his knuckles until he could pick it off, the brown-coloured flakes sticking in his fingernails. One eye was almost closed and it hurt when he tried to open it. He tried to get on a bus; he had the money to pay – his dinner money – but the driver wouldn't let him stay on. He told him the bus wasn't going anywhere until he got off. Then he closed the doors and drove away and all the passengers turned and stared at Liam out of the windows.

He wanted to get back to his nana's estate. Maybe if he found Mrs Donaghy and explained, she would let him live with her again. But with no clear idea of the direction he had to go in, he found himself wandering in aimless circles. When he saw a few groups of kids wandering desultorily along the street he knew it must be going home time. They weren't from his school; their uniform was a different colour. They walked past him as if he was invisible, but then he heard them laughing and he knew they had seen him really; they were just pretending.

It started to go dark and he realised it was going to take longer than he had thought to find his old estate. He would have to wait until tomorrow. When he saw a house with boarded-up windows he pulled himself over the wall and went to investigate. He was going to need somewhere to spend the night.

Getting in wasn't easy. His cut hand felt stiff and achey, and the boards over the windows were hammered into place with long nails. He pulled at the smallest plank until he had made enough of a gap to try to lever it off, and then he stuck the handle of a rotten mop into the gap and pushed. It didn't do much good; the handle snapped in half with a soggy, splintering sound, but he had made the gap a bit bigger and, after some more pulling, there was enough room for him to squeeze through. Around the edges of the window frame, triangular shards of glass stood guard. It was like climbing through an enormous pair of jaws into a big dark mouth. Once he was in he tried to pull the dislodged board closed after him and then, gloomily, he examined his fresh wounds. Tiny beads of blood were welling up in a line along his forearm where he had scraped against the glass teeth. Another bit had jabbed through his school trousers into his knee. He spat on his fingers and rubbed the dirty spittle into the cuts on his arms.

It was scary being in the dark room on his own. It was still light outside, but inside, with all the windows blocked up, it felt like night-time already, especially because the walls were all black, and there was a funny smell, like something burnt and mouldy at the same time, that bit at the insides of his nostrils. It felt much colder than outside, like being in a cellar, and there was nothing in there except an old chair with no cushions on it, just the elastic straps that were meant to hold the seat, all broken and hanging down on to the floor. He wished he could get back to his nana's place. And he wished his nana hadn't gone and died so he couldn't live with her any more. He listened, and underneath the silence he was sure he could hear scratching sounds, maybe coming from the next room, or upstairs. He couldn't tell. He was starting to wish he hadn't broken in at all, but now he was here he didn't know what else to do or where else he could go. Slowly, he backed himself against the wall by the window, where at least he could see some of the light from a street lamp outside, and sank to the floor. He would just have to wait until morning.

When the policeman found him he had messed his trousers and was sitting in his shame, shaking with fear. The policeman picked him up and carried him in his arms like a baby. He was kind. He seemed to understand about the humiliation, and ran a basin of hot water without any fuss or bother. Then he found a pair of too-big gym shorts in the lost property locker and left Liam in the police station lavatory to tidy himself up before taking him back to the foster home with his underpants and school trousers in a plastic bag.

ᦐ

Hannah stirs in her sleep. As the clock on the bedside table ticks and the dressing-table mirror quietly reflects the flowered paper on the opposite wall, her father walks into the room. He stands and looks at her, rocking slightly on the balls of his feet. She can smell whisky, can hear his raspy breathing. He has lung cancer, though he doesn't know it yet. He takes a step closer, reaches down and shakes her firmly by the shoulder. 'Wake up, Hannah Jane. Wake up!' She jerks her arm, pulling herself away from him, and briefly she opens her eyes and sees him standing there over her. His dark moustache and his waistcoat. He always wore a waistcoat. And then she sees through the night greyness the familiar pattern in the wallpaper, her wallpaper at *Swn Y Don*, and knows he has gone. Carefully, she eases on to her side, arranging her legs so that she won't wake up later with them aching, and drifts back into sleep.

14

'Wake up! Hannah Jane, wake up!' He has come back again. He is pulling at the quilt, this time, tapping her on the shoulder. 'Wake up! Wake up, now!' She opens her eyes and sees the white of his shirtsleeves against his black waistcoat. 'Quickly, now. Don't wake your sister.' She jerks awake and sits up in the bed. There is no one there. She is breathing heavily and she can feel her heart thudding in her chest. She leans back against the pillows and closes her eyes, waits for her breathing to return to normal. Well, she never thought she would see her father again.

❧

She looks awful, Marina thinks, looking up as Hannah comes through the kitchen door. Her face is grey, like overhandled dough and her hair, still messy from bed, looks thin and lifeless. Perhaps it is the dressing gown; old people always look so much older in dressing gowns, like they've given up on doing anything except lying in bed waiting to die.

'Hi,' she says. 'Sorry. We didn't wake you, did we?' It's only seven o'clock, but Oscar is already wide awake and hungry. Hannah pulls out a chair and sits down in it heavily.

'No,' she says, her voice flat and weary-sounding. 'I was awake anyway.'

Marina shoots her a glance, half concerned, half minding her own business. Hannah smiles and starts talking to Oscar, asking him if he slept well and what his mummy is making him for his breakfast. She speaks in that high, exaggerated, talking-to-children voice that is so useful for hiding behind.

Marina finishes making the toast and cuts it into triangular shapes before putting it on a plate. She feels awkward, standing in another person's kitchen, using their food, rummaging in their cupboards, even though this is how she has been living for months at Suzanne's place since things got really bad after Rob left. She makes a pot of tea and sets two cups and saucers on the table. Hannah notices the gesture. In return, she makes encouraging noises about the toast and jam to encourage Oscar to eat it up. Marina sits down to drink her tea and, for the first time, watches her son jabbering and waving his toast around at somebody else.

Rob hadn't wanted a baby. When she got pregnant he changed completely. He said he'd been happy with things the way they were, just the two of them, no worries. He seemed awkward around her, distant, as if he was embarrassed by the crazy situation they had created between them which was going to change everything. This coolness lasted for a few weeks, until he suggested she have an abortion, and then it changed to outright animosity when she refused to consider it. They should have

153

split up then, but Marina felt low, felt she needed him to be there. Even the way he was, he was better than nobody.

She was just starting the second year of university when all this happened. She completed the year, but after Oscar was born, it was impossible; Rob was hardly around at all and she stopped going to lectures after the first week of her final year. Eventually, she phoned the departmental office and asked to defer. It sounded hollow even as she was saying it, but it felt like less of a defeat than saying she was dropping out. Rob left for good soon after that, and things grew steadily worse. He had paid a month's rent in advance, but after that they had nothing. Marina didn't know what to do. She burned with nervous energy, building a wall between herself and Oscar and the outside world. She stumbled from bed to feed her son when he cried, and fell asleep again as he fed. When he was finished she burped him mechanically, put him down in his cot and climbed back into bed, whatever the time of day or night.

These black moods were not unknown to her. She had experienced them before, the same unforgiving mixture: buzzing thoughts spinning in her mind at night, her restless feet nagging at the bedclothes. And then such lassitude that turning over in bed or pulling in her cold arm from outside the covers seemed more trouble than it was worth. She recognised what was happening and eventually dragged herself out of bed and went to see a doctor.

It was in her already, the instinct for survival. It was what had saved her the previous times. But with Oscar's presence, his absolute need for her to be there for him, it doubled in strength.

Little by little, she improved. She started taking Oscar out in the buggy, wheeling him round Victoria Park and stopping at the lake to look at the fountain and the ducks. She went to the benefits office and made a claim, filling in all the forms the moment she got them home, refusing to let the leaden feeling overwhelm her until she had completed them, pushed them inside their envelopes and taken them to the post box. She knew that if she put the forms aside to fill in later, or tomorrow, they would never be sent.

In the end, she almost wished she hadn't bothered. She lost the flat anyway, while she was waiting for the housing benefit. Her landlord refused to give her any more time. On the day she was evicted, Suzanne came to help move her stuff. Where was Marina moving to, she asked. Marina shook her head and shrugged her shoulders, defeated. She had nowhere. They left all the furniture behind, because there was no space at Suzanne's flat, and they walked there in silence, carrying as much as they could of Marina's stuff between them.

ை

Oscar laughs and waves a triangle of toast in the air. Hannah leans forwards, magnifying her gestures, giving them sound effects, as she pretends to make a grab for his breakfast and gobble it down. He gurgles delightedly, jammy dribble running down his chin.

She remembers how Evan was with children. He was so formal with them that he scared them off. He was like a pantomime villain: the wicked guest-house keeper who eats up naughty boys. One summer she overheard voices on the landing outside a room she was cleaning and she stopped what she was doing to listen. *The one that gets closest before he turns round is the winner*, they had hissed in sticky, conspiratorial whispers. The children scattered when they heard the door creak open and ran into their rooms, but when they saw it was only Hannah they bashfully crept out from behind the half-closed doors and brought their seashell collections to show to her, holding out hinged cockles and razor clams on trusting palms. Not telling Evan about their game had made her feel complicit in it. She liked the feeling; she had felt the first stirrings of rebellion then, although she managed to keep them dormant for a good while longer, until he was nearly dead and it didn't matter any more.

Part of Evan's trouble was that he had had no experience with children. He was an only child, so had never had to grapple with younger brothers and sisters. His only cousins were years older. He didn't understand the physicality of childhood, the way you had to get stuck in and be demonstrative. When he caught her playing once, with the children of some guests or other, really playing, so that her hair had come loose and she had a happy flush in her cheeks, he asked if he could have a word with her and led her into the hall. Within earshot of the parents, he had told her, the tip of his nose pinched white, as it always was when he was angry, that playing with guests' children in such a way was not only undignified and unseemly but degraded the standing of the guest house and made *him* look foolish. When she tried to protest he had given her such a savage look that she

156

stopped mid-sentence and walked into the dining room to hide her brimming tears in the routine of setting tables for breakfast, a drill so familiar she could do it without thinking.

ço

'He likes you,' Marina says. It's true. With Hannah's encouragement Oscar has eaten all but one of the toast shapes. Marina feels a tiny twinge of jealousy: he is never this biddable with her. But then she smiles. It's like he is flirting, enjoying the attention of a new admirer. She watches the two of them, watches her son, rapt, his mouth hanging open, his eyes alive, fixed on the piece of toast hovering above his head, as Hannah weaves him a story about it dropping from the sky after falling from the hungry grasp of the man who lives in the clouds.

ço

Liam wakes up suddenly, jerking out of a dream which fades even before he realises he is awake. He sits up slowly, tearing the newspaper he has been lying on. The heels of his hands are black with rubbed-away print. His whole body is aching. He feels about a hundred years old.

It is dark inside the trailer, the only light a thin grey outline round the edge of the serving hatch. He crawls stiffly over to the door and pushes it open a crack. Nobody is about yet, but it won't be long. He leans back on his haunches and fishes his mobile phone from his pocket. 7.45. There will be people around soon; there always are. The early-riser types with stupid little dogs in tartan coats, who make it their business to notice things like broken padlocks. He doesn't want to get caught if some nosy parker decides to call the police. He needs to get a move on. He staggers to his feet and the movement makes him realise he needs to pee. He pushes the door further open and peers out again. He lowers one foot to the ground and is about to follow with the other one when he has a better idea. He steps back inside and pulls the door closed again. He'll leave a little something for the arsehole who wouldn't sell him a cheap-as-shit burger. With fingers still weak from sleep, he unfastens his flies and fumbles in his pants, and then takes aim carefully at the corner where he has been sleeping. For half a second, nothing happens, and then an arc of deep yellow piss hits the newspapers and splashes on to the wall. He lets out a long, slow, satisfied breath as he pees, watching the piss soak into the newsprint and leak across the floor in a slow, steaming puddle. The sweet and sour smell of warm urine and wet newspaper drifts into his nostrils. Serves the bastard right, he thinks.

Before he leaves he remembers something else and reaches across to the boxes of crisps, trying not to wet his shoes in his own pee. He pulls out a couple of bags and stuffs them into his jacket pockets.

Outside, he quickly pushes the broken hasp back into position, so the guy won't notice anything till he's right there, jangling his keys ready to unlock the place. He imagines his face when he sees he's been broken into, when he sees what's been left inside, and grins. It'd almost be worth being there.

It's getting lighter. He could find a café open somewhere, a greasy spoon, and get some breakfast down him. He has now been cold for so long he can't remember what warmth feels like. He doesn't believe it exists in this place; there's too much sea and wind. What he wants more than anything is milky, sugary tea and a plate of fried eggs and bacon. He sets off in the direction which looks most promising. If he finds a café he can pretend to read the newspaper until his circulation gets going again.

15

Hannah carries what is left of the breakfast dishes over to the sink, where Marina is starting to wash up.

'You don't need to do that, you know,' she says.

'Oh, I don't mind. Honestly. You've been so kind to us.' She dries her hands on her jeans and touches Oscar briefly on the top of his head, smoothing his hair before returning to the dishes.

Hannah so wants to pick him up and feel him, heavy and warm and wriggling with life, in her arms but she can sense Marina's guardedness. All through breakfast, she knows Marina has been watching her play with the child, as if she can't trust anyone to be alone with him. She wonders whether something has happened to make her so anxious, or if it is just that all mothers feel this way.

❧

When she has finished washing the breakfast things Marina wanders into the front room with Oscar. The old cards Hannah gave him are still strewn over the rug. She bends over to tidy them up, and as she does so, she opens one or two and reads the messages inside before making them into a tidy pile and putting them down on a side table.

She looks out at the bay. The sea seems brisk, glinting the watery sun in a thousand, brief shimmering spots that appear and disappear across its moving surface as she watches. It is so peaceful and quiet she feels she could almost forget about Dave and his money. She sits down in one of the armchairs in the window. She hasn't been able to just sit like this for months. At Suzanne's, even when there was no one else in, she couldn't really relax. She always felt uneasy if she switched on the TV for Oscar for half an hour. She could imagine Dave arriving home and sneering, telling Suzanne he'd come in and found her dossing in front of the telly instead of getting off her arse and finding herself somewhere to live. She would get out of the flat as early as she could each morning and trail Oscar round the shops in his buggy instead, or go into the library and read stories to him under her breath. Every few days they walked down Well Street and looked at the fish in the pet shop. Sometimes there would be rabbits, kittens, puppies and they would stand at the window watching them, shifting aside to make room when older children, clutching cones of hot chips from the chippy next door, crowded round for a look, their open mouths steaming vinegary patches of fog on to the glass.

She wonders why Hannah is doing this, letting her stay and not caring that she doesn't pay her. She feels bad. When she leaves, she thinks, she will leave some money anyway. There is

161

no point in worsening her guilt by ripping off a kind old lady, pretending she is penniless when she isn't.

⁊

When Hannah walks back into the dining room, her heart sinks. There are still a couple more boxes to sort through, but the pleasure she had taken in her task yesterday has gone now and it all seems totally pointless. There was absolutely no need to open that sideboard and drag everything out of it. It's not like she needs the space. Now she will have to ask Glynnis's husband to come round and make a bonfire of it all in the garden, and Glynnis will make all sorts of bother about it, rolling her eyes and tut-tutting, as if Hannah can't be trusted to take care of her own business. Well, she sighs, maybe Glynnis is right. Annoyed with herself for feeling so defeated so soon, she tips the last of the boxes into a half-filled bin bag, and then places the file with the letters inside on top and hurriedly ties the bag up. There, she thinks. That's it all sorted out and forgotten about. But she knows she can't leave it alone. Not now she has found those letters. The need to sit down and read them properly has been burning in her since she woke up. With a deep breath, she unties the knot she has just tied, lifts out the file and places it carefully on the table in front of her.

The first one is clearly a reply. It is from a Major James Croom, of the Salvation Army, thanking her father for his enquiry and giving details of a number of establishments that appear to meet his requirements. He also assures her father that officers of the

Salvation Army work, always, with the utmost discretion and sensitivity, both to the girls and to their families.

Quickly, she scans the letter beneath and the ones beneath that. They make arrangements, set dates, discuss the proposed duration of the young lady's stay. The 'young lady' is her. She swallows and reads each one over again. This brief flurry of correspondence must have taken place whilst she was in Chatham, confined for the most part to a small upstairs bedroom because her father's cousin was no keener to be associated with her situation than her father had been. Her hands are shaking again; she wishes they wouldn't. She laces her fingers together to try to stop them and closes her eyes.

ಬಿ

She stayed in Chatham for nearly three months and she could not believe, then, that her life could be any more miserable. The cousin's wife had produced no children of her own and the daily reminder of her lack of fecundity, waved beneath her nose in so unwholesome, so undeserved a manner, put her in a constantly ill humour. She seemed to like neither her home nor her husband and she moaned almost non-stop about both. When Hannah was put on a train back to London, with the address of a Salvation Army Mothers' Hospital in Clapton in her bag, Hannah was relieved to see the back of her. By this time, she had grown almost to full term, and her body felt pale and limp from lack of activity. Her confinement to the house meant also that now, clambering off the train at London Bridge, in the middle of the rush hour, a slow panic was spreading like venom though her body as she lumbered her solitary way through crowds of people she was no longer able to cope with.

From London Bridge, she took a taxi to the address written in her father's handwriting, which had arrived in the post three days earlier, and paid the driver with the money that had accompanied it. She had forgotten how devastated some parts of London were. Although the war had been over for years now, the scars of the Blitz were still open sores in the places she was being driven through. Whole streets emptied of buildings. Here and there, scrappy allotments scratched into the earth in strange empty spaces between buildings, up against walls where the ghosts of rooms and staircases still hung. It was early evening and there were people about, walking wearily home from another day at work. Stepping over the cracked paving stones, going about their lives.

When the driver stopped she looked through the window at the place where she was going to have her baby. It stood with quiet dignity behind a pair of arched iron gates. One of the buildings had clearly been damaged by bombs and still had a wooden joist supporting it in one corner. For a moment she wanted to tell the driver to drive her away again, but she had nowhere else to go and even if she wasn't ready to have the baby yet, her body almost was. There was no escape, no matter how hard she tried not to think about it. She climbed out shakily, paid the driver and let him carry her case to the main door. She waited until he was gone before ringing, although she pretended to so that he would drive away. She listened for the sound of

164

the engine starting up before she reached up and pulled the lever down hard enough for it to actually jangle the enormous bell that she could see through the fanlight. For those minutes before she heard someone on the other side of the door, sliding bolts across and turning keys, she had never experienced such smothering silence. She felt herself swaying, feeling giddy. Through an open window somewhere nearby she heard the mournful, echoing sound of a baby crying. For a disembodied moment, she feared she might faint. When the door swung open she felt almost grateful. Suddenly she was the centre of attention; a nurse rushed out and took her by the arm, another tutted and whispered something to her about supper. Whether she would like some now, or would rather rest first.

'Rest, please,' she whispered. The nurse smiled at her.

'I'll tell you what,' she said. Let's get you settled in and then I'll fetch you some hot chocolate. How's that?'

'Thank you.' She smiled weakly, glad that she would be left alone to sleep. The nurse led her up two flights of stairs and into a darkened room. In the gloom she could pick out beds on either wall. It looked like a hospital ward.

'I'm afraid we haven't the space for a room each,' the nurse whispered. 'But you might like the company, once you get to know the girls. They're all very friendly and, you know, everyone's in the same situation here.' Everything was very decorous and a little too cheerful, but the nurses spoke with genuine kindness; apart from the cab driver, they were the first people who had for months. Here, at least, she felt she was not in total disgrace.

The nurse led her to one side of the room, where an empty

bed stood waiting, the blanket smoothed as flat as an ironing board and pulled up to the pillow, with a wide band of sheet folded neatly over it.

'Your bag will come up later,' she whispered again. 'Try to get some rest, now. I'll go and see to that hot chocolate.'

16

After the disaster with the first foster family, Liam was placed with a new one. Again, he had to change school. He was so far behind, by this point, still struggling so hard to make sense of the sea of words swimming in front of him in his schoolbooks and on the blackboard, that he couldn't see any point in going. He started bunking off and jumping on to buses into town instead, diving on quickly as passengers got off and squeezing past the people coming down the stairs before the driver noticed. On the smoky top deck there was always a selection of tickets that had been tucked under the rail on the back of each seat by earlier passengers. Little square chits of green, orange, blue. He chose the right fare by colour as if picking sweets in a sweetshop, and held the ticket tight in his palm as he clouded the window with his breath and drew smiley faces and wrote his name over and over again, then watched it being slowly obliterated by condensation running down the glass. The buses stopped at the Pier Head, by the Liver Building.

His nana used to bring him down here, and take him on the ferry sometimes to see someone she knew in Greasby, over the water. She used to point out the Liver Birds perching above the huge clock faces at either end of the building, with their elongated legs and necks, and sprigs of laver seaweed pinched in their beaks. Laughing, in the phlegm-throated way she had, where, halfway through, the laugh would become a hacking, death rattle of a cough, she would point out the female bird, looking out across the river, waiting for her sailor's safe return, and then point to the male bird, looking backwards, to where the pubs were.

From the bus window he would stare up at the birds, remembering what his nana had told him, pressing his face against the glass as the driver rounded a corner and they disappeared, craning his neck to relocate them. And then, standing in front of the Liver Buildings, dwarfed by the huge façades, her voice would replay in his head, telling him how Liverpool would be destroyed if the birds ever flew away. When he was younger he had believed her, had thought the green birds had magic powers that would protect the city from any kind of catastrophe you could think of. The belief made him feel safe, as if he thought they would protect him too. But by the time he was wagging off school more often than he was going, he knew nothing would happen if they flew away. Things were leaving, being lost, all the time, and nothing ever happened to the people who had lost them. They just carried on. He had their measure now; he knew them for the frauds they were. They weren't even real birds, just invented ones, made of metal; they couldn't fly. If you looked closely, really squinted your eyes against the dazzle of the sky, you could see the wires holding them up. They were just like string puppets. Yet he always looked out for them from the bus, from the river, from wherever he could see them. In return, they ignored him and maintained their impassive gaze unperturbed, one scrutinising the grey buildings of Birkenhead on the other side of the river, the other turning its back, its verdigris-covered wings held open in the perpetual moment before impossible flight.

და

The baby was born in the early hours of the morning. The first pains woke her from a dream so insignificant and unconnected with her present circumstances that it took another spasm for it to register what was happening and that this was it: the baby was coming. She had hung on to the childish belief that hiding from what was happening could make it go away for as long as she could. Now she had to let go.

She endured the labour with an inexpressible mixture of pain and blankness she could only later remember in terms of the colour red. When she panted for breath between bouts of pushing and her face relaxed for a few moments, the light bulb hanging over the bed blazed red through her closed eyelids. The pain as she screamed the baby out was a constant, burning, streaming red, and the baby itself, as it was lifted away from her body hiccoughing into bright new cries, was red and angry, too.

And it was a boy. As they lifted it free and cut through the snake-coloured leash still tethering it to her, they told her. A boy. They carried him away. Him. She had already been told that her father had asked for arrangements to be made for adoption. She mutely accepted what she heard as if she were hearing echoes from a conversation in another room. Until she left the hospital, a nurse told her, she was free to nurse the child, if she wished. She wished nothing at all but the nurse was kind-hearted and brought him to her.

In her arms, he seemed to accept what she was told to offer him without curiosity or question. With the nurse's help, she settled him into the crook of her elbow and he took her nipple in his mouth as if it were just what he had been expecting. For six days she allowed this tiny, unsurprised creature to take possession of her; she fed him from her own body whenever she was told he was hungry; she sat rigidly still, her arms aching with the effort of not moving, whenever he chose to fall asleep in her arms. The nurses showed her how to clean him up and give him a fresh nappy when he needed it. In the hospital there was nothing else to occupy her. For six days she enslaved herself to him, forgoing her own comfort and care, so that the nurses fussed around her with a hairbrush, murmuring their disapproval as they tugged at her hair and told her to change her nightdress.

The night before she was due to go home, she sat beside his cradle and watched him as he lay there. He had managed to get his arms out from under the covers and was clenching and unclenching his tiny fists and waving them about on his little, doll-sized arms. His pink face was twitching and screwing up, his eyes moving beneath closed, gluey-looking lids. He looked like he was fighting in a dream, trying to hold off some attacker,

170

his creased-up face contorting with effort as he tried to find his way out of the mazy world he had wandered into.

As she watched him, spellbound, everything opened at once: fists, eyes, mouth, and he gulped at the air greedily like a surfaced diver. A long, creaking wail began to snake slowly out of his open, red-gummed mouth, not loud, but still penetrating in the padded silence of the sleeping ward. Quickly, she leaned over and lifted him into her arms. The wail paused and then started up again a little more quietly, dropping into a lower, less urgent gear. She knew just the way to hold him now, so that his head was supported as he fed. She held him in one arm, rocking him and clucking at him: ch ch ch ch ch, as she quickly unbuttoned the front of her nightdress and sat down. She pushed her nipple into his waiting mouth and felt the concentration of his whole body as he began to suck. She stroked his head, smoothing the soft hair, so much darker than her own. It's baby hair, the nurse had told her. It won't be his eventual colour. She wondered what his eventual colour would be, whether his hair would be like hers, light and slightly wavy, or dark and straight like Simeon's had been. She hadn't seen Simeon since the discovery of her pregnancy, had no idea whether he knew about it or not. She had refused to tell her parents who it was that had brought such shame on them. The skin on the baby's head was slightly flaky and sore in places. Cradle cap, the nurse had said. It would clear up in a few weeks. It was nothing to worry about. She cupped the tiny head in her hand. In a few weeks she would no longer be his mother. His head was so warm, resting in her palm. That, more than anything, was what she remembered. The heat he

171

produced, like he was already aflame with his future life, already living it at top speed.

The following morning, she handed him back to the nurse for the last time without protest and watched as the tiny, blanketed bundle was carried away from her down the ward. When he was gone she turned to the window and closed her eyes against the brightness of the day outside. She could still feel the tingling pain his champing gums had left imprinted around her right nipple. It was probably all for the best, the nurse had offered in consolation, but she had said nothing in return. In two hours her father would come to take her home.

∽

The job, he told her, had cost him no small degree of trouble to arrange, and for this he expected some show of gratitude. She nodded her wooden head, hoping faintly that he would take this thanks in arrears, because she didn't immediately know how to shape the words he required from her, let alone feel the sentiments they were supposed to express. After a silence weighted with expectation he shifted in his chair, making it scrape against the stone floor, and drew himself up to his full seated height. In order to make some reparation for the expense and trouble her recent situation had caused, he announced, his voice hitting some tonal harmony in the austerity of the kitchen and sounding plangently in her head as it ran up the walls and curved round the insides of the hanging pots and pans, she would give all of her weekly pay to him until further notice. She wished he had not chosen the kitchen for this interview. The hard seat of the chair hurt her where she was still swollen and sore from the birth, but she felt she couldn't ask for a cushion. This business will not be mentioned again in this house, he had said. We will have no cause to refer to it. This business. She felt she must will her body not to fail her, and she tried not to feel the bruised ache as she rose from her seat and left the room when he signalled that she could go.

She unpacked her belongings alone. Celia came into the bedroom to try and help her, but Hannah sent her away. It was early evening and the light was slowly fading. Everything in the room seemed heavy and sad. The remains of the spring day felt torpid and apathetic. Through the open window she could hear the unspooling skein of a blackbird's song and she traced the sound back to a tiny silhouette, perching on a chimney pot across the street. From that day on, she found the beautiful sound unbearable; it tripped her out of her life and if she wasn't careful it took her back to this moment, sitting awkwardly, painfully on the edge of her dark-counterpaned bed, unpacking clothes she had not worn for nearly half a year, as the light drained from the watery sky and a cool breeze made the hairs prickle and raise goosebumps on her bare arms.

෨

Marina notices Hannah jump as she comes in. As if she had forgotten there was anyone else in the house. She isn't sure whether she wants to be disturbed. She seems to be sorting through old papers and she has tears in her eyes. A couple of them have brimmed over and run down her cheeks.

'I've brought you a cup of tea,' she says softly. She looks around for a place mat and puts the cup and saucer down on the table in front of Hannah. She doesn't look at all well. 'It's none of my business,' she says, her voice hesitant and low, 'but are you all right?'

Hannah smiles and wipes the tears away with the back of her hand with a sniff. 'Oh yes,' she says. 'Don't mind me. I'm just a silly old woman.' She looks at the cup of tea. 'That's kind of you. Thank you.' She picks up the cup and Marina notices how unsteady her hand is as she lifts it to her lips.

'You would say, wouldn't you, if we were in the way?' She hates the idea that Hannah might be regretting her decision to ask them to stay. 'I'd understand, if you wanted . . .'

Hannah reaches forward suddenly and touches her on the wrist. Her hand is awfully cold. 'I'm so glad you're here,' she says. 'Both of you. Really, I am.'

17

Hannah didn't know her Uncle John very well. He was her father's older brother, and was the senior partner in a firm of solicitors. Theirs was not a close family and they met rarely, on only the most formal occasions. Hannah had seen him perhaps three or four times in her life. There was a familial resemblance, in the sense that seeing her Uncle John made her recognise things in her father's face which she had not noticed before: the broad, flat bridge of his nose; the shape of his eyes; the jut of his chin. Yet, where her father had bulk – a robustness and a certain firmness to his flesh – his brother seemed to have just bones and skin. He was taller, but he lacked her father's physical presence and bullishness, preferring to get things done in a quiet, efficient manner.

She began work at his offices the day after she returned home from the Mothers' Hospital. There was no question, now, of her staying on at school until she was sixteen to get her school certificate. Not after the shame and expense she had caused. And she needed to earn money, to reimburse her father.

The clothes she had worn before her pregnancy were too

tight around the waist, but she had no others, so she left the top two buttons of her skirt unfastened and wore a long cardigan to cover the gaping V at the back, even though the weather was too warm. She felt self-conscious and imagined she could hear the other two office clerks whispering and giggling behind her back as she sweated in her woolly prison. Her breasts were still full and heavy and leaking milk. During a mid-morning break on her first day, she sat on the lavatory and cried quietly from the pain the fullness caused. There was nothing she could do to ease it; rubbing seemed to make it worse. She sat hunched at her desk and folded her arms across her chest every time anyone spoke to her, pinching the skin at the tops of her arms as hard as she could bear to keep herself from crying. Before long her arms were dotted with bruises.

The work was easy. It was filing, fetching and carrying, and typing letters. But her mind was not there. Standing at a filing cabinet drawer, she remembered the feel of the baby's head, the fine-as-fluff fuzz of dark hair he had been born with, and forgot whether M came before or after P. In the middle of a letter she would feel the sudden prickle of attention as the other girls noticed the silent typewriter, her hands hovering motionless over the keys as her eyes burned unseeing into the sheet she was typing. Each time it happened they nudged each other and smirked.

It wasn't that she couldn't do the work – her typing was fair and, although she didn't yet know shorthand, her education had been solid and she learned quickly. She just felt as if everything

176

she was doing was taking place somewhere else, and that the fingers she watched fumbling through piles of legal briefs and tying and untying pieces of coloured ribbon were somebody else's. It felt like she was working in a submarine world, where movement was slow and difficult and sounds muffled as they travelled to her through a kind of thickened water, compressed with the heaviness of the thousands of fathoms pressing down on top of it.

ॐ

She returned home after her first day with a shorthand manual and an exercise book, and instructions to have the rudiments mastered by the end of the week. The first one home from work, she sat down at the kitchen table and watched her mother put the kettle on and scoop tea into the teapot. Celia would be home soon, she told her, but their father would be slightly delayed. Her youngest brother, still in his school uniform, was poring over the latest copy of *The Eagle* comic, his head sunk low over the page, his fingers furiously twirling a section of his fringe round and round as he read. She could hear him breathing, the rapid in and out of a child's breath.

'George, love. Go up and get your sister's slippers for her,' her mother said, as she scalded the tea with water from the kettle. George kept reading, the fingers still twisting his hair.

'George!' She stepped across the kitchen to him and yanked his hand away from his head. 'Stop that. You'll pull it out! Now go and get your sister's slippers.'

George slid slowly off his seat and walked out of the room, still reading the comic.

'How was your first day, then?' her mother asked. It was the first time they had been alone together since Hannah's return. Her voice was soft and Hannah's eyes filled with tears.

'I . . . I don't know,' she said. She noticed a flicker of alarm cross her mother's face. 'I mean . . . it was fine. Just, you know, the first day.'

Her mother nodded and relaxed a little. She carried the teapot to the table and poured milk into two cups. Then she rattled the tea strainer from the drawer and sat back down again.

She seemed to be avoiding looking directly at Hannah. It made Hannah feel even more self-conscious about her appearance, about her enlarged breasts and thickened middle.

'I might need to get some new clothes,' she said, almost in a whisper. 'Would Father mind, do you think, just this month?' The wary look crossed her mother's face again. 'Only a few things,' she reassured her. 'It's just I'm still quite—'

Her mother stood up abruptly.

'My skirt doesn't—'

'I can see for myself, Hannah,' she interrupted. Her voice was suddenly sharp. Hannah felt something like panic beginning to flutter in her throat and more words came tumbling out before she could stop them, about the pain in her breasts and how she couldn't bear it any longer, she was going to burst if it didn't stop soon and please could she help her and she had heard her name out loud two or three times before she realised her mother was saying it and that she wanted her to stop.

'Hannah! Stop this at once. Hannah! There is a child in the house; have you forgotten?' Hannah looked up at her mother, standing over her, through bleary eyes. She was speaking in an urgent near-whisper which was threaded through with something almost like fear. 'For God's sake, stop this!' She sat down again, but the tips of her fingers were white where she gripped the edge of the table. The sound of creaking footsteps meant that George was coming back downstairs with the slippers. She leaned forward: 'I am sorry for what has happened to you, God knows I am, Hannah. But you cannot behave like this.' She stood up to leave the room as George came in, slippers in one hand, his comic in the other. Without taking his eye from the page he held the slippers out to Hannah and slid back on to his seat. 'The water's on,' her mother said; her voice had recovered its composure and sounded tight and final. 'Go up and get ready for your bath now, Hannah.'

She left her alone in the room with her brother. He was lost in the fantastic, battle-strewn world of Dan Dare and the Mekon, oblivious to everything going on around him. He was the only one who had acted perfectly normally when she walked back into the house after an unexplained absence of four months. To him, she was almost a grown-up, and grown-ups had their own ways which he didn't question. His own world was far too involving for him to have any time to spare on anyone else's. His life was filled with feeding his rabbits, building toy aeroplanes and arranging the bits of shrapnel and parachute silk from the war, which he still proudly displayed on his bedroom windowsill. That wasn't to say he was indifferent to his sister's

179

return: quite the opposite. Of all the family, he was the most strident in his welcome, possibly because it wasn't clouded by the circumstances of her absence. He had put down what he was doing and run to her, unrestrainedly glad to see her, naively unaware of everyone else's discomfort. She loved him all the more for that.

Part Two

18

Marina stops to catch her breath. The wind has been building up all morning. It is hugging the coastline, whipping along the promenade and she has been pushing the buggy into it head-on. Oscar is zipped into his too-small anorak with the hood pulled up, and she has velcroed his mittens as tightly as she can on to his hands so that they won't work themselves loose and blow off. Belted and buckled safely into the buggy, he waves his padded arms sadly, as helpless as a beetle on its back, waiting for providence to set it on its feet again so that it can scurry away. Marina turns the buggy round so that he is facing the way they have come and the wind is behind him, then crouches down in front of him to roll a cigarette. The tiny circle of his exposed face has a wind-rouged bloom, his nose is running and his eyes are watering so much his long eyelashes have clumped together wetly and he has tear tracks running down both cheeks. She smiles at him and he gurgles and jiggles his arms stiffly, like a hand-puppet. She puts the cigarette together quickly, a few stray strands of tobacco dropping into Oscar's lap as she rolls it into shape, others being taken by the wind and waltzed away. When it's made, she pushes it between her lips and holds it there gently as she grabs both of Oscar's feet and wiggles them in the air. He laughs a big open-mouthed laugh that shows his two new teeth, and blows a big snot bubble from one nostril. She uses the bit of jumper cuff poking out from her coat sleeve to wipe his nose, then lights the cigarette in the shelter of the buggy before standing up. He jounces his arms and legs in protest, wanting her near to him again; he moves his mouth, saying something that is almost words, but it is whipped away by the wind and she doesn't hear it.

She leans over the railings, letting the wind catch the smoke the moment it leaves her lips so that it leaves no trace of itself hanging in the air. It is a persistent wind, nagging at her hair and blowing it across her face no matter how much of it she catches in her hands and tries to batten down, retying it as tightly as she can with her elastic band. She can feel it slipping inside her cuffs and up her trouser legs, brushing coolly against her skin as it slides between layers and through the separate fibres of her clothes.

She feels a tap on her shoulder and turns round. It's a girl, not very different from herself.

'Got a spare ciggie, have you?' she asks, jerking her head at the cigarette between Marina's fingers, burning lopsidedly because of the wind. Marina nods and digs around in her pocket before pulling out the folded-over packet of Old Holborn. 'The Rizlas are inside,' she says, passing it to her.

Just as she is holding it out, and the girl is reaching forwards, poised to take it from her fingers, something happens. The noise and the pummelling of the wind are so all-consuming that she doesn't see or hear it coming. A person is just suddenly there, on the periphery of her senses, moving with the wind, so that, later, when she is telling the policewoman what happened, she falters, not sure exactly how it happened because it's all caught up in the sound of the wind in her ears.

She twists round, trying to see who or what is there, but her eyes can't catch up. As she turns she instinctively reaches out to catch hold of the buggy. A protective, conditioned response. But she is already too late. She stumbles forwards, her hand closing on nothing, as the faceless stranger swoops in front of her, catches hold of the buggy handles and pushes it at top speed away from her, the wheels skittering noisily as they spin madly against the tarmac.

For just a moment, she freezes. It is a millisecond, something indivisible, not enough to matter or make any difference. But later she tortures herself about this: saying over and over to the policewoman, then to Hannah, that she wasn't quick enough, that by the time she caught up with what had happened and started to run after him he was already too far away, running with the wind behind him, moving further and further away. Her legs pounding against the ground, her arms scratching at the air, trying to drag herself forwards more quickly, as the distance between them widens, her hair streaming out in front of her, screaming herself hoarse.

She doesn't remember when she stopped running, or when she dropped on to the ground, defeated, howling, and was helped by a passing dog walker who had been coming in the opposite direction.

But as the passer-by helps her to her feet and sits her down on a bench, she realises that this is it. This is her punishment. The man is middle-aged and bumbling, and although he has a mobile phone, he doesn't know how to use it. He fumbles with the buttons through his gloves, his dog yanking at its lead. Marina sits rigidly on the bench, unable to move or help. This is it. This is what she has been waiting for since yesterday. She had been right not to feel safe. Dave has found her already, hasn't he? And he has taken Oscar away, because she stole his money.

19

Hannah has decided to make a bonfire in the garden to get rid of all the rubbish she has thrown out once and for all. She has put the Salvation Army letters in the bin too. Let it all burn, she thinks. Let it go. When everything is reduced to ashes they can be tipped on to the compost heap and one day spread on the garden. She likes the idea of that: the detritus of the past somehow fuelling the future. It is as it should be.

The wind has built up since yesterday, and she can see the shrubs on the front patio juddering in their pots, their leaves flipping up with each gust and showing paler undersides. Out across the bay, the familiar outline of the Great Orme seems hard and sharp-tuned in the unforgiving winter light. Still, she will have to brave the weather. She goes into the hall and puts on her old gardening jacket and digs out a thick pair of gloves.

Tiger Valentine follows her as far as the back door and sniffs at the gusty air before thinking better of it and slinking away. Undeterred, Hannah strides across the lawn. She is looking for a metal dustbin which Evan had bought years ago for burning old papers in. Bills paid, copies of receipts and bookings, old monthly accounts books, sundry letters and order forms and God knows what else. Every year he would go out and set fire to another load, only each year the pile grew smaller and smaller until it wasn't worth the bother any more. The bin hasn't been used for years.

She finds it behind the shed and drags it out into the middle of the lawn. The grass is so overgrown that the wind is shimmering through it, making it seem liquid and flowing. Slightly breathless, she lifts off the funnelled lid. A sudden gust catches inside the rim and jerks it in her hand as she lowers it stiffly to the ground. Inside, the bin is lined with a layer of sodden ash, stained brown by the blooming rust covering the surface of the metal. A damp, earthy smell rises from inside, heavily tinged with smoke. She supposes all this will have to be emptied out, otherwise nothing will burn.

The telephone shocks her out of her thoughts. She hears it trilling faintly in the hall. 'Damn,' she says, abandoning the dustbin and rushing back inside, leaving the back door wide open. It hardly ever rings these days. She hurries down the hall and catches it just in time.

'Hello?'

'Oh, good morning. Am I speaking to Mrs Hannah Thomas?'

'Yes,' she says, trying not to puff and pant into the receiver. It's a stranger's voice, rather formal, although local. He asks if there is a Miss Marina Wilkinson living at the address and she replies suspiciously that there is, but who is it that wants to know. How stupid, she thinks, as soon as the words are out of her mouth. I shouldn't have said yes until I knew who it was.

188

It occurs to her that she hadn't, until this moment, even known Marina's surname, hadn't thought to ask it.

'It's the police, Mrs Thomas. There's been an incident, I'm afraid. Miss Wilkinson has asked if you would kindly come to the station.'

'What sort of incident? What do you mean? What's happened?'

After the policeman has explained and rung off Hannah stands there for a moment in the hall, unsure what to do next, before replacing the receiver soundlessly in its cradle. Someone has taken little Oscar. An attack on the promenade. Out of the blue, he says. They have Miss Wilkinson at the station but she is not coping very well. Could she come as soon as possible? An uneasy memory flares up, like a cloud passing overhead, as Hannah remembers the man who was hanging around last night. Could he have had something to do with it? With a shudder, she goes back into the kitchen and locks the back door, throwing the bolts across for extra security.

≈

The policewoman is writing down Marina's statement as if it were really possible to replace what has happened with words. As if saying 'I started to chase after him but he was running too fast and I couldn't catch him up' bears any relation to the events of the last hour. She looks at the woman's hand as it moves slowly across the blank form, shaping what is unendurable into bold, blue biro letters. As if that can explain it, shrink it down into something understandable, when she knows it is impossible.

Sitting here at a table in a small square room, putting it all into words when she should be out there, looking for him. Some disjointed part of her notices that the policewoman is writing the whole thing in capital letters, as if to stress the urgency of the situation, but it slows down the process of her writing it all down even more. Every couple of lines she reads out what she has put and waits for Marina to nod before she continues.

Marina feels as if she will explode if this goes on much longer. She wants to shout out again that this is a waste of time, that she needs to go and find her son, that he needs to be fed and he will be frightened, so frightened, without her, but they keep telling her to stay calm, that they already have enough people looking for him, that the best help she can give is by doing this. How can there be enough people? she sobs. How can there be, if I'm not out there looking for him too?

There is a knock at the door and the policewoman excuses herself. Alone, Marina looks hopelessly around the room. She doesn't know what to do to stop herself from tipping over into the bottomlessness of the panic which keeps grabbing at her when she is not being made to concentrate on describing Oscar – giving the factual details that will identify him to a rescuer who has never seen him before, a saviour he will not recognise – or trying to remember what the man they keep calling 'the abductor' looked like. With no specific thing to grab on to to keep her afloat, she feels herself being sucked down. She can hear muffled voices outside the door. The policewoman comes back in again and says that her friend is here. For a moment, as she flails back up to the surface, she has no idea who she is talking about, but then she remembers that they asked for someone they could call, someone nearby who could come and be with her until Oscar was found. Her parents, perhaps. She had said no, there was no one, and then she had remembered Hannah and given them her name. Perhaps she would come.

⁓

Hannah follows the desk sergeant to whom she has given her details, and sits down gratefully on one of the hard, waiting-room seats he indicates, breathing heavily. She has told him, too, about the young man she has seen lurking outside the house. Just in case. He jots something down on a pad, saying 'It may be significant', but he doesn't sound convinced.

She is still in her gardening jacket, didn't think to change it before rushing out. Marina is in one of the interview rooms with a colleague, he tells her. She is giving her statement.

Hannah nods, a sick feeling of dread rising in her chest and up into the back of her throat. How could somebody just snatch a baby in a pushchair? Why would they do it? She grasps the desk sergeant's arm as he goes to leave her. 'They will find him, won't they?' she whispers. 'She will get him back?'

'We are doing everything we can, Mrs Thomas, everything we can,' he says, putting his big hand over hers for a moment before leaving her alone.

But what if he isn't found? she thinks, unable to let the possibility fade. What if he stays lost? What then? She can't bear to think of it: another little boy lost, never to see his mother again.

191

What will happen to him? What will they do to him, these people who have stolen him away? And what will happen to his mother?

The desk sergeant returns with a cup of tea from a vending machine. He places it gently on a table at the side of her, pushing aside some leaflets to make room. It is kind of him, but she can't drink it. She thanks him anyway.

They seem to be taking an awfully long time with Marina. She stares hard at the door they must have taken her through. Even in a quiet town like this, it's all keypad locks on doors these days. Nothing is safe. A young officer, tall and lean, in his shirt-sleeves, comes through and she sits up in her chair expectantly, but he picks up some forms then taps a code into the keypad and disappears again. The sound of his shoes squeaking on the lino slips round the door before it snaps shut behind him.

She looks around the waiting area to try and calm herself down. She will need to be sensible when Marina comes out, will have to be strong for her sake. How impersonal, how bleak the place is, though. The upholstery on the seating is stained and the lino stuck down in places where it has worn with brown parcel tape. A couple of large noticeboards break the monotony of the walls, thinly covered with lost dog and cat notices. Somebody has made an effort to make a display on one of them from the many leaflets about protecting your home against crime and security marking your belongings, but it isn't convincing. Huge stretches of the pinboards are bare, their surfaces dimpled with the drawing pins and staples left over from past notices, torn too roughly down. Here and there, coloured snags of paper are still caught there and stand out like tiny marker flags.

Please find Oscar, she thinks. Please don't let him be lost. Unconsciously, she crosses her arm over her chest and, finding the loose flesh of her upper arm, pinches hard in the place which, more than fifty years ago, was covered in the bruises she had made there.

෨

When Marina appears through the locked door Hannah jumps up from her seat and goes to her. The girl's tears, temporarily staunched, break through again and she leans into her open arms, her grief unstoppable. Hannah closes her eyes and strokes her arm. Firm, regular strokes, pressing into the flesh.

'They will find him,' she says, trying to keep her own tears unshed.

෨

Back at home, Hannah can do nothing to calm her. She tries sitting with her but the girl cannot be still; her fingers flutter round her face and pull at her hair. She stands and walks to the window then out of the room and back in again. Hannah offers her tea, brandy, anything she likes, but Marina looks at her as if she doesn't understand. As if she is an orphan, a refugee, who has no idea where she has been brought, who needs, more than anything, to return to a world she can take part in. The power of her distress cuts her off. Although Hannah can take her in her arms, can sit beside her and hold her face between her hands,

193

intoning they will find him, they will find him, until the words are drained of meaning, she knows that Marina is drifting over dangerous waters, within sight but further and further out of reach with every minute that passes.

Standing in the kitchen, Hannah shakes two iron tablets from the bottle she has put by the kettle and swallows them with the last of her tea, almost cold. They stick slightly in her throat and she feels the lump travel slowly towards her stomach. She sinks on to a chair and puts her face in her hands. If the child isn't found, that girl's life will be destroyed, she thinks. Just like that. She seems tough in some ways, but it is only because she has had to be. That kind of hardness is eggshell-thin and hers is already crazed with fine cracks. Hannah knows this better than Marina could ever guess. She shivers as a draught scoots under the back door and skims across the tiles, catching at her ankles. It's a harsh day, she thinks sadly, too harsh for a little one to be out on his own. She has never been religious, has never seen the point in a God who inflicts on his people such casual cruelty, but she prays to him now. 'Please,' she begs. 'Don't ruin this poor girl's life. If you've any mercy, bring him back.'

⁊

'Why not go and lie down?' she says to Marina. 'Try to get some rest.' And then: 'You'll need to be fresh for when he comes home. He'll need you to be.' She notices herself using the word 'home' but brushes the observation away. This isn't their home, she thinks. Even less so now, after what has happened.

She persuades her at least to go upstairs and lie on the bed. She knows the girl won't sleep, but it gives a fleeting sense of purpose as she leads her upstairs and opens the door for her.

Marina walks into the room and sits down on the edge of the bed. Oscar's discarded pyjamas are still lying on the counterpane. She picks up the little top and holds it in her lap, looking without seeming to see it. She looks beaten. She mustn't look like that, Hannah thinks, and she wants to slap her senses back into her. She mustn't let it beat her. She sits down beside her on the bed and puts her arm around Marina's hunched shoulders, shaking and squeezing a little to banish the look from her eyes. So thin, she notices, underneath all the layers of clothes.

Marina sniffs. 'I always knew I'd lose him,' she says. 'Right from the beginning.'

Hannah says nothing.

'He was too good for me.'

Hannah strokes her hair, whispers 'They'll find him. They will. He will be all right.' It occurs to her how empty these words are, these well-meaning comforters, slipping automatically out of her mouth, before she has time to think about what she is saying. But even if she had thought about it, this is what she would have said. Even if it is not true, what else is there to say at a time like this?

There had been no comfort for her, even if it was just words. Not after she left the hospital. It was like nothing had happened. The whole sorry business was never to be mentioned. That was what it had been, a sorry business. There was never any

195

acknowledgement of a baby, another person involved as well as Hannah. She had even almost forgotten that herself until she was married and everything started to unravel.

She pulls herself back to the present. 'He isn't too good for you. Never say that. He—'

'I always knew,' Marina interrupts her, still stumbling, blinkered, along the same track. 'I tried to keep him. I came here, I . . . I knew it would happen. First it was the Council. Social Services. They were going to take him away. That's why I came here . . . So they wouldn't find him. But I . . . I only . . .' She can't say any more, can't tell Hannah what it is that is making her so sure. 'The police won't find him. The people that took him, they're too clever for that. They'll take him somewhere where I'll never think to look, and I'll never know what happened to him. That's my punishment. I . . .'

Surely she doesn't mean Social Services would do something like this, Hannah thinks. It's a ridiculous idea. It is hard to make out what Marina is trying to say, but she sounds so fixed, so resolute. A deadness already moving beyond resignation. Hannah recognises it only partially, the numbness real enough to her, but Marina's despair seems to be tinged with a kind of wilfulness which she cannot understand, as if, with the absolute strength of her conviction, she might almost prevent Oscar from being found. It is frightening, but it is perhaps a way of protecting herself, Hannah thinks. By choosing to believe the worst thing possible, she is allowing for it, isn't she? Facing the fact that it could happen. Maybe it is a sign of how jaded young people have become in this modern world, how preternaturally conscious they are of the breadth of possibility, the absence of limitations. Hannah keeps her arm around her shoulders knowing that, for all its good intentions, it is a useless gesture, and lets the girl's words flow over her like water.

The child will be found, she repeats over and over in her mind, forcing herself to think positively. He must be. Marina cannot be mired in this defeated state for long without lasting damage. And thinking like this galvanises Hannah into a more robust determination, as if, by convincing herself, her faith will balance the scales of Marina's fatalism and bring the child back to his mother unharmed.

20

Liam has to get away from this place. It's messing with his head. He is going mental with the constant wind and cold and miles and miles of grey sky. It's too empty, too open. It makes him feel edgy; he needs the closed-in security of the city, the familiarity of places he has always known. It is half wild here; there is a rawness which is making him feel more and more uneasy.

It is Sunday now and nothing is open. He is hungry; he hasn't eaten anything proper since the burgers the girl bought him yesterday. He walks up and down the streets looking for somewhere, anywhere, to take shelter and get some hot food, but all he finds is a newsagent's just about to close. He dashes in and buys coke and a couple of Snicker bars which he eats ravenously as he walks. He thinks: if he's ever going to get out of here he needs to find a petrol station and buy as much petrol as he can with what's left of the money. Then he will go back to the car, if he can remember where he left it, and see if it will start. With this purpose driving him, he feels his heavy mood lift a little. Night is still a long way off, he thinks, and when it comes he will be home again in Liverpool, safe in his own bed.

ᕤ

It's the crying that makes him turn his head. He glances down the alleyway between two shops where the sound seems to be coming from. It's a narrow passage, with two wooden gates side by side at the bottom. Pushed up against one of the gates is a child's pushchair. He can't see the child because it has been left facing inwards. If it wasn't crying you would walk right past. You wouldn't even look down the alley, and if you did throw it a quick sideways glance as you passed, you would think it was just an old, knackered buggy that someone had dumped there. You wouldn't think there was anything in it. He looks up and down the street. There is nobody about. But somehow, the thought of stepping into the alleyway and walking towards the crying makes him feel as if he would be trespassing. It occurs to him that someone might have gone inside one of the buildings to open the gate from the other side, and he looks for signs of life. One has a padlocked iron gate across its doorway, the other has a roll-down shutter covering its entire frontage. Both places are dead, closed up for the weekend. Towns like this don't open up on Sundays. They spend the day shut up indoors. He would too, he thinks. If he lived here.

In the mouth of the alley the close acoustics make the baby's crying get suddenly louder. He doesn't like the way the pram has its back to him and he can't see the child's face. What if there is something wrong with it? He tries not to, but he can't help himself picturing it, bloodied and dehumanised. It's a horrible image; he doesn't know where it has come from. It frightens him, makes him not want to look. He wishes it hadn't been crying and he could have walked past without noticing it. Somebody more able to help might have come along then and known what to do, and he would have known nothing about it. Still, there's no point thinking like that now. He's got to do something and that's that. He can't leave it there, crying. He walks closer, his palms sweating suddenly, and puts a tentative hand on one of the handles. When he looks over the top, all he can see is a hood, no face. He takes a deep breath and backs the pushchair from its parking spot, then swivels it around so that he can see inside.

The crying jerks to a standstill. In the flash of silence, he sees its face. It's normal. Nothing wrong with it. He takes a deep breath. It's just a baby, an ordinary baby in a pram. No ghouls, no faceless black holes.

It looks back at him, its surprised eyes locking with his, and then the moment dissolves and the crying starts up again worse than ever. In the tight space, Liam tries to ignore the sound but it is impossible to block out; it goes on and on and on. He squats as low as he can, feeling the wall pressing against his back, his knees knocking into the child's seat. He tries smiling and making comforting noises, but the look on the tiny, tear-streaked face is one of absolute terror and his attempts to reassure it only seem to make the situation worse. When he tries to touch its arm it gasps and recoils as if he has burnt it with a lighted cigarette. It's like trying to befriend a wild animal that's turning somersaults behind wire mesh, equally terrified of every chequered face that leers close because it doesn't know the difference between its captor and the friend who has come to set it free.

He leans as far away from it as he can, until the back of his head rests against the wall. 'All right,' he says. 'Calm down.' The child doesn't react other than by turning its face away from him. It obviously preferred being alone, he thinks, and he stands up slowly. He wishes he could just walk away from it. Push it back down the alley where he found it and leave it there. Someone else's problem. But he can't.

He lingers at the mouth of the alley, unsure what to do, and then walks back down towards the baby again. It looks like a boy. He wonders whether it has any identification, like dogs do, but he is scared to look in case it screams even louder. And anyway, even if there was an address, he wouldn't be able to read it.

He looks at the kid again. There's something about it. It isn't just any kid. It looks familiar; he recognises it from somewhere. And then, with a surge, he remembers. It's the kid from yesterday, with the girl who bought him the burgers. He's sure of it. He tries to remember what the child had looked like as it bent down to investigate the tomato sauce that had squelched out of his burger bun, bouncing its bottom up and down with excitement.

He stands up and scratches his head. He could be wrong. He hadn't really taken much notice of the kid; he was more interested in the girl. But it's the right sort of size, and he's pretty sure it was wearing a red coat.

So where's the mother? Where is the girl who hadn't wanted to tell him her name? If it is her kid. And even if it isn't, what's it doing here on its own? It can't be right; something weird must have happened somewhere for it to end up in an alley.

If it would stop screaming just for a minute he could try to think. He is angry with himself for not being able to walk away, and he drags the pushchair out of the alley roughly, almost tipping it over. Once it's out on the street the noise softens without the mossy walls to bounce between and the child even seems to calm down slightly, as if it had been frightening itself more with its own echoing cries.

What was the name of the girl's kid? Did she tell him? If she did, he can't remember. He looks up the street again, praying for a passer-by who can help. A woman, who can take over, who will lift the child out of its pram and magically soothe its tears away, the way women can. He is useless. He doesn't know what to do with it, and he hates kids anyway, can't see the point of them. But it's lost and scared, and he can understand that, so he has to do something. Guiltily, as if it is radiating from every pore that he has no right to be in charge of a baby, he starts pushing it up the street. The wheels make a gritty, catching noise and keep lurching to one side. He feels self-conscious, jerking the child lopsidedly up the road, making the crying come suddenly louder at each ungainly jolt. He doesn't know where he is taking it. Maybe if he walks around for a bit he'll find the mother. She might be wandering around near here, looking for it. Or if he doesn't find her, he'll find someone, someone who can help.

࿎

He hasn't gone far when a car pulls up silently alongside him, the quiet engine blocked out entirely by the noise the kid is making. When he notices it he jumps, thinking he is seeing things. He almost grazes it with the side of the pushchair as he tries to steer it out of the way.

'Excuse me, sir.'

He turns round. It's a police car. He hadn't even noticed. Here's his chance to hand the kid over. For the first time in his life, the sudden dry mouth feeling he usually gets when he's accosted by a policeman is flooded with relief.

'Excuse me, sir. Could I have a word, sir?'

Another one gets out of the passenger side. They're both uniformed. Liam turns the buggy round and pushes it towards them, his relief making a smile break out on his face.

The officer who has just got out comes closer in such a way that Liam lets go of one of the pushchair's handles so he can make a more comfortable distance between them. A meaty hand immediately replaces his as if staking a claim and its fingers curl round the rubbery grip as if he owns it. Liam notices the fuzz of blond hairs sprouting from the back of each finger.

The other one does the talking. 'Excuse me, sir. Is this your child, sir?'

'No,' Liam says. 'I just found it. Just now.' He lets go of the other handle, as if to demonstrate how much it isn't his child, and the blond one commandeers the buggy, wheeling it a few feet away and fiddling with his walkie-talkie. It looks faintly ridiculous, a policeman in full uniform wheeling a baby around. Liam is still smiling, glad someone else has taken charge, absolving him of the responsibility.

What happens next is a muddle. The one asking the questions doesn't seem to be listening, and when Liam tries to point out where he has come from, explaining where he found the pushchair, he won't let him get past to show him. He steps to one side, barring the way, and Liam stops, confused. His smile has vanished and, instead, the urge to lash out is tickling the tips of his fingers as his efforts to explain are frustrated. He looks around, feeling suddenly cornered, although there are only the two of them and the other one is still talking into his radio. He can't make out what he is saying, and all he can hear of the responses from the other end are the interference and sudden cut-outs. It sounds like how he is feeling: his words are coming out chopped up and wrong and the policeman doesn't seem able to communicate except through questions. Liam has never been any good at answering questions, has always found that the more direct they are and the more obvious the answers seem to everyone else, the foggier and more tangled up they are for him.

Another police car pulls up behind the first one and more uniforms pile out. One is a woman. The pushchair and its bawling contents are wheeled over to her. Liam notices that they push it in the road, rather than go past him on the narrow pavement. Over his questioner's right shoulder he watches the female one fiddle with the fastenings and lift the child out. She disappears into the back of the car with it and the pushchair is folded into the boot. After a flurry of slamming the car drives off.

That should be the end of it, he thinks. They can take the little boy back to his mother. Everything will be all right.

When the main one turns back to him with a pair of hand-cuffs he freezes, stunned. He can't mean them for him, surely. The kid is safe now; what else has he got to do with it? But the policeman gestures for Liam to hold his wrists out in front of his body so that he can fasten the cuffs round them. When he holds back he can't believe what he is hearing. The familiar words from the TV: 'You do not need to say anything but anything you do say which you later rely on in court . . .' come spilling out of the guy's mouth as he manhandles him into the cuffs. The blond one is there right behind Liam, a cautionary hand on his arm, as if warning him not to try anything.

'But I'm not going to court,' he butts in. 'I've done nothing wrong. What are you arresting me for?'

Eventually he gives in. He's made the mistake of resisting arrest before and it got him into more trouble than the thing they were nicking him for. He is furious, but he swallows his anger as well as he can. They'll soon see he's done nothing wrong and they'll let him go. Then he can give them a right mouthful.

As he climbs into the back seat, the blond one is still there behind him, waiting to close the car door.

෨

205

His dad had made a run for it. But then his dad had done something wrong. After he was caught in Dublin, they brought him back to Liverpool with a police escort and he was kept in prison until the trial. They didn't offer bail, and even if they had, who would have paid it? After what he'd done, no one wanted him walking the streets. Liam was too young to go to the trial, but his nana went on the bus into town every day of the court case until it was over and Jim Kelleher, the man who had murdered her daughter, was safely behind bars.

As he sits in the back of the police car, she comes into his mind. He pictures her watching the proceedings, straining forward in her seat, drinking everything in, the same way she did every time the case was mentioned on the telly and she shushed everyone in the room and twiddled with the volume knob. She said she couldn't follow half of what was being said, all those legal terms, but maybe she had felt her concentration might recover something of her lost daughter, as if it could glean some lingering particle of her life still catching the light as it fell to the ground.

It had angered his nana that they even bothered with a trial, wasting taxpayers' money when everyone knew what he'd done. He wasn't even denying it. He had pleaded guilty and offered no explanation for his actions, as if none were owed.

'That bastard,' she said, over and over to Mrs Donaghy, forgetting Liam was still in the room. 'They should lock him up and throw away the key.'

When the verdict was reported on *Look North* his nana's body went rigid, her back as straight as a fence-plank. She had been in the courtroom that morning and didn't want to hear it all over again. 'Switch it over, Liam,' she had ordered him, and he had jumped up and pushed in one of the buttons at the bottom of the TV set and his dad's face had disappeared.

21

Although Hannah is used to being alone, she feels the emptiness of the waiting house like a damp bat in daylight, flapping forlornly from room to room, looking for a place to settle. But she has been here alone for two years; surely all that she has grown accustomed to in that time cannot have been erased by just one day of youthful energy about the place. She remembers this morning, how nice it had been to come downstairs to an occupied kitchen, with breakfast already under way. And how the same thing might have been repeated tomorrow, slipping into the comfortable ease of routine. They mean nothing, she thinks now. These things, these habits we surround ourselves with. They can be swept away as easily as the tide obliterates messages scrawled with a stick in the sand. Their reassurance is a lie, embroidered from nothing but human aloneness. It is all self-deceit. We have no control over any of the things that matter.

☙

Hannah's slide into despair had not been as instantaneous as Marina's has been this afternoon, but it had happened eventually. She couldn't stop it. When her father's bad stitching came undone and the viscera of her pain came tumbling out in one ugly, bloody mess, there was nothing to contain it. The howling emptiness she felt for the child she had given away two years earlier couldn't be accommodated inside the fortress she had built around herself; there wasn't room for it. She felt she would explode. But explosion was out of step with the times. Her pain came out half-strangled; she exhausted herself with the effort of holding it in. Little by little, her strength gave out and the foundations of her defences were flooded; solid earth turned to liquid mud.

Lying in bed, day after day, she craved the child she had so obediently entrusted into someone else's care. She went over and over the six days they had spent together at the Mothers' Hospital until she feared she would wear out the memory. She wanted to go there, to demand the baby back, as if the nurse had carried him away from her down the ward moments ago and he was still there, a few rooms away, only walls between them. Occasionally, she felt it might be possible to reverse time, to rewind it like unused thread back on to a bobbin, until she reached the precise moment she wanted to undo and, instead of handing him over to the nurse, she would clutch him against her body and turn away.

When Evan tried to drag her back to the present, she hated him. He was a stranger. When he forced himself on her she wept silently afterwards, terrified she would conceive his child. She

209

didn't want any other child. If an imposter grew from Evan's sweaty exertions she knew she would hate it. This fear swirled in her mind at night, round and round in a torturous vortex, until it forced her out of bed. She prowled around the dark house, feeling the nearness of something terrible. As she paced up and down the kitchen, where Evan wouldn't hear her footsteps, the seeping cold from the tiles unfelt on the soles of her feet, it crept nearer and crouched in the corner, watching her.

If only she hadn't been so complicit in concealing everything, hadn't worked so hard at damming herself up. But it was a different world then, a different life. A shamed family was a shamed family. Unmarried pregnancy, mental illness. It didn't matter. It all had to stay hidden away, out of public view. Nobody must ever know.

When she came home from the psychiatric hospital she could tell Evan felt he had been cheated. He had been sold a rotten apple, a windfall that looked perfectly rosy on one side but which was hollowed out and wormy underneath. Just as her father had been given a bad daughter. It was like they both thought she had done it all on purpose.

She is buried so deeply in her thoughts that the jangling telephone in the hall makes her jump. By the time she reaches the hall Marina is already at the bottom of the stairs gripping the banister rail. She is staring at the ringing phone, her face awash with terror and hope, both mixed together. She cannot speak, but her eyes implore Hannah to pick it up. As Hannah answers, Marina sinks on to the bottom stair, her legs no longer able to support her. She can hardly process what she is hearing when

Hannah repeats what she has just been told – that they have found Oscar, that he is safe. She is still waiting for the worst to come.

'Marina! They've found him!' she says again, coming closer, touching the girl's shoulders, wanting to shake her out of the horror she has glimpsed. She smiles; she understands, but her face is glazed, as if she cannot now forget the loss, will always carry it with her.

ᦂ

She hears him before she sees him, as the policewoman carries him through the door. His tired, panicky crying. They have never been apart for so long. When she sees his face, its mask of despair, she thinks he has been made to grow up too quickly. She takes him from the policewoman who is holding him out to her and presses his cheek to her chest. She buries her face in his hair and breathes him in. Later, when she is feeding him, she feels something has changed. He is relaxed again, the drama already forgotten, but an important boundary has been crossed and she can feel the difference it makes to their relationship. He has been taken away from her and has come back safely. He has survived the unimaginable, as he will have to all over again when he goes to nursery, when he starts school, each stage one more step away from the dependence she would love them to share indefinitely.

Whilst she was lying down earlier, the silence in the room pressing in on her ears, she had not known what she would do. She had been so sure he was gone. Now she feels as if she has been physically picked up and shaken. She looks at her hands, her feet, and isn't sure if they are really hers. When Oscar drinks her milk she is astonished that her own body has produced it. She examines him carefully, going over every inch of his skin, looking for the tiny markers which identify him as her son. Can he really have been brought back? She feels nothing is certain.

22

They put him in an empty room and leave him there. It is small and almost square, with a Formica-topped table, like a canteen table, and blue plastic chairs with metal legs. He sits down on one. In the corner, more are stacked up, and the stack leans slightly into the room, as if it might topple over. There is no window; the room is drowned in over-bright fluorescent light. It makes the backs of his hands look almost dead.

They think he has taken the kid; they won't believe him when he says he found it. They won't tell him exactly what he is supposed to have done: presumably they think he already knows. In the car he kept asking what he had done wrong, but they didn't seem to be listening. The one driving shot him an annoyed glance in the rear-view mirror and told him to save it for the station.

He doesn't like this waiting. And in this room, it feels as if he has been cut off from the rest of the world. The light is buzzing slightly; it is all he can hear. Nothing seems to be coming from outside the room – no voices, no echoes or thumps carrying through the walls or the ceiling. It's as if the room has become disconnected from the rest of the building, and is floating somewhere on its own. He imagines opening the door and the floor ending at the threshold. Looking down at the disappearing world as he spins up and away from it, like Dorothy in the Kansan tornado that took her to Oz.

He goes to the door, angry that they think they can keep him waiting without telling him anything. As he reaches for the handle, the door opens.

Questions. They want to ask him some questions.

'What questions?'

'Sir, if you would just sit down and give me some details. The sooner you start helping us the sooner we can get this cleared up.'

'And then I can go?'

'Just answer the questions.'

They ask him everything: what his name is, where he lives, how long he has been here, why he came here, whether he has been on the promenade today, what he was doing at eleven o'clock.

'I don't fucking know what I was doing at eleven o'clock. I was . . . fuck knows.' He suddenly lifts his arm and waves it arbitrarily round the room, making the policeman opposite him glance nervously at his colleague. 'I was just . . . wandering around the streets. I didn't make notes. Didn't think anyone'd be interested.' He leans forwards earnestly, putting both hands flat on the table. 'Look, I didn't do it, whatever you think it is that I did. I didn't. I've told you. I was trying to find a place to buy something to eat and I heard it crying. I looked down the alleyway and there it was. Honest, I never done nothing but pull it out of the alley and try to find its mam.' He looks imploringly at the two officers. 'Honest to God. You've got to believe me. It was on its own. What was I supposed to do? Leave it there for some passing head-case to find and interfere with? Is that what I should have done?' He has risen from his seat as he has been saying all of this. The two police officers stand up, too, on the other side of the table.

'All right, let's just calm down,' one of them says.

Liam exhales angrily through his teeth as he sits down heavily in the chair. It's all right for them to say keep calm. They're not the ones being accused.

He slumps as low in the seat as he is able, every part of him rebelling against what is happening. Why won't they just believe him and let him go? But they haven't finished with him yet.

'Stay there,' the one in charge says. He murmurs to the other one and goes out of the room, leaving the two of them alone. Liam folds his arms, leans his head as far back as it will go, and stares up at the polystyrene tiles on the ceiling.

෨

They are having an early tea when the phone rings for the third time in one day. They have a suspect, the voice at the end of

215

the line says, when Marina picks up the receiver. He fits the description.

'What description?' she asks. 'I told you I didn't see anything. Only his back.'

'What about the witness?' Hannah asks, when she tells her they have caught someone. 'The man who called the police. He must have given them a description. Maybe he saw more.'

Marina thinks. He had been walking towards her, pressing into the wind. He must have seen the attacker sail past. Perhaps he saw the hooded face she had not seen.

She pauses, a teaspoon laden with mashed-up boiled egg halting in mid-air and hanging there as she remembers. Just a longish coat, and a hood pulled up – that's all she can see when she concentrates on it. The stronger details are not visual; they are to do with the swooping way he appeared, like a hawk seizing its prey, and then swept away before she had time to take a breath and cry out. Fluid and smooth, in a way which she had found unaccountably frightening, as if it was an accustomed action. But the policewoman taking her statement had only frowned at her when she tried to explain this. 'If you didn't recognise the abductor, Miss, how can you be sure he has offended before?' She tried to say that wasn't what she meant, but the policewoman didn't understand. Her statement required facts not feelings. Concrete observations. *He was wearing blue jeans and an army surplus jacket. He was five feet ten inches tall with close-cropped hair and a tooth missing.* How could anybody notice such things all in a moment? It seemed her description of what had happened was useless to them. As she went over what she remembered, she knew she was saying the wrong things. The policewoman stopped writing; she just sat and let Marina finish, let her pour it all out in her own, incomprehensible way, and then, planting her elbows purposefully on the table, and uncapping her biro, as if to say now let's get down to business, she took her right back to the beginning and started the excruciating process of translating Marina's experience into something else, something that might bring her baby back.

Oscar whimpers, his mouth trembling in expectation of the mashed-up egg on the end of Marina's forgotten teaspoon. Marina quickly completes its journey, angling it as she pulls it from his mouth, so that it comes out clean. As he chews, she uses the spoon to scoop up the bits that dribble on to his chin and feeds them back in without him noticing.

'Yes, maybe he saw something,' she says. But now that Oscar is safe she doesn't want to dwell on it. She almost fears time has become unstable and might double back on itself if she looks behind her. She has got Oscar back this time, but if they have taken him once they can take him again. Maybe this was just a warning, a 'We know where you are' calling card. She can't relax yet.

ᘒ

Liam goes back to the beginning so that the officer can check what he is saying against the notes he has already made. 'I was trying to find a place to buy something to eat—'

'You say you know the child's mother?' The officer is glancing ahead through his notes, not listening, and he suddenly squints at something he has written down, as though he doesn't remember writing it. He adjusts his glasses on his nose and leans forwards on his chair, making it squeak under his weight. Then he shoots an expectant look at Liam.

'I don't *know* her. I met her yesterday. She bought me some food.'

'And why did she do that, do you think?'

'How should I know? Maybe I looked hungry.' Liam is tired of this. He has said everything he has to say. Why do they keep asking him the same questions over and over? He can't stand it. He is sweating so much that dark patches have appeared on his T-shirt under each arm. Everything he says seems to come out wrong, seems to make him appear not to be telling them everything, to be concealing something. He is starting to feel as if he must be guilty, after all.

'And you say she gave you some money?'

'Yes.'

'Did you ask her to give you the money?'

'No.'

'You didn't ask her if she had any change? A couple of quid spare? You didn't threaten her?'

'No. I told you. She just gave me it.' He can hear the anger stiffening his voice, making it come out louder and tauter. He takes a deep breath and releases it slowly through his nose in a steady stream until his lungs are empty.

The policeman consults his notes again and Liam flops

back in his chair. His back is aching from last night on the trailer floor. He presses his chin down as far as it will go, until it is touching his chest, and then swivels his head up slowly, first one way and then the other. He massages the back of his neck, pressing his fingers into the knobs of bone at the top of his spine. The policeman looks up and a momentary kindness flickers across his face. 'Shouldn't be too long now,' he says.

Liam wants to laugh out loud at the ridiculous situation he has got himself into. Ever since getting that fucking letter and taking off without stopping to think what he was going to do about it. Why the hell hadn't he just stayed where he was? Was he that scared of seeing his dad again? Or was it something else he was scared of?

'Right.' The policeman straightens up, apparently satisfied with the notes. 'I just need a few more details. You say you left your girlfriend's home after an argument. Is that right?'

Liam nods.

'Could you say yes or no. For the records.'

'Yes.'

'Could you tell me her address. We might need to contact her.'

Liam tells him.

The policeman starts writing and then pauses. 'Could you spell that, please?'

'No.'

The officer looks up wearily. 'I'm afraid I need you to spell it. It really isn't in your interests to be obstructive.'

219

'I'm not being ob-whatever-you-said. I can't spell it.'

'Can't, or won't?'

'Can't.'

∽

Hannah shows the officer into the guests' lounge where Marina is waiting for him and pulls the door quietly closed behind her.

Marina hasn't let Oscar out of her sight since his return. She sits him in her lap, now, and he stares open-mouthed at the policeman. The young officer clearly isn't used to children and doesn't know what to do when Oscar starts jigging up and down in his mother's lap and making strange noises. He clears his throat and raises his voice above the atonal singing.

They need her to corroborate something, he explains.

'Oh,' she says. She has had the stolen money tied around her middle since she got out of bed this morning. She had completely forgotten it was there, but now it feels uncomfortable and bulky. She wishes she had put it somewhere safe in her room. Under the carpet, or up the chimney. She is too conscious of it and is suddenly worried it is making her seem guilty. Perhaps Dave has reported it missing after all. She hadn't thought he would, but maybe he has told the police his girlfriend's lodger has done a runner with his rent money. And if he has, he will have given them a description, too.

But no, she is being stupid. There's no way he would have gone to the police. Not Dave. Snatching Oscar is far more his style. Still, she gives the policeman a caged, defensive look as he sits down and takes out his notebook.

He wants her to tell him about yesterday.

'What about yesterday?' she snaps.

He looks up sharply, a little startled. 'Oh, nothing to worry about, Miss. If you could just tell me what you remember about yesterday afternoon, from about three o'clock.'

'Oh,' she says again. She thinks. So he isn't interested in yesterday morning. She relaxes a little, but her voice is still brittle as she describes her walk along the promenade, her meeting with Hannah, and the burgers she bought for a guy who didn't have enough money. She doesn't mention the money she gave him. As she speaks she stares over the policeman's shoulder out at the bay. She is still scared he will ask why she is here, why she left London, and she finds it easier to stay calm if she doesn't look at him. But it is the burger guy on the promenade who catches his attention. She notices the change in his voice and pulls in her gaze to glance at him, but the light from the window has turned him into a silhouette and she can't see his face.

'What did he look like?' his voice asks. 'How was he dressed?'

'Why d'you want to know?' she asks. And then it occurs to her: 'You don't think it was him?'

'I'm afraid I can't discuss details, Miss—'

'You do, don't you! You think he took Oscar!'

'Miss, if you could just tell me everything you remember, it

221

would assist us enormously in tracing the culprit. I'm sure you want him brought to justice just as much as we do.'

'Yes, of course I do. But—'

'So, if you could just tell me everything you remember . . .'

Marina sighs, defeated. They are wrong. That guy didn't take him. It was one of Dave's mates; she knows it was. She can even vaguely remember someone, some dodgy bloke who called round at Suzanne's flat once or twice while she was staying there, who was tall like the one they are calling 'the abductor' was, who she can imagine running in the same, swift and silent way dressed up in a long coat and a hood. But how can she tell that to this young policeman? Reluctantly, she describes the guy at the burger van, explains how she bought the burgers for him.

'And did you give him any money?'

Marina looks startled. 'A bit, yes.'

'Why did you give it to him? Did he ask for it?'

'No. He looked like he needed it.'

ᖆ

When they are finished, the policeman stands up to go. 'Obviously we will keep you informed of any developments,' he says. 'We are taking this crime very seriously indeed.' As if to demonstrate just how seriously, he reaches out to Oscar at this point and jiggles his waving arm awkwardly up and down, looking half afraid that it might come off in his hand. Oscar looks at him in open-mouthed surprise.

As Marina shows him to the door, he says that the crime was probably drug-motivated. When Oscar was found, he explains, her bag had gone from the buggy handle. This, he says, is significant. They are seeing more and more of this kind of desperate crime. It probably wasn't Oscar they were after at all. Just her money. She glances at him as he says this, wondering again whether he knows something, but his face reveals nothing but helpfulness, nothing to raise the alarm.

When he has gone she closes the door and walks back into the guests' lounge. She sits back down in the same chair. It wasn't the guy on the promenade; she knows it wasn't, and she feels guilty, knowing that it must be him they have got in some police cell being questioned because of her. It is all her fault. All of it. Nothing of what has happened is arbitrary. She has always believed vehemently that what a person does or does not do counts in some way. Maybe it's the dregs of the Christian stuff her parents fed her when she was growing up, everything a sin or payment for a sin. As if the whole of a person's existence was reducible to a kind of book-keeping exercise. The credits and debits of a lifetime's choices. If she hadn't taken the money, she wouldn't have got this guy into trouble. If she hadn't taken the money, Oscar would not have been taken from her. It is all her fault. She carries Oscar up to their room, closes the door quietly behind her, and unties the sock from round her middle. Oscar sits on the floor watching her as she pulls out the money, her hands shaking as if every moment she fears the policeman will come back and catch her red-handed. Hurriedly, she finds a loosened bit of carpet in one corner and tugs it

223

gently free. When she has stuffed the bundle of notes underneath she pats it back into place and presses it flat with her foot.

ൟ

Whatever he says, he seems to dig himself deeper into the trench of his own guilt. To cover up for the fact that he was driving without a licence, he says he got the train. What time train? they ask, and he tells them he can't remember. How much did his ticket cost? They bombard him with questions. But you told us you had no money? How could you afford to buy a ticket? Do you have a credit card? Can you show it to us?

In the end he tells them the truth. He is worn down and getting confused, tangling himself up in his retailored versions of events until he can't remember what bits he has left the same and what bits he has changed. Enviously, he eyes the notes they have in front of them which remind them so unequivocally of everything he has said. It isn't fair; they can use what they have written down to trip him up and he has nothing but his memory to rely on.

They sit up and listen, though, when he tells them about the car as if the confession proves something. If he has been lying about this, then might he not have been lying about the kid, too? It is just too convenient, too lucky, that he was simply walking past. They start on him all over again: 'How did you know where to look for the kid? Were you following its mother?'

'I wasn't looking for him. I told you; I just found him. When are you going to let me go?'

They won't answer his questions. It is like when he was tiny and the police came and found his mother lying motionless on her bed. He was taken away and nobody would answer any of his questions then, either. When can I go home? Did they wake up my mam yet? Is she coming for me? They had tried to be kind to him, but they took him away and looked at him funnily when he said he wanted to go home. He got scared and started to cry. He didn't like their black uniforms, and their smell – a mixture of car seats and aftershave and sweat – it made them seem bigger than they really were.

'Mr Kelleher? It would help us if you were a little less reluctant to assist us with out inquiries.'

He snaps himself back to the present. 'What?'

The policeman clears his throat and repeats his question slowly. 'Would you tell me, please, the location of the motor vehicle?'

Liam lets a laugh escape before he has time to check it. It hangs in the silence, derisory, mocking, or that's how it will be taken. And it is mocking, in a way. He can't stand the way they speak. Everything exact and clipped and just so. How is he supposed to know the location with the kind of precision they want? It's on a road is all he knows. By a tunnel. He explains this, but the laugh already has his questioner on the defensive. A tightness has crept into the police officer's voice, clipping his words, pulling them taut as guy ropes. He has run out of patience.

'And you didn't make a note of exactly where you left it? You didn't think that little bit of information might have been useful when you decided to go home? Hmm?' He pauses for effect. 'Or were you just going to steal another car?'

Liam stands up, sudden anger rising to his throat. 'I never stole it! It's my mate's car, I told you. Why are you trying to—'

The other one springs from his seat so instantly it seems as if he has been waiting there, tensed, for this exact moment to arrive. He tries to get Liam to sit down again but Liam shakes him away, his anger bursting out of him. 'Get off me, for Christ's sake! I've told you everything I know. Just let me get out of here.' He flails around, his arms spinning like windmill sails, repelling their attempts to restrain him. 'Get off me! I know what you're trying to do. Just let me go!'

One of them must have rung a secret buzzer, because another one comes rushing in to help. Liam sinks down into the chair, defeated. 'All right, all right. I'm sorry.' He holds his hands up, palms outwards, submissive. 'I'm sorry. I've told you everything I know. There's nothing else I can say. I just want to go home.'

He feels as if he has been in this room, in its false daylight, for hours. They lead him out but, instead of letting him go, they take him into another, much narrower room with nothing inside it but a hard bench.

'Hey! You can't do this! You can't lock me up.' The anger rushes up again, flushing his face, making the veins stand out in his temples, as he realises what they are doing. They grapple with him, forcibly walking him, stiff-legged and resistant, into

226

the room. 'I haven't fucking done anything!' he shouts. 'Hey! Are you fucking listening to me?' But they bundle him inside and push the door closed. He stands, unsure what to do, as the observation grille slams shut less than a foot away from his face.

23

The wind has gained a new source of energy and blows with more determination than ever as the short winter day starts to darken prematurely with the heavy rain clouds that have been ballooning over the bay all afternoon. Hannah switches on the radio to listen to the weather forecast. It was like this the day Evan went out for his last walk. She had switched the radio on then, too, as evening descended, her husband still not back. The tiles that blew off the roof in that storm are still missing. The dark watermarks on the ceiling in her old bedroom and the study spread and grow with each successive rain, each time pushing beyond the dried tidemark rings, and leaving fresh ones further out. She has abandoned that upper floor now, not needing the rooms, no longer having the energy to climb the stairs. She sleeps in one of the old guest rooms on the first floor in a single bed.

As she gazes out of the window, a lazy drizzle starts up, firing oblique drops at the pane, like slow, silent arrows. She thinks about her child, her son. This morning she was so angry with herself for having disturbed old memories, she wanted everything got rid of, burned in that old incinerator as quickly as possible. But now, something has shifted. It's hardly perceptible, but she thinks she can sense a kind of freedom. No, not freedom exactly; during the past two years she has spent alone she has already discovered what that is like. No, it is more a slackening, a loosening of something inside herself which allows her to look around, and to think about things she has never dared think about before.

Her son will be a man now. A fifty-three-year-old man. For the first time in all those fifty-three years she alights on this thought and rests there, butterfly-still, hardly daring to breathe. It is difficult; the old fear of being discovered hovers over her, keeping every part of her body and mind tense, ready for flight. She feels like a trespasser; she has never allowed herself to be here like this, standing quietly at the very perimeter of her life and peering out. She can barely recognise what she sees. He is fifty-three years old. He is tall and slender, his body still that of a much younger man. Or perhaps he is broad across the shoulders, like her father was. He is deep-voiced, perhaps, and maybe balding a little. She feels almost shy thinking about him like this, bashful, as if she is considering a potential lover. And age is a strange thing. If she met him now, they could be mistaken for the same generation, for siblings, lovers, friends. Yet she would be his mother, he her son. The thing that doesn't fit with these thoughts, though, is that what she has kept hidden all these years, the secret kernel she has preserved and has allowed to petrify inside herself, has not moved with the years; it is still a six-day-old baby. She has frozen him, fixed him for ever at the very start of his life, so that the man he is now, the stranger whom she might pass in the street without recognising, is not the same baby grown up, but an altogether different person, as if there are two of them, living their lives in parallel.

The wind gathers force, rattling the window frame, and the rivulets plaiting themselves down the glass turn to hailstones which ricochet like gravel being flung against the window, a broken string of pearls suddenly bouncing away in all directions, coming to rest on the soil, or lodging in the gaps between the flagstones.

She has left it too late to grasp all of this. There probably isn't the time left in her life to grieve the loss of the child properly, let alone accommodate the man. She will never know him. But still, it does little harm to think, to wonder. Or, if it does, no matter. What point is there in protecting herself from it any longer? She has been covered up enough in her life; she is sick of it. Let her thoughts give her pain if they must. She has borne worse.

᠖

They have been back to tell him they are keeping him until morning. They don't listen any more when he says he didn't do it; they just close their ears. There's a storm coming, they say. At least you've got a bed for the night. Be grateful.

He can hear the wind but only just. The walls are so thick, the one window so tiny, that everything from outside is dulled and distant. But the building seems to be creaking and groaning

230

now and he can hear noises which sound like they are in the walls, sweeping noises, scraping sounds, and bumps and knockings which seem to be above him, in the ceiling.

His mouth feels swollen and dry with so much explaining, his spittle thick and stringy. Eventually someone brings him a sandwich in a plastic packet and a polystyrene cup of sugary tea. He tears at the sandwich packet and eats the contents in huge mouthfuls, the dry bread sticking in his throat, the bright pink ham salty-sweet on his tongue. He gulps most of the tea just getting the bread down and his thirst is no less once it is gone. But he is exhausted, and the food in his stomach calms him enough to let him lie down on his side, close his eyes against the harsh light, and drift into a dull and anxious rest.

෨

He wakes suddenly, something – voices – breaking through the thin meniscus of sleep and dragging him back to the surface. He blinks his eyes open, but something is wrong. Nothing happens; he can't see. He shuts them again, squeezing the lids tightly together, screwing up his whole face with the effort, and then reopens them. Still nothing.

The lights have gone out.

He sits up and listens. There is nothing. Maybe it wasn't voices that woke him up. Maybe it was the darkness itself, its heavy, velvety touch pressing against his skin.

It must be late, because there is no light coming through the tiny window either; he can just make out its shape as his eyes adjust a little – a rectangle of blue, vertically striped with the repeated shadows of a row of bars.

He would like to stand up, to go to the door and call for help, but he doesn't trust his feet to find the way. He can't judge how far away the door is any more. He takes a deep breath, trying to stay calm, but in such heavy darkness the breath sounds loud and clammy in his ears. He mustn't panic. Nothing will happen.

He can hear the whispering again. This place is making him imagine things. Why the fuck don't they put the lights on? What has happened out there? He manages to stand up and shuffles across the room as if his feet are tied together. His outstretched hands touch against the cold wall and he follows it round until he reaches the door and then bangs on it as loudly as he can, his hands balled into fists. The sound explodes in his head and reverberates there, as if the darkness has thickened the air and made it resinous, holding any noise captive. His breath is coming quickly, panting and shallow inside the airless shroud he feels hugging the contours of his face.

He stops banging and listens: there is no sound from outside. Nobody comes. There is almost no point having his eyes open – apart from the shape of the window, he can see nothing – but if he closes them he feels there might be something behind him, beside him. He keeps them wide open, blinking rapidly, each blink renewing their bright film of tear fluid.

Still, nobody comes. He leans his back against the door and slowly lets himself slide down it until he is sitting on the floor.

ග

It started with the whispering. He recognised both their voices in the next room, trying not to wake him. But he was already awake, woken by the little cry of annoyance his mother gave when the power cut started and his little bedside light fluttered out.

The power cuts had been happening every day for weeks because of the miners. He didn't quite understand what the miners did to make the lights go out, or, really, what miners were, but his mother had bought lots of packets of candles and put them in the kitchen cupboard. When the lights went out at bathtime she lit them and stood them in mugs along the end of the bath where all the shampoo bottles were kept, behind the taps, and he watched their little yellow flames bobbing in a line, making the tiles shine and reflect, and lighting up the room so that it looked different. They made his mother's face look different too. Softer and harder at the same time. Like she was a statue made of hard stone with corners and dark bits, but like she was all warm and cuddly as well. The candlelight even made the bathwater seem different. He could feel it more against his skin, could smell the bubblebath and feel the soft bubbles between his fingers. And if he took a handful of foam and held it up in his palm his mother would go one, two, three, and they would both puff out their cheeks and blow and the foam would fly up into the air in hundreds of bits and stick in their hair, making them laugh and forget all about there being no electricity.

He didn't mind the power cuts coming at bathtime. When he was in bed it wasn't so good, though. He didn't like the dark when his mam wasn't there. She had taken him to Woolworth's and bought him an early birthday present: a big blue torch with a handle on top and a slidy switch that you pushed forward with your thumb to make it come on. He kept it on the floor next to his bed and he knew that if he ever felt scared he could dangle his hand down for it and switch it on. He could shine it round the room and see the yellow apple-shape of its beam on the walls and ceiling. Or he could hold it under the covers and make a warm tent until the lights came back on. But he never had to use it because every time it happened his mam came and lit a candle and sat with him until the next thing he knew it was morning and the sky was light and happy again.

When the little lamp by the side of his bed went off, he lay still and concentrated on making out the shapes of his toys lined up on the windowsill. His mam would come into his room in a minute and then he wouldn't be scared. He just had to wait for her. The streetlight outside made an orangey glow in his bedroom and he could see the ears of his panda teddy sticking up, and the extendible ladder half-extended on the top of his fire engine. In the corner of the room was the pushalong dog his nana had given him when he was a baby learning to walk. He never played with it any more, but it was comforting to see the familiar outline, standing sentinel, unconcerned.

His parents' whispering continued uninterrupted, as if they hadn't noticed that the electricity had stopped. And as Liam lay there listening, they slowly got louder, as they stopped whispering and started using their proper voices, quiet at first, but with sound in them, not like whispers, which were all see-through and empty apart from the esses. They sounded just like his parents' everyday voices, like normal talking, except faster, and with words he didn't understand. And then they started to turn into telling-off voices. Louder and angrier, like when he had done something wrong. He wondered whether he had done something wrong, but he couldn't think what. He pulled the sheet over his head and thought about reaching for his torch. Soon, the voices had turned into shouting, his father's more than his mother's. His father had a bigger voice than she did; it was always big. Big and brown, even when he wasn't angry, whereas his mother's voice was usually yellow and tinkly, and never got much above orange even when she was really cross. But now, his father's voice was black and his mother's, straining shrilly, was edging into red.

∾

He doesn't want to think about this, doesn't want to be made to remember it. But the darkness is doing it to him, getting inside him: up his nose and into his lungs, into his mouth and down his throat into his stomach, filling him up with itself, forcing him to look.

∾

There was a kind of crash, muffled through the wall but still loud enough to make Liam jump, and his mother's voice stopped. Just like that. He wriggled down further under the covers and put his hands over his ears, trying to block out what was happening. But he could still hear his father's voice, no longer making words, just a long, low growl, building up louder, to a roar, like the lion in his picture book. He imagined his father's mouth, the top lip drawn back and wrinkled into a snarl, and then suddenly wide open, with a line of shining white teeth, and a fang on either side, the hot breath of his anger. He could hear their bed squeak, and more animal sounds, like crying, like . . . he didn't know what any more. And then everything went quiet. That waiting. That silent waiting, after all the noise and thunder. He heard his father moving about the flat, clumsy in the darkness, dragging against the walls, bumping into things, as if the flat had suddenly shrunk and couldn't contain him any longer. He was muttering all the time under his breath, Liam could hear his voice, not stopping, just going on and on until there was the sound of the front door opening and closing and he was gone.

The lights didn't come on again. He waited and waited, but his little bedside lamp stayed unlit. He wanted his torch, but he was too scared to put his arm out of the bed now. He huddled in a tight knot in the centre of his mattress and waited for his mother to come and comfort him.

ॐ

The lamp dims and brightens again, flickering uncertainly before it finally goes out. Round the coast to the east, the glimmering

236

lights which dot the familiar shape of Llandudno's promontory are extinguished in a series of waves, like the successive phalanxes of an advancing army in miniature, until the dark hump of the Great Orme is reached. In a matter of seconds the whole stretch of coast is in darkness. As Hannah continues to watch, her eyes adjust and the blackness slowly resolves itself into land and sky, the solidity of rock and earth hunkering down more strongly into itself, dark against the turbulence in the air above. Between roiling clouds brief patches of luminescence break through and then disappear. There is too much activity in the sky for the stars to show themselves tonight and she can pick out only one or two in the whole troubled expanse.

Slow to react, she doesn't move until the uncertain wail threading its way from upstairs rouses her. Oscar. She pushes herself up from her chair to go and look for some candles.

She finds a half-used box in the kitchen cupboard. Marina follows her into the kitchen with Oscar astride her hip, wailing lugubriously in his pyjamas. Without putting him down, she lights them from her cigarette lighter, dribbles wax on to two saucers and stands the candles upright in the centre of each one. Without saying anything the two women go back into the guests' lounge and Marina sits in the empty armchair opposite Hannah, the agreement to sit out the loss of power together unspoken. Slowly, Oscar quietens down and grows sleepy again in his mother's arms.

Hannah looks out towards the Great Orme; Marina, on the other side, stares without recognition at the small dark shape of Puffin Island. Their visual paths cross unnoticed as the candle flames dance and lean slightly in the draught from the window and their two reflections lean in the opposite direction as if in a conflicting air current.

ॐ

He can't remember everything. He was six years old; his memory was still on the cusp of permanence in some things, although he can remember other things from years earlier. Selectivity. Perhaps, even at the age of six, he had known it would not be useful for him to remember that night too much. As he got older he found it more and more difficult to put the pieces of his mother's last hours back together from the fragments he still retained. Each new experience seemed to overlay it, making it gauzier and gauzier, as if another curtain was dropped in front of his eyes each time something new happened, obscuring his past life. What was it, exactly, that made his mother and father go away? When enough time had passed for his nana not to get angry with him, or dissolve into never-ending tears at the merest mention of it, he would gently probe for answers which could halt his sinking memories and somehow keep them within reach. His nana would get a misty look and say his mother was with God, who would look after her better than they could and his father would go to the other place when the time was right. And then she would change the subject, saying it was better for him not to know. After she

238

died and he was taken to the foster home, there was nobody left to ask.

෴

The slidy switch of his torch was difficult in the dark, but he managed it and, as the switch suddenly budged with a loud click, the light shot across the room and hit the curtain. It was scary being out of bed in the very darkest dark he had ever known, but he had called and called for his mother and she hadn't come. If she wouldn't come to him then he had to go to her. Nothing else mattered.

The beam of his torchlight wobbled across the wall in a wild zigzag until he got it under control, and then it trembled on the carpet in front of him. He had to carry it in both hands, carefully held out in front of his body.

His bedroom door was open a chink as it always was; it helped him to sleep better. He pulled it wider and stepped into the hallway. As he swung his torch round, the circle of light lurched on to the wooden stand hung with coats and scarves by the front door. It looked alive; he moved the light over it and horrible black shapes like cut-out silhouettes crawled across the wall behind it. He started walking. The shapes swayed with each step, making him feel unsure of his footing, as if he were on the rocking deck of a ship. When he reached his parents' bedroom door he stopped and steered the torch round so that it shone full on it. It was closed. He angled the beam upwards and the doorknob's shadow stretched away from him and slid on to the wall. To turn it he needed both hands; he would have to put his torch down.

Carefully, he placed it on the carpet and then reached up and grasped the doorknob with both hands. It was slippery and difficult to turn, but he tried as hard as he could, and then he pushed against the door. Nothing happened. He let go and started to whimper. Why didn't his mother get out of bed and help him? He tried again but the same thing happened, and the twisting hurt his hands. He gathered all his strength in one more desperate effort. He held on as tightly as he could and as he felt the handle budge slightly, he hurled his whole body at the door. It swung violently open and banged against the wall. He fell into the room.

There was absolute silence. He picked himself up, retrieved his torch and carried it over to the bed.

'Mam?' He pulled at the covers, trying to tug her awake. He lifted up the torch, standing on tiptoes, and shone it on her face. She was fast asleep, lying on her back outside the covers and still in her clothes. He reached across for her hand, half clambering on to the bed to reach it, the torch dropped, forgotten, on the floor. 'Mam, Mam?' He pulled her hand, but she wouldn't wake up, so he took a handful of bedclothes in each fist and pulled himself on to the bed, feeling his way to her face. He touched her cheek and followed the curve of the bone up to her eye. It was closed. His fingertips brushed her eyelashes. He crawled in as close to her as he could, but still he shivered outside the covers. He wished they could both be inside them, underneath the warm blankets together. He lay down with his face next to her ear. He could smell her perfume and the washed smell in her hair. The pillow smelt of grown-ups. He squeezed himself as close as he could, wanting her to wake up and lift him under the covers for warmth, but she wouldn't, even when he put his hand on her shoulder and shook. Eventually he gave up and just lay still. When he fell asleep the lights were still out.

ॐ

Hannah breaks the silence. 'Are you all right?'

Marina mishears, her thoughts unable to move beyond the sleeping boy in her lap. 'He's fine.'

'You,' she insists. 'What about you?'

Marina looks across at her, her face cliffed and angular in the candlelight. Hannah thinks she isn't going to speak, but she does. 'I thought I'd lost him,' she says quietly. 'For good. I thought that was it. I would never see him again.' Her voice is soft and calm. Hannah nods, remembering the distraught Marina she had tried and failed to comfort earlier. She looks down into her own lap. Her hands are resting there, one hand unconsciously gripping the opposite wrist, the tips of the thumb and middle finger touching each other. The skin on the back of her hands looks so old; the elasticity is gone and instead it has a soft, silvery cast, spotted with brown liver patches. She wants to tell her about her own child. This stranger.

ॐ

Marina cannot shake the feeling that what has happened is some kind of deserved punishment and is going over and over how Oscar has been put in so much danger because of her. She strokes his head softly. She doesn't deserve to have him. Grimly, she thinks how much her feelings of guilt would please her parents. How glad they would be to know that their self-righteous puritanism had filtered through and found a root-hold in their daughter's rebellious masonry. Her whole life has been like this: the constant, nagging feeling of badness, of wrongness, hanging over her, making her always guilty, always waiting to be found out and punished. But she has never allowed anyone the satisfaction of seeing that this is how she is; she keeps it folded within herself.

As far as her parents are concerned, she is a lost hope, filled with the demons that tempted her away from the life they had wished for her. When she was young, they never looked behind the defiant glares, the answering back, the incessant batting away of their most deeply held beliefs with the hatred and sarcasm with which she protected herself.

When she moved to London, she cut herself away from her upbringing and allowed herself to be swallowed up by the city, thankful for the anonymous comfort it offered. The whiff of guilt still trailed after her, though, occasionally tugging at her nostrils, a reminder of what she had run away from, but amongst all the other smells the city harboured, it was easier to drown it out. She carefully unfastened the crucifix which had hung around her neck all her life and threw it symbolically into the Thames from the middle of Waterloo Bridge the day after she arrived. A kind of peace descended as it disappeared into the water and she imagined it slowly sinking, settling into the muddy riverbed with all the other rubbish that had been thrown in there over the centuries. Once freed from her shackles, she allowed herself to drift freely, noticing how little heed everyone else around her paid to the continuum that played on and on, almost inaudibly, just beneath the surface: 'You shouldn't do that.' 'You shouldn't have that.' 'You shouldn't think like that.'

After her first spell of depression she went to see her parents. She had lost weight, had dark circles round her eyes and was trembling by the time her father came to fetch her from the station, in the same boneshaker of a car she remembered from her childhood. But her time away from home had only distanced them further. They didn't believe in depression, they told her, sitting side by side on the living-room sofa. It was an invention of the modern world. It hadn't existed in the past, had it? Where was depression in biblical times? She shrugged her shoulders, but the bombardment continued: she hadn't been taking pills, had she? Drugs were just a way of avoiding the truth. She should know that. If she felt bad, there must be a cause; she must have done something wrong. You didn't just feel bad for no reason; it didn't make sense.

'Sense?' she had screamed at them then. 'You talk to me about things making sense?' They had blinked at her, like animals, she thought. Pathetic, frightened rabbits. She almost felt sorry for them. But then they had linked their hands, a show of unity in the face of their raving daughter, and sat there, taking it. Maybe

243

they were trying to look meek. Maybe they were genuinely frightened, shaken by what she was saying. But to her they were impassive. A brick wall. 'You think you know everything,' she shouted, unstoppable. 'What about me? Just me?' But she hadn't been able to put into words what she felt. They were strangers. When she left they promised to pray for her, said they had never stopped praying for her. 'Fuck you!' she had shouted before she slammed the door, and she had caught the next National Express coach back to London.

But it was all connected. She could see there was a pattern, even here. It was on that coach that she first met Alan, Rob's best friend since their schooldays. It was Alan who had introduced them to each other a few weeks later. And just as she had rejected her parents, so Rob had rejected her and Oscar. Rejection matched rejection; loss matched loss.

Her parents don't even know Oscar exists. When she found out she was pregnant she decided they would never know about him. That way, he could never become a part of their reductive moral accounting; he would remain untarnished by blame and guilt, outside their range.

Her mind drifts back to the money she has tucked under the carpet. She knows now that she cannot keep it. But what should she do with such a huge bundle of notes?

಄

There is a tiny *pink*, like a bubble of sound from underwater, and the cell blinks into light. Liam is still sitting hunched in front of the door. He clamps his eyes shut, unprepared for the ache of such sudden, dazzling brightness which bleaches everything in front of him. He feels as if he has been stripped naked, and shivers with the sense of exposure. Outside the door, he hears footsteps and then a voice at the other side.

'All right in there? There's a power line down with the wind. Emergency generator's running now. Everything all right, is it?'

Liam groans in reply. Evidently satisfied, the owner of the voice carries his footsteps away and a door bangs shut. Liam reopens his eyes just a slit, filtering the light through his lashes gradually, allowing his eyes to adjust. Swaying slightly, he gets to his feet. He presses his palms against the door and lets his head hang down between his arms, trying to compose himself. He takes one deep breath and then another.

When are they ever going to let him out of here? He can't spend the rest of the night in this tiny room alone. It has already made him think too much. He unsticks his clammy hands from the door and tries banging and shouting some more. The sound of his voice makes him feel as if his head will crack open; the inside of his skull has been thickly painted with a layer of sick, yellow pain. Eventually someone comes but can't tell him anything. He asks for some Aspirin and crawls back to the bench.

He is cold without his jacket, but he needs something to cushion his throbbing head. It is as if the thoughts, the memories this place is stirring up, have caused the pain, scratching around in his head making it bleed into itself. Lying on his back he bends one arm across his face to shield his eyes from the burn of the fluorescent strip light.

☙

When the morning came, he was still there, lying next to his mother in the growing daylight. The curtains were still open and by midday, when his nana came round and knocked at the door, he and his mother were lying together in a pool of warm sunlight.

He couldn't open the front door on his own. He spoke to his nana through the letter box. Mam was sleeping, he told her. She wouldn't wake up.

His nana called out to her in a voice that juggled worry and annoyance together, unsure which one to discard. Her mouth was pushed up so close to the letter box that he could see her tongue red in her throat, shaping his mother's name: 'Bernie! Bernie!' She banged on the door and rattled the knocker. Liam leapt out of the way, the sudden noise jangling in his head. She called out instructions to him through the letter box in a voice that sounded strained and upturned at the edges. He didn't like the sound of it; it made his head feel funny. There were other people there by then, he could hear their voices weaving together with his nana's. The man and woman from the flat next door. 'Go and stand by the kitchen door. Don't move,' his nana's mouth ordered in its new voice. He did as he was told and waited. 'Don't move,' the voice shouted again, and then the banging against the door started, and he saw it moving,

246

bulging inwards before, with a splitting crack, the lock gave way and the man from next door came bursting through the opening.

What happened next was difficult to piece together. It was when he started to realise something was wrong and everything got mixed up. His nana making horrible noises that went on and on and lots of people everywhere. Policemen came and walked in and out of his mother's room in their big, shiny shoes, saying quiet things he couldn't hear. Another one stood at the front door with his legs wide apart and his arms folded, blocking the entrance. For a while, nobody seemed to notice Liam in all the confusion and he squeezed himself behind the front door, hiding in the folds of his mother's coat hanging on the coat rack, so that all that was visible were the bottoms of his pyjamas and his bare feet.

A police lady with a police skirt and solid-looking black legs came and found him in the end. She had the same kind of shiny shoes, but she didn't have a hat on like the others. Her hair was scraped into a tight bundle on the back of her head. She crouched down in front of the coat stand and gently moved the coat away from Liam's face so that she could see him. She smiled a big friendly smile at him and offered him her hand. He wasn't sure whether he should or not, but he looked around and there was nobody to tell him not to, so he unclenched his fist and placed his hand in hers. It was fatter than his mam's, and smoother than his nana's. When she asked, he showed her where his bedroom was and she took some clothes out of his drawers but she didn't help him to get dressed. Instead, she

247

took him out of the flat still wearing his Spiderman pyjamas with his coat on over the top. She picked him up and carried him out through the front door and down the concrete steps. He hung on to the stiff collar of her police lady's uniform and looked over her shoulder, jolting with every step, his nana's noises getting quieter and quieter.

He went with her in the back of a car. He had never ever been in a car before, had often begged his mam to take him for a ride in one, but now he didn't want to get in. He tried to clamber out, and started crying when he knew his efforts were useless. The police lady didn't seem to notice his feet kicking and kicking at her black skirt as she strapped him into the back seat. He never went anywhere without his mam or his nana.

They said they had to make sure he wasn't hurt. He didn't know where he was. A man made him lift his arms in the air and whisked the pyjama top over his head before he had a chance to put his arms down again. He looked at him and then he pressed a cold thing on his back and front and felt his ribs with his hands. Liam started crying again when the man took his pyjama trousers off and made him lie down on his front so that he could look at his bottom. The police lady was holding his hand and another lady was there too. Afterwards the new lady helped him get dressed in the clothes the police lady had put in a bag and then they gave him a glass of milk and a biscuit. He tried to tell them he couldn't have the milk because he only drank milk out of his red plastic beaker. The lady tried to help him, but the glass bumped against his teeth and some of the milk spilt down his clean clothes and he started crying again. He wanted to go home and have his milk at the kitchen table with his mam, like he did every morning. He didn't know how to drink in front of strangers; the milk wouldn't stay in his mouth. He didn't want it without his mam. They used kind voices but it didn't help. Eventually he put his hands over his eyes and closed everybody out.

24

'I had a baby, once,' Hannah says, her voice small, almost childlike, as it fits itself around the unfamiliar words. It is surprise, more than anything, that she feels in the half-second before Marina replies. Surprise that the words are finally out.

'Really?' Marina turns from the window and looks at her, waiting for more.

'Yes. I . . . I had a son, like you.' Hannah takes a deep breath and fixes her gaze on the topmost point of the Great Orme. Suddenly it is difficult. So difficult she isn't sure she can say any more. The words feel so leaden, each one of them a dead-weight to be heaved out of her mouth separately, and trundled across the floor like a cannonball.

Marina shifts in her chair, being careful not to wake Oscar. 'Hannah?'

Hannah bites her bottom lip and nods her head slightly, not breaking her gaze out across the dark bay.

'Hannah? What happened?'

Slowly at first, then more and more sure of herself as she finds the words to mould around what happened, she tells her.

All of it. Simeon. Her father. Chatham. The hospital. The letters. The baby. Her son.

Marina listens. Afterwards, they sit in silence. The wind still whistles outside, catching in the loose guttering, making it judder and rattle. A trickle of wax overflows the molten pool at the bottom of the flame and runs down the outside of one of the candles. Halfway down, it slows and stops, its transparency hardening and thickening.

ॐ

The lights in Llandudno come back on first, seeming to flicker uncertainly as if roused from sleep. Marina and Hannah watch in silence as the sequence spreads outwards. The lamp in the corner of the room comes back to life briefly but then the bulb fizzes and pops and it goes out again. The street lamp outside the window reasserts itself as custodian of the small circle of pavement around it and lights up the drizzle still slanting down.

The storm, the darkness, and Hannah's revelation on top of the day's events, have coloured the two of them, drawing them together somehow. They both feel it. Marina leans forward in her chair. In the darkness, Oscar is almost invisible against her body.

'Did you ever think about, you know . . . trying to find him?' she asks.

'Find him? No. I . . . Until yesterday, I – until I found the letters, I mean – I hadn't thought about it . . . him . . . at all. I tried not to.'

'Would you want to find him?'

'I don't know.'

As Marina stands up and switches on the main light, Hannah feels again that something has changed between the two of them, some connection has been forged. She is glad she has told this young girl her secret. Is glad that there is someone else alive, apart from poor Celia, who doesn't even remember her own name nowadays, who knows what happened.

But she feels sad, too. Everything is too late. Marina is young. She cannot expect her to understand how impossible it would be for her to try to find her son now, after so long. She has missed almost his entire life. And yet. She watches as Marina walks back to the window and carefully blows out the candles. So natural, she notices, the way she carries the child. As if he is a part of her, moulded to her body.

And yet. Looked at another way, she supposes it is never too late for anything until the day you die, and that isn't going to be happening for a good long while yet.

But her new friend, the sharer of her secret, will leave tomorrow. She hasn't said so, but Hannah knows it. This whole evening together has been like a goodbye. Perhaps that is why she was able to tell her. Because after tomorrow she knows she will be gone. How lovely it would have been, though, if they could have stayed for longer. If today had never happened and she had been able to help Marina the way Marina has helped her.

ജ

The morning is clear and calm. Hannah wakes early and is already up and dressed when Marina comes downstairs. As she had feared, she is carrying some of the bags she arrived with. She is leaving, creating as much distance as she can between herself and the place that nearly stole her son from her.

'Where will you go?' she asks, trying to keep the disappointment out of her voice.

Marina shrugs. 'I dunno,' she says. 'I can't go back to London. I . . .' She stops suddenly and throws her a nervous look which Hannah notices. And then, 'Maybe I'll go to my parents'. For a while. Just till I get myself sorted, you know?'

Hannah nods slowly. Marina is still so cautious with her, so guarded, despite what they have shared. She doesn't sound like she wants to go to her parents'. Hannah wonders why. Maybe they don't get on. Maybe they disapprove of her having the child. She is very young, after all. Perhaps they are old-fashioned and think she should have married first. As if being married made a blind bit of difference.

If only she wasn't in such a hurry to leave. It would be so wonderful to have them stay for just a few more days. The place, empty again after the two of them have gone, will be so much more empty than it was before. Just herself and Tiger Valentine, and Glynnis a couple of times a week. Suddenly, she can't bear the thought of being alone again.

℘

They wake him up from an aching half-sleep, rattling the lock and swinging the door open. As he drags himself into a sitting position, they stand expectantly at either side of the cell door, waiting for him to pull on his jacket and stand up. Blearily he stumbles after them, weaving along the corridor on uncertain legs.

They take him back to the interview room and inform him that the car has been found. It is being returned to its owner and Liam will be charged with driving without a licence. There will be a court appearance in a few months.

'So can I go now?' he asks, once they have told him all of this. 'Or do you still think I took that kid?' He can scarcely put one word after another, he feels so exhausted. The thought of deep, dreamless sleep hangs in his mind, taunting him. Even so, he can't contain his anger over what they were suggesting yesterday.

The young policeman clears his throat and looks at another sheet of paper. 'We won't be needing any further help from you with those particular inquiries, Mr Kelleher.'

'Oh, right. I see. So you found him, did you? The guy that *actually* took him? Instead of the guy that was trying to help? Yeah?' He juts his face forwards aggressively; he can't help it. After an unearned night in a police cell he can't stop himself having a go. They have no idea of the hell they have put him through, leaving him in that dark little room all night. No fucking idea. The sooner he can be on his way back to Liverpool the better.

'I'm afraid I can't divulge any information about police

cases.' He gives Liam a blank-faced look, as if to show just how closed the subject is. Wanker, Liam thinks, but he manages to keep it to himself.

'Fine,' he says. 'Whatever you like. Just so long as you know it weren't me. That's what counts. So what have you brought me in here again for?'

The policeman clears his throat. 'There is something else,' he says slowly. 'It shouldn't take too long. I'd just like to ask you a few more questions.'

'Jesus Christ! You're not serious?'

The policeman nods.

Liam sighs dramatically but the policeman ignores him and carries on.

'I don't think we have anything currently in your statements about your whereabouts the night before last. Could you take me through your movements of the evening in question?'

ஒ

Marina goes back upstairs. She is sad to leave this room, with its beautiful, sky-infused light, and its closeness to the sea. She is sad to leave Hannah, too. Such a kind person. She hasn't encountered many people in her life who will offer her something without the hope of something in return. There's Suzanne, of course, although now Dave is on the scene she has changed. But most people want something out of her. Money, sex, obedience, Oscar. She gives her baby a squeeze and lays him in the middle of the bed whilst she collects up their few scattered belongings and stuffs them back into the last of the bags. The others are already waiting in the hall.

The police have caught the people who took Oscar. There were two of them, working together, the officer told her, puffing a little after climbing the steps up to the front door. The girl who asked her for a light wasn't just anyone. She had distracted Marina deliberately, so that her accomplice could take the opportunity to steal her bag while her back was turned. There have been reports of it happening before along the promenade. Mostly they pick on out-of-towners and elderly people, he said, standing, awkwardly huge, in the narrow hallway. In her case, matters had been complicated because the bag was hanging over the handles of the pushchair and, rather than try to disentangle it, the other half of the duo had simply run past and taken the lot. They probably didn't even notice Oscar until they were well away and stopped to tear open the bag and take whatever money there was. They must have dumped him in the alley as soon as they realised, and he was found soon afterwards. As he explained, Marina tried to remember what happened to the girl. She didn't remember her following the other one, disappearing up the promenade with Oscar, but it was all such a blur, she couldn't really remember. She was certainly gone by the time the man with the dog helped her up from the ground where she had fallen.

The policeman sounded sad as he explained. She wondered whether he had lived in this town all his life. Whether he remembered it from a time before she was born, when people flocked to the North Wales resorts every summer, spending their hard-earned holidays by the seaside in the days before skateboards and hooded sweatshirts were invented and teenagers didn't yet hang around the streets after dusk, drinking cider. Maybe he found it frightening, the way the place he had grown up in had changed. As he left, he lingered on the threshold, his policeman's hat upside down in his hand. He had grey hair, a bald spot on his crown, and the shirt under his uniform looked a bit crumpled like he hadn't had time to iron it properly. He was just an ordinary man. Hesitating on the top step, he turned round to face her.

'I must say, Miss Wilkinson, I'm truly sorry this has happened to you here. I hope you won't judge us all too harshly for it.' He sighed and she smiled at him.

'Of course not,' she said.

She watched him go down the steps to his car. He made her feel sad. He seemed weary, as if he didn't understand the world any more. As if it had picked up speed and left him behind. He climbed into his car and put his hat on the passenger seat. As he started up the engine she closed the door.

ରୁ

Hannah wonders, with a growing sense of anxiety, what she will do once Marina and Oscar have gone. At some point she will have to clean out that dustbin and have her bonfire. But she can't face it today, and anyway, the rain will have made a mire of the back garden. Better to wait.

She thinks back to last night. How, as she sat there in the

darkness, watching Marina with her child, she had realised something about herself. Seeing this girl, this stranger, stroking the little head that rested against her arm, she had almost felt like she was watching herself, a projection of what could have been if her life had been different. It was so close, she realised. After so many years. It hadn't faded at all. She had felt again the warmth of her own baby's head, the soft, fine hair. Her arms had remembered the weight they supported as she carried him to his hospital cradle and gently laid him to sleep, and as she lifted him up and calmly handed him to the nurse for that one last time. She had realised, for the first time in her life, that she was a mother. Whether or not she knew her son, it made no difference. She was still his mother.

❧

Marina sits on the chair by the bedroom window and pushes it as far open as it will go. She wants to breathe in as much sea air as she can and store it in her body, so that she can sip away at it, breath by breath, when she needs to. She can't bear the thought of her parents meeting Oscar, would rather run away somewhere else and start all over again. But without the money, without the luck that brought her Hannah, it is just not possible. And she has had enough of running away. She will take the memory of the sea with her, and she will weather her parents, will force herself to, for Oscar's sake. She won't allow them to penetrate. She will be strong. She will find some kind of job, something temporary. Anything – it doesn't matter – and when she has saved enough money, they will make a fresh start in a new place.

Now that she knows what happened yesterday was nothing to do with Dave, she should feel easier about the money, but she doesn't. Almost fearfully, she crouches in the corner of the room and peels back the carpet. The money is still there, all nine hundred and something pounds of it, pressed flat against the floorboards. Part of her had wished it would just disappear overnight. Reluctant even to touch it, she picks it up quickly and pushes the carpet back into place. She feels sullied by it, knows she would not enjoy or want any of the things it paid for if she keeps it. Perhaps if she sends it back, her conscience will stop worrying at her. That's what she will do, she decides. She will post it to Suzanne with a full confession. That way, Dave won't be able to say she took it herself. She wouldn't put it past Dave to knock Suzanne around if he had half a mind to, and if that happened to her friend because of what she had done she would feel terrible.

So. She is ready. There is nothing else to keep her here now. Sadly, she closes the bedroom window and straightens the curtains. She picks up the bag waiting by the door and hoists it on to one shoulder, then lifts Oscar off the bed.

'Come on,' she says. 'Time to go.'

ல

The old lady hugs her at the door and she can see the moisture in her eyes. She wishes she didn't seem so sad.

'Let me know how you get on,' she says, her voice not quite steady. 'I would love to hear from you. And from you,' she says, bending down to Oscar, who is wriggling excitedly in the pushchair, his arms and legs as busy as a whirring clockwork toy. She kisses her hand and touches it lightly against his cheek.

Marina bumps the buggy as gently as she can down the steps and comes back up for the two bags she will have to carry. 'Thanks for everything,' she says. 'For letting us stay. And yesterday, you were brilliant. I would have gone mad if you hadn't come.' She goes back down the steps and waves, and picks up Oscar's hand and waves that too. Hannah waves back, trying not to let her disappointment show. Marina mouths another 'Thank you' and turns to go.

ᴥ

She watches them from the front door, not moving until they are out of sight. Then she goes back inside and closes the door. The hall is so quiet she can almost hear the dust stirred up by their departure settling back into place on the stairs, on the banister. It is Monday morning. She thinks of all the other Monday mornings people must be having. Workers in a modern-day London she has never known, crammed into offices with flickering computer screens and fluorescent lights. Schoolteachers, calming their pupils' excess weekend energy, trying and failing to make them concentrate on their times tables. Shopkeepers, nurses, publicans, miners, hairdressers. All of them busy, occupied, surrounded by other people.

She walks slowly into the guests' sitting room and sits in her armchair in the window.

She mustn't let herself drift again. She has spent so long not really living at all. Now that she has this opportunity to live when she thought she would die, she mustn't waste it. But it is easy to say this. Easy to make resolutions. If she is honest, she is a little frightened. She doesn't know *how* to live her own life. She doesn't know what she must do to get herself going again. It's all very well to throw away a few things and give the appearance of managing, but it isn't as straightforward or as easy as that. Her pregnancy, her father, Evan, the isolation of the past two years. She sighs. She must go back to being fifteen years old, if she is going to pick up the reins where she first dropped them. How will she be able to do that? In the silence her brief new friend's absence creates, all her self-doubt comes tumbling down on her at once.

Oh, if only they had stayed a little longer. There is clearly something troubling Marina; she has come here to get away from something. In her distress when Oscar was lost, that much had been clear. And now she is running away from what has happened to her here. Maybe bad things dog her. Maybe she feels she always had to be on the run, always looking over her shoulder. But it isn't right; she shouldn't have to live like that.

Suddenly, she has the answer; she knows how to start up her life again.

Without being aware that the thought has started to shape itself, she is already acting on it, getting up out of her chair and rushing through to the hall and pulling her coat on as quickly as she can. She doesn't stop to think. She picks up her keys from the hall table and stuffs them into her pocket. Her handbag is upstairs; it will take too long to go and get it. She leaves with nothing but the keys in her pocket and pulls the front door closed behind her.

෴

The waiting room at the station is empty. Its stillness feels so at odds with the turmoil in Marina's head, where the events of the past few days spiral round and round, unable to find a way out. She is holding the ticket to her parents' town between her finger and thumb and staring at it. How can it have come to this?

There are twenty-five minutes to wait until the next train. She knows she should warn them she is coming. Leaving the bags piled on the bench, she wheels Oscar to the door and peers up the platform. There is a payphone at the far end. But the thought of dialling the familiar number, the one she memorised as a child, and hearing her father or her mother on the other end is so appalling she knows she won't do it. She goes back to the bench and sits down again.

Once, when she was eight or nine, she climbed into the apple tree in her parents' back garden and fell out. It wasn't far to fall, but she landed badly and had to have her arm in plaster. She remembers it hurting, remembers the funny cracking sound the bones made inside the skin and the fear she had that she would never be able to do anything properly again, because it was her useful arm that had cracked, the one she wrote with at school, the one she used to eat her breakfast cereal. The doctors and nurses had been kind to her. The nurse had given her a lollipop for being brave, but her mother took it off her, right there in front of the nurse, and said that she and her husband didn't believe in rewarding disobedience.

She imagines Oscar in all his moods: inquisitive, lively, boisterous. Fretful and frightened. Noisy and messy, with his endless chatter and love of playing with his food rather than eating it. With her, he can be all of these things; it doesn't matter. And he is her son, not her parents'. If she goes back and lives with them again, she thinks, the price will almost certainly be Oscar. They won't take him away from her, of course not, but they will have him just the same. While she is out at work her mother will slowly chip away at him. If he plays with his food she will take it away. When he cries, she will not run to him immediately. His singing will go ignored and eventually dry up because he will get no pleasure from it any more. It isn't cruelty; it isn't anything close. But Oscar will change, will start to move ever so slowly away from her and will become a different little boy.

Of course her mother would dismiss such a suggestion, would tell her in a clipped voice that the changes were called growing up. She would insist on calling her Maria, no matter how much she asked her not to. Everything, with her mother, is about having the upper hand, and it exhausts Marina. She knows how it will be. Now that Marina has a child, mothering will become

263

a competition, but it will be an unfair competition, because her mother will make sure she always comes out the victor simply for having gone through the experience first.

Marina isn't sure she can bear all of this. If she goes back, she may never have the strength to leave. Her parents have always taken all her energy to resist, and with Oscar she will have to work twice as hard if they are ever to extricate themselves again.

She glances at the clock. There are six minutes until her train. Is she going to be able to do this? Is it really her only choice? She stands up and walks to the door again and glances up and down the empty platform. Maybe she could go back to London, after all. It's a big place. They could lose themselves there. They wouldn't have to go back to Hackney. But she doesn't know any other parts of London, doesn't know anyone, apart from Suzanne, that she could stay with for a couple of nights until she found a place. She would be starting from scratch. And going back to London would mean keeping the money. She would have to.

No, London is impossible. It is riddled with complications and the whole idea of returning and trying to settle down somewhere new seems so insurmountably opaque that she knows she won't be able to do it. The city that was once her escape has already spat her out as waste. It is such a forbidding place, she has realised, once you are no longer a part of it.

Her eyes search out the wall clock again. Two minutes. She sits down, perching on the very edge of the seat, every muscle tensed. She can't do it. She looks at Oscar. 'I can't,' she whispers.

When the train slides up to the platform she watches, immobile, as its doors open and a few people get off. Nobody gets on. She hears the beeping and then the doors glide closed again, and it pulls away. She doesn't move. Her whole body is prickling with the heat of her anxiety; when she unclenches her fists the creases in her palms are shiny with sweat. In the silence that follows the train's departure she can feel her pulse still throbbing in her neck.

༄

Hannah is out of breath when she reaches the station. There is still a stiff wind, although nothing like last night, and it has been pushing against her, slowing her down, the whole way. She can't see Marina on either of the platforms. Maybe she's in the waiting room, keeping out of the wind. As quickly as she can, she walks across the footbridge to the opposite platform. There is nobody about. A uniformed guard is standing, arms folded, legs slightly apart, just behind the safety line painted along the length of the platform for when the intercity trains pass through. She hopes he isn't standing there because Marina's train has just left. Pointlessly, a spark of anger at him flares and then withers. It isn't his fault if she is too late. She rushes past him and into the waiting room.

She is there, sitting with her head bowed, so that she doesn't notice when Hannah walks in.

265

'Marina?'

Marina lifts her head. She has been crying; her eyes are red and still swimming with tears. On the benches around her lies the debris of her life. Three bulging bags: the sum total of her possessions. Hannah walks towards her and moves one of the bags out of the way so that she can sit down. Marina's hands are held together as if in prayer and squeezed between her thighs. Her breathing is tight and rapid. Hannah takes hold of her wrist, pulls one of her hands free and takes it on to her own lap.

'Marina, listen. I've got something to say to you. Before you leave and it's too late, I just want to make sure.' She takes a deep breath. 'I know what happened yesterday was awful, and I won't be offended if you want to get away from here as fast as you can. I wouldn't blame you. But you don't have to run away, not if you really don't want to.' She looks up at her, squeezing the girl's thin hand between her own gloved hands before she continues. 'You would be very welcome, both of you, more than welcome, to stay with me. If you wanted to. Not as guests. I mean properly, as . . . as your home.'

∽

They're doing him for the burger van. They have no evidence it was him, no one saw him breaking in, but that weasel-faced git it belonged to had remembered his face and given the police a description.

They trick the truth out of him, tripping him up with their

266

clever questions, making him forget what he's said and contradict himself until they've got him in a corner. He has been in trouble before and this could be enough to put him inside for a few months. In prison, just like his father.

'You've had quite a party, lad, last few days,' the copper says as he leads him to the exit. 'You need to keep yourself out of trouble for a while.'

◈

The leftover gusts of last night's wind ruffle his hair as he walks, but he doesn't mind it now. He's just glad to be out of that place, free. He should make the most of it while he can. He wonders what it will be like if he goes to prison. It won't be for long, like his dad, but still. It was bad enough being locked up for just one night. He never wants to go through anything like that again.

He has nowhere else to go, so he wanders towards the promenade again. Ever since waking up, something has been roiling round in his head, not letting him alone, and he needs to concentrate on it to work out what it is. He finds a sheltered seat facing out towards the sea and sits down. He unbuttons the top pocket of his jacket and pulls his father's letter out. It is in an even sorrier state than before, creased and battered and slightly blue at the corners, where the dye from his jacket has rubbed off on it. It looks so pathetic, so small and incapable of doing anything at all.

But it has set him thinking. It is the only proper letter he has ever received in his life, not counting benefits stuff and court demands. His father is the only person who has considered him important enough to write to. If he thinks about it, there's no one, really, who'd miss him if he did go inside for a bit. Yes, Steve and Gary would have to find someone else to make up the rent, but they wouldn't come and visit him. And Julie. Well, he has blown it with her before it had a chance to become anything. Just like he always does. A part of him has always been scared of getting too close. And maybe, he thinks now, maybe it's just too risky. If his dad could do what he did to his mam, well, isn't it possible that he could end up like that, too?

He takes a breath, lifting his chest and filling his lungs to capacity. The thing is – and he can't shake himself free of this idea; it is like a pitbull, hanging on to him no matter how hard he tries to pull himself away from it – he is his dad. No matter what he did, he is still his dad, and he is all he's got. There's no one else. All his life he has moved from place to place, from friendship to friendship, never stopping long enough for anything permanent to take hold. His whole life has been one big fucking waste of time. He is nothing. He serves no real purpose to anybody. He's no good at anything. OK, maybe he can be funny, sometimes; he can make girls laugh, but so what? Apart from a few laughs and a few shags, they won't miss him when he's inside. Nobody will.

He looks at the letter again, holding it tight between his fingers, so that it doesn't get yanked away by the wind. His dad has written to him. Suddenly, that feels important. He wants to say something to him. Has already said it, in this letter, if only Liam had the guts to tear open the envelope. And if only he could fucking well read what it says inside.

಄

Hannah suggests they walk home via the promenade to tire Oscar out for his afternoon sleep. She knows Marina will be wary of going there, but, if she's going to stay here she will have to overcome her fear. It's best she face it straight away rather than let it grow. Nevertheless, she notices her wavering, worried face and puts a hand on her shoulder. 'They've caught the people that took him,' she says. 'He'll be safe. I promise.' Marina nods, but the worry crease in her forehead doesn't uncrinkle completely as they turn and walk down towards the seafront.

And then, as they approach the shelter where they first met, two days ago, Marina stops suddenly.

'What's wrong?' Hannah stops beside her and waits for her to answer.

'There,' she says. She points at the shelter. Hannah squints her eyes and looks. There is someone sitting there. A young man. Her stomach lurches. She recognises him; he looks like the one she told the police about yesterday, the one who was hanging around two nights ago.

'It's him,' Marina says. 'He's the one that found Oscar.'

'How do you know?'

'I just do.'

Well, perhaps I'm mistaken, Hannah thinks. It is hard to tell one young person from another these days, they all wear such baggy grey clothes, and their faces are so difficult to see with those hoods pulled up all the time. She glances at him again. No, she can't be at all sure it is the same person as her skulker. Already, her memory is fuzzy.

Marina turns to her. 'I . . . I'd like to go and thank him. Would you mind?' She pauses, uncertain, and then seems to make up her mind about something. 'If you like, you could take Oscar home?'

Hannah notices the slight question in her voice, the way it rises at the end, unsure of itself. She wants to talk to the young man on her own, she thinks. That's understandable. 'Of course,' she says. She touches her arm. 'We'll get the kettle on ready, won't we, Oscar?'

ॐ

He is holding something in his hands and studying it so intently that as she approaches he doesn't notice her until she is almost in front of him. Her shadow falls across him and he jumps.

'Sorry,' she says.

'Oh, it's you. Shit, I was miles away.'

She sits down, perching a little awkwardly on the edge of the seat. 'I heard what happened,' she says.

'Oh yeah?'

'Yes. I'm really sorry. I . . . I did try to tell them it wasn't you, but they wouldn't believe me.'

'They never do, pigs,' he says, a wide grin suddenly spreading across his face, cracking it in half in a way that makes Marina smile too.

'No, they don't.' She looks down at her feet, suddenly lost for words.

'The little kiddy's OK, is it?'

'Oh, yes. Yes, Oscar's fine. He's with . . . my friend,' she says. 'Look, I just wanted to say thank you. For, you know, finding him. And I'm really sorry about what happened. It's really crap, what they did to you. All you did was try and help. I'm really sorry.'

'It wasn't your fault, was it?'

'It feels like it was.'

'Well it wasn't, so don't worry about it.'

There is another silence, as Marina tries to think what to say next. He is still clutching the thing in his hand. It's an envelope with a handwritten address. A letter. She shivers. A polystyrene cup rolls under the side of the shelter, a plastic stirrer rattling around inside it.

Marina clears her throat. She isn't sure how to say this. 'Look,' she says eventually. 'I was wondering whether I could, you know. Well, return the favour in some way. As a thank you, I mean.'

'Oscar,' he says. 'It that the kiddy's name?'

She nods.

He sits staring out at the sea. She isn't sure whether he heard what she said, but then he seems to decide something. As she watches, he unpicks a corner of the envelope in his hand and

271

slides his finger inside to tear along the edge. He pulls out the letter inside, folded up so small that the envelope seems too large in comparison, and then he turns to face her.

'There is something you can do,' he says. He holds out the letter. 'You can read this.'

She doesn't understand. 'What is it? What does it say?'

'It's a letter. From me dad. I dunno what it says.'

'Why don't you read it yourself?'

'I can't, can I?'

'Oh, right.' She doesn't know what to say. She takes the letter from him. It is a single piece of notepaper that has been folded into quarters. The paper is so thin she can feel the texture of the handwriting, like Braille, and she can see the words without unfolding it, their message doubled in on itself and reversed. Being careful not to tear it, she unfolds the sheet and smoothes it on her lap. 'You want me to just read it through, out loud?'

'Yeah.'

She reads it. It feels weird to Liam, hearing his dad speak to him through someone else's voice. It's a short letter. When she has finished he asks her to read it again. He listens as carefully as he can, trying to memorise it as the girl's voice mixes in with the sound of a seagull screaming past above their heads, and the faint sound of traffic somewhere in the town behind them.

His dad isn't coming to find him. Not if he doesn't want him to. So all that panic, his crazy flight from Liverpool, was completely for nothing. He is coming out of prison, but he doesn't say when. Just soon. He doesn't offer any explanation for what he did. No apology. He doesn't even mention it. There seems to be no real reason why he has written, aside from the fact that he now can. Liam never knew that he couldn't.

'Fuckin' 'ell,' he says. 'Like father, like son, eh?'

Marina laughs. 'Well, I suppose you could always learn too. If you wanted, I mean.'

'Yeah,' he says. 'Maybe.'

She hands the letter back to him and they sit in silence. Without the kid there, he notices how awkward it is to think of things to say. He would like to tell her she is the first girl he has ever admitted he can't read to, but he doesn't say anything.

She turns to him and smiles, a nervous, girlish smile that makes her look even younger than she probably is. 'I guess I should go,' she says. 'I'm glad I bumped into you again, though.' She pauses, and throws her glance out to sea again, as if to draw courage from it. When she turns back he isn't sure what she is going to say. 'Look, I don't know how long you're going to be around for,' she begins, ' but . . . well, if you need anything else . . . you know . . . I've decided to stay here, so . . .' She tells him where she is staying. Just in case, she says. And then she looks down at her knees, as her words dry up.

'Well, it's my turn, now,' he says, grinning at her. 'I owe you one, don't I?'

ஒ

When Hannah reaches home, she unlatches the gate, and noses it awkwardly open with the pushchair. She unhooks Marina's bag from round the handles and carries that up the steps first, and unlocks the front door before returning for Oscar. He watches her intently, his little round face following her every movement as she busies herself with the luggage and rummages in her bag for the keys.

Carefully, she bumps him up the steps backwards, one by one, trying not to jolt him. It isn't easy. It has never struck her before, just how much work it is, looking after a child. She has a lot to learn. As she manoeuvres him through the front door, his little head cranes round in the seat to watch her, the tiniest hint of worry flickering in his eyes. But he doesn't make a sound.

She knows how significant it is that Marina has let her take charge of Oscar, even for such a short time. It is a gesture, a thank you, she is sure of it. And there is no better thanks she could have given her.

Inside, she quickly unbuckles the straps across his chest and between his legs and lifts him out of his pushchair. He doesn't wriggle or push himself away from her. He lets himself be picked up. As she carries him into the guests' lounge to wait for Marina, she bounces him up and down in her arms and he gives a little smile, although she can still see the ghost of a frown hovering over his forehead. After the adventure he has had, he doesn't want to be away from his mother for long.

She sees the old Christmas cards she gave to him the day before yesterday, in a pile on one of the side tables. She picks them up and lowers him on to the rug, crouching down in front of him, holding out the cards. This is what her own life might have been, she thinks, watching the little boy's face light up as she shows him the different pictures. If, all those years ago, she had been given the choice. But still, if things had been different, she would not have been here right now, with Oscar.

He slaps his hands against the floor, impatient, and she realises she is just crouching there, looking at him.

'Look at this one, Oscar,' she says. 'Look at the snowman's funny nose.'

He reaches out his pudgy hands to take it, and waves it in the air, with a sudden torrent of nonsensical chatter. She reaches forwards and strokes his cheek with the back of her finger, delighted she has done something to make him happy. She is going to enjoy her life from now on.

❧

While Oscar has his afternoon sleep, Marina tips out the sodden ashes from the dustbin in the garden, and carries out Hannah's bin bags full of rubbish. One by one, the two women tear the bags open and feed the fire Marina has started with armfuls of paper. Little burnt bits fly up with the smoke, and the wind catches them and dances them under the eaves, and then up over the roof, past the chimney and away.

Hannah looks around the bedraggled garden, all sodden and grey. Dead leaves that fell in the autumn are caught everywhere in the branches of the apple tree, and here and there, a brown, shrivelled fruit still dangles from its stalk. When the spring comes, maybe she can tidy the place up a bit. The roses need some attention, too. Maybe she should just pull them all up and buy some new ones. Why not? Marina and Oscar could choose the colours. The ashes from the bonfire can be thrown round their roots to help them grow, and perhaps these burnt reminders from the past can be, if not forgotten, at least put to some practical use, feeding the roots of their future garden.

CLAIRE ALLEN

The Mountain of Light

'A book to be savoured ... here the ordinary is overlaid with that intangible magic that lies just below the surface of the everyday' *Time Out*

The Mountain of Light, a London Indian restaurant, is Balu's great love, the delicious *kulfis* and *dansaks* he devises in its kitchen his sole connection to the land of his childhood. When a young woman, Sarah, rents the flat upstairs, she, her boyfriend Jude, and Hari, a waiter, begin to gather after hours to chat around Balu's tables, though Jude's jealousy of Hari threatens their circle. Meanwhile Jozef, an elderly Polish man, begins to reveal a heartbreaking story to Sarah, and so inspires a journey that will lead her to discover where – and with whom – she really belongs.

'A touching tale of unexpected friendships and the heartbreak their collapse can cause ... tenderly written' *The Big Issue*

'I loved it ... I felt under its spell from the beginning' Margaret Forster

0 7553 0741 0

headline
review

MANETTE ANSAY

Blue Water

Aboard their sailboat, *Chelone*, Megan and Rex Van Dorn look like a couple living their dream. But when people ask, 'Do you have children?' Meg doesn't know how to answer. For their only child, Evan, was killed in a car accident, and behind the wheel was Cindy Ann Kreisler, Meg's one-time best friend.

The couple's only plan, as they set sail, is to put as much distance between themselves and Cindy Ann as possible. But when Meg returns to shore for her brother's wedding, she is forced to face the ties that bind her to the woman who has wounded her so badly. As Meg well knows, Cindy Ann has secrets and sorrows of her own – which date back to the summer of their brief friendship.

Praise for Manette Ansay

'Ansay is a powerful storyteller with lyrical gifts' Amy Tan

'Witty and perceptive . . . Anne Tyler meets Amy Bloom with added value' *Eve*

'A writer with a gift for a persuasive and shapely narrative' *New York Times Book Review*

'Intense and deeply affecting . . . this heartbreaking novel resonates with wisdom about life's hard truths' *Publishers Weekly*

0 7553 2989 9

headline
review

You can buy any of these other **Headline Review** titles from your bookshop or *direct from the publisher*.

FREE P&P AND UK DELIVERY
(Overseas and Ireland £3.50 per book)

The Interpretation of Murder	Jed Rubenfeld	£7.99
The Vanishing Act of Esme Lennox	Maggie O'Farrell	£7.99
Markham Thorpe	Giles Waterfield	£7.99
The Lost Art of Keeping Secrets	Eva Rice	£7.99
The Chase	Candida Clark	£7.99
Anansi Boys	Neil Gaiman	£7.99
Passion	Jude Morgan	£7.99
The Mathematics of Love	Emma Darwin	£7.99
The Red Carpet	Lavanya Sankaran	£7.99

TO ORDER SIMPLY CALL THIS NUMBER

01235 400 414

or visit our website: www.madaboutbooks.com

Prices and availability subject to change without notice.